*The wait wou...
when he finally ... make love
to Maggie.*

And he knew as surely as he knew the sun would rise in the morning that he would. And she would love him back.

Before now, he hadn't been sure how Maggie would feel about his attentions. Then he'd seen the light in her eyes as they gazed into his soul. She hadn't pulled away, and her response had told him more than volumes full of words could have.

Maggie wanted him as much as he wanted her. He hated that he would have to wait to make her his. He didn't just need time to heal; he needed to find out who he was.

Rance closed his eyes and hoped to dream. Not the same dream that had haunted his sleep in recent days.

He wanted to dream of Maggie.

Dear Reader,

Once again, Intimate Moments offers you top-notch romantic reading, with six more great books from six more great authors. First up is *Gage Butler's Reckoning,* the latest in Justine Davis's TRINITY STREET WEST miniseries. It seems Gage has a past, a past that includes a girl—now a woman—with reason to both hate him and love him. And his past is just about to become his present.

Maria Ferrarella's *A Husband Waiting To Happen* is a story of second chances that will make you smile, while Maura Seger's *Possession* is a tale of revenge and matrimony that will have you longing for a cooling breeze—even if it *is* only March! You'll notice our new Conveniently Wed flash on Kayla Daniels' *Her First Mother.* We'll be putting this flash on more marriage of convenience books in the future, but this is a wonderful and emotional way to begin. Another flash, The Loving Arms of the Law, has been chosen to signify novels featuring sheriffs, those perfect Western heroes. And Kay David's *Lone-Star Lawman* is an equally perfect introduction. Finally, enjoy *Montoya's Heart,* Bonnie Gardner's second novel, following her successful debut, *Stranger In Her Bed.*

And, of course, don't forget to come back next month, when we'll have six more Intimate Moments novels guaranteed to sweep you away into a world of excitement and passion.

Enjoy!

Leslie J. Wainger
Senior Editor and Editorial Coordinator

Please address questions and book requests to:
Silhouette Reader Service
U.S.: 3010 Walden Ave., P.O. Box 1325, Buffalo, NY 14269
Canadian: P.O. Box 609, Fort Erie, Ont. L2A 5X3

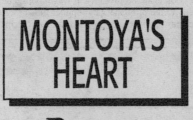

MONTOYA'S HEART

BONNIE GARDNER

Published by Silhouette Books

America's Publisher of Contemporary Romance

SILHOUETTE BOOKS

ISBN 0-373-07846-3

MONTOYA'S HEART

Books by Bonnie Gardner

Silhouette Intimate Moments

Stranger in Her Bed #798
Montoya's Heart #846

BONNIE GARDNER

lives in Alabama with her husband of thirty years and two spoiled cats. She has two grown sons, who are serving in the air force. She loves to cook, garden and, of course, read.

She has finally figured out what she wants to do when she grows up. After a varied career that included such jobs as a switchboard operator, draftsman and an exercise instructor, she went back to college and became an English teacher. As a teacher, she took a course on how to teach writing to high-school students. That course showed her that she would rather do it than teach it, and a new career was born.

To Mud, as always.
To Dad, for helping me get the farm stuff right.
To Wayne, who keeps my computer running.
To Ava, who reads, and Kathie, who proofreads.

Chapter 1

Rance, wake up.

He struggled out of sleep, responding to his mother's voice though he knew it had to have been a dream. As a child, Rance Montoya had dreamed repeatedly of the mother who'd disappeared, but as a man, he'd thought he'd outgrown it. Yet in the three nights he'd slept on the cot in the kitchen of this old home, the dream had begun again. It wasn't a bad dream; it was almost comforting, in an odd sort of way.

Rance, wake up.

He heard his mother's voice again as he struggled to face the morning. Why had memories of the last time he had seen her overtaken him so strongly since he'd come home?

A dog barked, and Rance realized that must have been what called him from sleep. He swung his legs over the edge of the cot and groped for the jeans he had dropped the night before. Rubbing his tired eyes, he went to check on the dog.

The pregnant, mostly Irish setter bitch had been curled up under the front porch when he took possession of the house three days before. Rance had made a halfhearted attempt to find out who her owner was. But the house's proximity to the interstate highway suggested that she had most likely been abandoned when her owner was unable—or unwilling—to cope with the expected litter. She was friendly enough, and Rance couldn't turn her away in her present condition.

The dog whimpered and looked up listlessly as Rance peered into the nest she had dug in the cool red earth under the house. Rance patted her gently and felt her nose. It was cold and wet.

"It doesn't look like it'll be long now, little mama." Rance palpated the dog's swollen belly. He didn't know what he was looking for, but it seemed like the thing to do.

He wished he could offer her a cool place to nest, but the burrow under the porch was probably cooler than any spot indoors. The house had been built in the days before air-conditioning, and Rance hadn't been there long enough, or had the money, to install it.

But at least it had stopped raining. Maybe he could finish painting today, before the three suites of furniture he'd ordered arrived tomorrow. Rance shrugged in the sticky, warm air. Until the humidity went down, nothing would dry, inside or out. The rain had ended a four-week dry spell that threatened crops in the rural Alabama county. Rance might have appreciated the moisture more if he was actually working the farm right now, but as far as painting was concerned, the rain was nothing but an inconvenience.

Rance tended to the dog's needs, then stepped out onto the overgrown front lawn and gazed up at the house. He had saved for most of his adult life to buy the farm. Not just any farm. *This* farm. After twenty years in the air force, saving every spare penny from his pay, he'd finally accumulated the money to reclaim most of the Hightower family's original holdings. Holdings that had been lost when he was too small to realize what had been going on. All he knew was that his mother had blamed one man. Then she had gone, too. Now that he was back, he would find the answers he sought.

He studied the old house and sighed. "Two-story southern pyramid-style home with second-story sleeping porch and wraparound veranda," the real estate brochure had said. He had recognized it immediately from the picture, down to the incongruous Victorian tower haphazardly attached to the northwest corner. The place had once been called Hightower's Haven. Later, when Luther Hightower used the farm as collateral in a business venture that eventually failed, it had become known as Hightower's Folly.

Rance looked up at the turret that identified the house. Horace Hightower, the original owner, had insisted upon the tower as a testament to the family name, though it was out of place on the simple wooden home, with its wide porches and fading white paint. Rance didn't care that the house might look out of place in the piney hills near Mattison, Alabama. He had dreamed of this land for the better part of thirty years. Now it was his. All he had to do was make it live again.

And he had one other mission. He had to find a man he knew only as Drake, who was connected somehow to everything that had gone wrong with Hightower's Haven. Rance didn't know why Drake was so important, but he did know that his father had committed suicide and his mother was gone. And everything seemed to point to Drake. In Rance's book, they had a score to settle.

Maggie Callahan wiped a flyaway strand of hair from her eyes with the back of her hand and glanced out the window toward the tower she could just see above the trees across the narrow country road. She looked down to her kids in the tiny yard she had carved out of the old cornfield at the entrance to her parents' farm. Such an ordinary sight. Yet there had been moments—days—when she believed nothing would ever be ordinary again. How wonderful it was to feel normal after so long a time.

The rain had finally stopped, and the sun was trying its best to pry a path between the clouds. With luck, the sky would clear and the Annual Popwell Family Reunion and Independence Day Extravaganza would go on as planned. The recent tinder-dry conditions had almost caused the cancellation of the Popwells' traditional fireworks display, but rain had come just in time.

The farmers might be grateful that the rain would save their crops, but Maggie Callahan was happy that her family tradition could take place. She needed every bit of normalcy she could find these days. Coming home had seemed so easy. Now, making a good life seemed so hard.

Even though Chet's air force duties had taken them all over, she and Chet had made a point of bringing their family home every July, if they could manage it. Then Chet had died in a senseless training accident, and nothing had seemed the same after that. Now she was trying to regain the equilibrium she'd lost in the past few years. Coming home was the first step.

Maggie had missed the Fourth of July festivities for the past couple of years, and now she looked forward to the family reunion it promised.

Sometimes she wondered if she had done the right thing in taking her kids so far from their friends, and the busy suburban life they had known in tidewater Virginia. But not on days like this. She knew the clean country air and small-town values in Mattison were far better for them than the pressures of life in a more urban town where the drug culture was rapidly gaining a foothold. She couldn't imagine bringing the kids up anywhere without an extended family to depend on. But she'd forgotten about the isolation of living on a farm ten miles from nowhere.

Buddy was at that crucial time in a boy's life when he needed a man to look up to and emulate. Who was she kidding? Buddy needed a father, but he wasn't likely to get one. Sure, Maggie's dad helped with her son. But at sixty-four, he had a hard time keeping up.

The distant ding of the kitchen timer called Maggie out of her introspection, and she headed inside to turn it off. She had a cake to frost and two dozen deviled eggs to finish making before noon. Pushing her thoughts aside, she hurried to the oven.

Rance paced the worn hardwood floor. He had never been one for sitting around, and just waiting for the humidity to lessen so that he could paint was enough to drive him to distraction.

Suddenly, a staccato sound sent him diving for cover. It had been years since he was actually in combat, and then it had been more as a spectator than a participant, but a career's worth of military training had honed his reflexes. As his pulse rate returned to normal, he tried to identify what he'd heard. It wasn't hunting season, at least not legal hunting. And he didn't think there would be much game around here. Not in the summer, anyway.

Just when Rance thought the noise was over, another volley shattered the Sunday-morning quiet, and he realized that it wasn't gunfire that he heard. The sound had a familiar quality. He knew he'd heard it before, but couldn't quite identify it.

He glanced toward the screen door just in time to see the rusty-colored dog hurtle up the porch steps toward him, wild-eyed with fear. The unexpected noise might have startled Rance, but it had absolutely terrified her.

Another burst of sound reached his ears, and Rance finally identified it and its source. He glanced through the trees and toward the narrow country road.

For the dog's sake, he would have to silence it if he could.

"I hear somebody bought the old Hightower place," Tess Hampton announced as she breezed in and made herself comfortable on a high stool in Maggie's cramped kitchen.

Maggie didn't comment on her sister's announcement, but continued stuffing yellow filling into egg halves. She had noticed that the For Sale sign that had stood, faded and worn, for what seemed like forever was gone, but she had dismissed it, assuming it had simply fallen down.

"You don't have anything to say about somebody moving into the house nearest you? I'd have thought you'd be the first one over to visit." Tess dipped a manicured finger into the egg mixture and popped a dab of creamy mustard-flavored filling into her mouth.

A series of loud crackles and pops interrupted Maggie's train of thought. "Did you have to give them that batch of noisemakers? I've been trying to keep them out of their own stuff all day."

"Lighten up, sister of mine. It's the Fourth of July. You're supposed to make noise."

"They've been making noise all day without any help from outside sources," Maggie countered as she arranged the eggs neatly on a platter. She stretched plastic wrap over them and placed the tray in the refrigerator.

"Are you finally done?" Tess made no attempt to hide her impatience.

"Yes, big sister, I'm finished." Maggie followed Tess into the living room, where they settled themselves. "What do you absolutely have to have my undivided attention for?"

"The hunk who bought the Hightower place, of

course,'' Tess replied as she tucked a sandaled foot under her and adjusted her designer sundress. "Have you seen him yet?"

"No, I didn't even know he existed until you mentioned him about five minutes ago. And who said he's a hunk? In fact, who said he's a he?'' Maggie looked over at Tess and wished she didn't look so decidedly frumpy next to her taller, older sister. Then she dismissed the thought. What did she care what she looked like? Only family would be in attendance today.

"Mary Lou saw him when he went in to register the deed at the county probate Office in Pittsville. He's about forty. Retired military, I think she said, and he supposedly paid cash for the entire one hundred acres.''

"Consider the source, Tess. You know Mary Lou lusts after anything in pants. He's probably a grizzled old sergeant with his belly hanging over his belt. Besides, he won't stay any longer than any of the other half-dozen or so people who bought the place in the last thirty years.''

"Maybe. Maybe not. If nobody tells him the place is haunted, maybe he'll stay,'' Tess suggested.

Maggie laughed humorlessly. "Nobody will have to tell him. I can guarantee Luther Hightower's ghost will introduce himself right quick.'' She shivered in spite of the July heat. "I still get chills thinking about when…''

Tess chuckled. "We dared you to spend the night there?'' She laughed again. "I'll let you in on a secret. Tom, Truman Higgins, Nancy Nelson and I provided the ghostly sound effects.''

Making a wry face, Maggie looked over at her sister. "I knew that. Your silliness was uninspired and predictable.'' Something else entirely had spooked her. Something she still couldn't explain had driven her from the empty house twenty years before. "I expected you guys to try something, but you were nowhere in sight when I took off like a bat out of hell at 2:00 a.m.''

"Are you trying to tell me it really is haunted?"

"We're a little old to be believing in ghosts. But I know I felt something that night. And it was more than just a case of the willies. Call it a ghost if you want."

"What happened to the idea that country life was supposed to be peaceful?" Rance muttered as he flung open the door of his used red Ford pickup. He had driven by the neat double-wide trailer that sat just off the road several times in the past few days, and he hadn't seen so many kids there before.

He parked the truck, then stalked over to a gawky boy who was obviously the ringleader and snatched away a string of firecrackers before the kid had a chance to light them. "Set off another one of these and I'll break your arm," he warned.

Then he remembered what day it was, and some of the fight left him. He could stand one day of the racket, but the dog had nearly clawed the screen door off trying to get into the house and away from the noise. The stress was not going to ease her delivery.

The group of kids, ranging from about ten to the teens, stopped what they were doing and stared. Rance stared back, wondering if he should apologize for his gruffness. "Is there an adult in charge around here?" he finally managed.

The biggest boy of the bunch acted as spokesman. "Yeah. Who wants to know?"

"That's enough, Tom." A long-legged blonde stepped out of the trailer onto the front stoop. "You'll have to excuse my son. He sees too many movies." She walked down the short flight of steps and offered her hand. "I'm Tess Hampton. This is my sister's home. Can we help you?"

Rance stuck out his hand and started to say something, but stopped as a woman with a cloud of flaming red hair stepped onto the stoop behind Tess. She wiped her hands on a towel as she shot a killer glance at the group of kids in the yard below.

In spite of the cool beauty of the other woman, this second one got Rance's attention. Her complexion was like peaches and cream sprinkled with brown sugar. And where the other woman was tall and lean, this one was shorter and softer. At least to his discerning eye. Rance guessed she was the sister.

She wasn't as beautiful as Tess, but Rance appreciated the way her curves filled the orange-and-gold-print summer outfit she wore. She looked accessible and real.

The sight of the two women knocked the rest of the bluster out of him, and Rance shoved his hands into his pockets. "I have a problem with all the noise your kids are making." Five kids and two women looked at him expectantly, and Rance felt suddenly more awkward than a decorated military officer should in the face of mere civilians.

"Go on into the backyard, kids. This is grown-up business." The redhead shooed the gaggle of kids away. Grumbling their protests, they headed around to the back of the house.

Rance didn't know how to proceed. He hadn't had much to do with civilian women in the past, and he didn't know what to say. He'd learned some stock statements to use when it was necessary to converse with the other officers' wives. But none of them would do here. He was accustomed to issuing orders and having people jump. Polite requests didn't come easy.

"I just bought the old Hightower place down the road," he began.

"Yes?" The redhead's eyes widened when she looked Rance square in the face. She damn sure wasn't making it easy for him.

Something squealed shrilly in the backyard, followed by

the rattle of a string of firecrackers. Rance resisted the urge
to duck, and tried to ignore the noise.

"You see…I have this pregnant bitch at my house—"

"What you do in the privacy of your own home is your
own business, Mr., uh…" The redhead waited.

He got the message. "Rance."

"…Mr. Rance," she continued. "But you could find a
nicer way to refer to your lady friend. There are children
around."

The blonde snickered.

What the hell was the redhead talking about? Then he
noticed the twinkle in her luminous turquoise eyes.

"Dog," he said. "I've got a pregnant *dog* at my place
who's due any time now, and all that noise isn't helping
her."

"Enough said." The redhead called to the herd of kids,
who were now peering curiously around the corner of the
house. "Put away all those noisemakers."

Tess finished the instructions. "You can take them over
to Grandma's."

"Aw, Mom…" came the collective refrain.

"Gather up your stuff and go on over. Now! Maybe
Grandma won't mind the noise. Let's not upset Mr.
Rance's dog while she's trying to have puppies," the red-
head said.

Rance watched as the group of kids pocketed their para-
phernalia and picked up their strings of firecrackers. With
dejected looks, they trudged down the red dirt lane, leaving
him alone with their mothers.

He groped for an excuse to leave. He had accomplished
what he'd set out to do, but now he wasn't sure how to
get away from this awkward situation. "As you were
ladies," wasn't going to work.

"I'm sorry I spoiled the kids' fun," Rance remarked
lamely. He looked down to where his booted toe had
scuffed up the rust-tinged dirt, then quickly looked up

again. Carrot-red hair and turquoise eyes compelled him to linger.

"Believe me, you did me a favor." The redhead smiled. "Now I can have some peace and quiet. At least until later, when we commence with our Annual Popwell Family Reunion and Independence Day Extravaganza. But don't worry about the noise. We'll be about a mile off in the woods by the pond." She gestured in a direction some distance away. "Your dog shouldn't be able to hear us."

"You're welcome to join us," the blonde interjected.

"Thanks. No." Rance looked down at his paint-spattered T-shirt. "I'm in the middle of painting. And I've got—"

"The bitch?"

Was the redhead teasing him again? "Yeah."

"Well, maybe some other time," the blonde suggested. "Oh, and if you run into trouble with the dog, give us a holler. My husband, Tom, is a veterinarian. He can take a look at her."

Rance was too near drowning in the turquoise pools that were the redhead's eyes to care what Tess had just said, but he saved himself before he was too far gone. "Thanks," he finally said, and turned. He climbed into the truck and pulled the door shut. With a wave, he started the engine and backed out to the main road.

"Damn," he muttered as he shifted into first gear. "I didn't get the redhead's name."

He was certainly no grizzled, potbellied sergeant, Maggie thought as she watched the truck retreat down the paved county road. His belly was flat, and his muscles had molded the tight T-shirt just like a washboard. And his black hair, though lightly streaked at the temples, was far from gray. This was a man unlikely to be run off by a ghost, real or imagined. She drew in a deep breath to stop the unexplained flutter she felt in the region of her heart.

"What a hell of a man," Tess announced from somewhere behind her as the red pickup turned into the lane about a quarter mile down the road.

Tess's comment brought Maggie back into the world of the here and now. "Really, Tess. You're a happily married woman."

"I can still look, can't I? Just because I shop doesn't mean I have to buy." Tess turned and looked evenly at Maggie. "Maybe I was in the market for a gift. You know, something for someone else. If you get my drift." Tess looked down at her manicured hands. "I didn't notice a wedding ring."

"Only you would look for a wedding ring on the hand of a man who'd just threatened to break your son's arm. Besides, his hands were in his pockets."

Tess laughed. "I saw how you stared after him when he drove away. You're interested." Maggie rolled her eyes at Tess's statement, but the message had struck far closer to the target than she was willing to admit. "And he didn't mean it, anyway."

"Mean what?" Maggie usually had no trouble following her sister's meandering conversations, but today was something else. And she sure wouldn't admit that she couldn't think straight because her mind was stuck on her handsome new neighbor.

"He didn't mean he was going to break Tom's arm. Big Tom threatens like that all the time."

"Yeah, but you *know* Tom. You just met this Rance character today. And what kind of a name is Rance, anyway?" Maggie remembered the way his black eyes had snapped with heat and anger and then cooled down, and she felt an unaccustomed warmth deep within her. "He could be an ax murderer."

"Well, if I need any axes murdered, I'll know who to go to."

"Tess, I'm serious. We don't know him from Adam.

What were you thinking—inviting him to the folks' tonight?''

"Just being neighborly."

"He's not your neighbor." Maggie snorted. "You were meddling."

"So sue me. I knew he wouldn't come."

"And what made you so certain he wouldn't come?"

"The whelping dog and the paint," Tess answered smugly.

"So now you're psychic. He didn't mention painting until after you invited him."

"No, I'm not psychic. Or psychotic, before you go accusing me of anything else. I'm just a very observant person," Tess replied.

"Don't go pulling that 'Elementary, my dear Watson' stuff on me."

"Margaret Rose Popwell Callahan, you wound me to the bone. And you would have noticed the paint, too, if you hadn't been staring into those gorgeous black eyes and flirting."

"I did not flirt."

"It looked like a pretty good imitation, then."

"You're the flirt in the family, Tess, though I can't understand why. You have quite a hunk of your own, you know."

"Southern women always flirt. It's in our job description," Tess answered defensively. "You should try it."

"I guess I'm out of practice after fourteen years away."

"You'll be sorry when the hunk goes looking elsewhere."

"I don't need a matchmaker."

"You need a man. It's been two years now."

"I don't need a man. I already had my one great love. I have to adjust to living without him."

"Maggie, you're still a young woman. There's no reason for you to spend the rest of your life alone."

"I've adjusted to my life, Tess. Get a life of your own, so you'll stay out of mine."

"Okay. I promise to drop it for now," Tess conceded. "But I think Mr. Rance Whatever-the-Rest-of-His-Name-Is has definite possibilities."

Maggie threw up her hands. "I give up."

Rance looked down at the dog and her brood of nursing pups, nesting in a cardboard box in a corner of the kitchen. The makeshift mattress on a pile of rags and clothing included his favorite running suit. He had thought twice about tossing it in there, but the dog needed something soft to rest on. It was time he got a new one, anyway.

He had never witnessed birth before, animal or human, and he was still struck by the wonder he'd seen. The dog had looked up at him with her beautiful, trusting brown eyes and gone about the business of giving birth, in spite of his bumbling attempts to help. And now she was a mother.

It had taken two long hours for the dog to deliver her litter of four tiny pups. After what they'd been through together, Rance knew he would have to keep her. And he knew he couldn't go around calling her Dog forever. Or bitch. He laughed as he remembered the silly exchange with his attractive red-haired neighbor. He would have to come up with something to call the dog. And the redhead, too.

He sorted through a list of likely names for the dog, all Irish, in honor of her predominant bloodline. All the names he'd come up with seemed very appropriate for an Irish colleen, but not for a rusty-colored Irish setter. Rusty. No, that was too masculine. But he supposed it was appropriate. Rusty. That was it. Rusty, for the color of the dog's silky hair.

The dog whimpered and looked up at Rance with soulful eyes. She turned her head toward the window, in the direction of the Popwell place. It was dark now. Had they begun their annual extravaganza? Rance couldn't hear anything, but Rusty had better ears than he.

Rance reached down and rubbed the soft red fur on Rusty's head. "Your name is Rusty now, girl. And I'm going to take good care of you. Do you like that?"

The dog whimpered her assent.

The window was open in deference to the sultry July heat, but Rance crossed the room and manhandled it down. The wood was old and warped, just another thing on his list of many to be fixed. Rusty seemed to settle as Rance closed the kitchen door quietly behind him, shutting out the sounds he couldn't hear. Satisfied he'd done all he could to make the dog comfortable, he stepped through the empty front parlor and out to the front porch, into the steamy summer night.

Yes, the Popwells had begun their annual extravaganza. He could see the flares of the rockets exploding above the trees. He just couldn't hear anything. Rance leaned against the wooden roof support and watched what he could of the fireworks display. As he looked, he took a wooden match from his pocket—the last vestige of the bad habit he'd kicked—and chewed on the rough sliver of wood. It wasn't as satisfying as a cigarette, but it was healthier.

The show lasted about thirty minutes, but Rance remained on the porch long after it was over. He lingered and imagined being included in the family fun. He had been invited, but he'd been right to refuse. Not because he had to paint. Not even because of Rusty. That kind of family gathering was too intimate for someone who didn't belong.

But he did belong here, Rance reminded himself. He had finally found and bought the place that had been the driving force behind everything he did in his life. He might have tried to please his grandfather Montoya by taking his name, but he hadn't been able to forget his birthright. He still carried the genes, and he hadn't been able to ignore the force that had drawn him relentlessly toward this run-down house and his mission.

A sound from the road drew Rance from his deep thoughts. The headlights of a car winked through the pines that stood between the house and the road. Then another set of lights. And another. More traffic was hurrying down that road tonight than Rance had seen in the four days he'd been here. The Popwell family must be going home.

His thoughts turned to the two family members he'd met earlier that day. Two sisters: one slim and blond and the other one shorter and plump and vibrant, with billowing waves of curly, red hair. He thought of their children, and the husbands he hadn't met. He'd once longed to have a wife and a houseful of kids, but his quest to claim Hightower's Haven had been all-consuming, and had gotten in the way.

How could he have asked for the hand of a woman when he had nothing to give in return?

Now, when he'd nearly achieved his goal, the first woman to catch his eye had kids and a husband. Rance tried to forget that glowing nimbus of coppery hair. He plucked the match from his mouth and snapped it in two. Then he tossed the pieces to the weedy yard below.

Rance Montoya had been struck by a completely unfamiliar emotion today, and he didn't know how to deal with it. He shook his head vehemently, as if to dislodge her face from his mind's eye. He still wasn't ready to build his life with any woman. Certainly not this one.

He had to locate and confront the man who had cheated Luther Hightower out of his future—and Rance out of a family. All he had to go on was the hazy memory of a whispered name, but it was enough. And Rance Montoya would find that man if it was the last thing he did.

The man he knew only as Drake was from somewhere near Mattison. It wasn't much to go on, but it was enough.

Chapter 2

Maggie glanced out the window and sighed. The rain on the Fourth of July had been a crop-saver, but the continuing wet pattern with its soaking rain had caused farm work to take a temporary back seat. And for Maggie, it had brought an increase in business to the county library in Pittsville, where she worked. With little to do but wait for the life-giving rain to end, every farmer and his wife and children had come to town to pick up supplies and visit. Most of them had stopped in to the library to chat.

Maggie looked up from the cart of books she had been shelving to see her new neighbor in the doorway. Her breath caught as he looked around, got his bearings and strode purposefully over to the circulation desk. He was the last person Maggie had expected to see in the library.

Rance was more dressed up than the usual library patron. Unlike the locals, who would slip into their best jeans and whatever plaid shirt had the fewest tears and the most buttons, Rance wore a pair of crisply pressed charcoal gray slacks and a formfitting royal blue polo shirt. The deep, clear color of the shirt gave his tanned skin a coppery glow.

The shirt did nothing to conceal the rippling of his muscles beneath the clinging fabric. Her stomach fluttered, and Maggie was embarrassed to realize that she had been staring. She looked away as he asked Mrs. Larson for an application for a library card. Searing heat in the area of her face told her that she was blushing, and she would be damned if she would let anyone know what she had been thinking. Trying to ignore the memory of his pantherlike stance, Maggie forced herself to get back to work.

Her mind not completely on what she was doing, thanks to her distracting neighbor, Maggie took more time than usual to shelve the morning's returns. By the time she'd finished and headed back to the circulation desk, he had disappeared.

Maggie took a seat behind the desk and began to log in a new batch of books. Maybe without Mr. Rance's distracting presence, she would be able to get her work done. But one thing was for sure. By the end of her shift, she was going to find that application form and see what her new neighbor was all about.

Surely even a small-town library like Pittsville's would have the information he needed to fill in the gaps about Hightower's Haven and how it had come to be haunted. Rance wasn't even sure it *was* haunted. He certainly hadn't noticed anything unusual, aside from his recurring childhood dreams. But something had given rise to the rumor. He knew bizarre occurrences had begun in the sixties, after his father died and the family lost the farm. He knew, too, that his mother had disappeared without a trace. But everything he did know had been gleaned from whispers overheard when he was a child. He needed more than just a last name to find the man who held the answers. And after he did, he wasn't sure what he would do.

Maybe the answers would be enough.

He'd asked for and been directed to the periodicals section. In a jumble of indexes, he searched for the location of back issues of the local weekly paper. There was a daily paper in Montgomery, forty miles away, but Rance doubted they would have cared much about what happened in rural Pitt County. Even thirty years ago.

Except for the current issue, and copies of each issue from the month before, there was no evidence that old copies were on file anywhere. At least, Rance had found no index that alluded to that. Surely back issues of the county's only paper would be available. Rance uttered a frustrated exclamation and slammed the periodicals guide closed. He shoved himself away from the work area beneath the indexes.

Rance turned to leave, but halfway to the door he noticed a sign that stated If You Can't Find It, Just Ask Us. It Has To Be Here Somewhere.

At least they had a sense of humor about it, Rance thought as he changed his course and headed back to the desk.

The matronly woman at the circulation desk looked up. "Can I help you, Mr. Montoya?"

That the woman had remembered his name surprised Rance. But only for a moment. This was a small town, and newcomers were noticed. Especially if they were as different as he was.

"Yes, ah…" Rance looked at the name tag the lady was wearing. "Yes, Mrs. Larson. I was trying to find some back issues of the *Pittsville Partner*."

"Well, Mr. Montoya, we don't get many calls for back issues of the *Partner*. I'll see what I can do." Mrs. Larson shoved her bulky figure out of her chair and ambled toward him.

"Just how far back were you wanting to look?"

Rance told her.

"Gracious. Why do you want to look that far back?"

Should he tell her? Rance had intended to keep his purpose a secret. At least until he was able to untangle the threads of the Hightower family's tarnished past. Then he realized that he didn't have to reveal everything to the waiting librarian. As the new owner of the old Hightower place, he had every right to be curious about what had happened there.

"I just bought the old Hightower place," Rance told Mrs. Larson. "And I guess I'm just curious to know what happened back then."

A series of emotions played across Mrs. Larson's grandmotherly face and ended with indecision. She gnawed her lip. "Then you've heard it's supposed to be…"

"Haunted?" Rance chuckled. "I've heard that rumor."

"Have…have you had any…any manifestations?"

"No, ma'am. Everything's just as ordinary as can be. The most unusual thing that's happened is that I've been adopted by a stray dog."

"I hope it stays that way. Several other families who've tried to live there left in an awful hurry."

"So I've heard," Rance agreed amiably. And he had heard. At the lumberyard, and the paint store, and the grocery store when he went in for groceries. The only place he hadn't heard the rumors was the real estate office.

"You know, it's odd, now that you mention the Hightowers. Somebody came in and told me about noticing flowers on Luther's grave." She shook her head. "Nobody's tended that grave in thirty years, and now…"

Rance managed a shrug. It had never occurred to him that anyone would notice his simple gesture of respect. "Do you have the issues I need, Mrs. Larson?" He didn't have time for gossip; he had work to do.

"Gracious me, I don't rightly know. As I told you, there's not much call for back copies of the *Pittsville Partner*."

"I don't imagine there is," Rance commented blandly. "We do have back issues stored, but it may be hard to locate what you want."

"Well, ma'am, I have plenty of time today. Just point me in the right direction, and I'll start looking."

"It's not that." Mrs. Larson wrung her hands and looked flustered. "Our filing system is not exactly scientific. It may not be real easy to lay our hands on the specific issues. You see, they're not on microfiche, like you'd expect. We have the actual issues. In storage."

She got a thoughtful look on her face, and Rance hoped it meant she was coming up with a solution to his problem. "Now that I think about it, there was one other time that flowers showed up on Luther Hightower's grave, after Rose and the boy moved away. About thirty years ago..."

A woman approached Mrs. Larson, disrupting her rambling thoughts. "Excuse me, Mr. Montoya. I have to help Mae Ellen." Mrs. Larson scurried away.

It was obvious that he wasn't going to get anywhere here. Maybe if he tried the newspaper office. Then he stopped short.

Mrs. Larson was moving toward him, motioning to someone. And that someone was his red-haired neighbor.

Maggie responded to Mrs. Larson's insistent beckoning by putting down the dust rag she'd been using on the shelves. Aware that Mrs. Larson's urgent summonings usually meant some sort of wild-goose chase, she was in no hurry to see what the librarian wanted.

Until she saw who was standing beside her.

Curious to find out what her new neighbor had to do with Mrs. Larson's frantic gestures, Maggie picked up her pace, pausing at a table to pick up several magazines that had not been returned to periodicals.

Clutching the magazines to her chest, Maggie drew to a halt beside the two people. She turned to her neighbor.

"Hi. It's nice to see you again," she said before turning to the older woman.

"Oh, Maggie, you and Mr. Montoya know each other?"

"Yes. He's my new neighbor. We met last Sunday." *Montoya,* Maggie realized, would explain the dark skin and the unusually angular planes of his face.

"Oh, that's right. I had forgotten that you live near the Hightower place."

Maggie was too busy appreciating her new neighbor in his best clothes to listen to the librarian's chattering. "Good morning. And how is the...?"

"Bitch?" Rance finished, and grinned. "She's fine. She delivered four healthy pups around dark on the Fourth. Now that we've been through childbirth together, I guess I'll keep her."

Mrs. Larson interrupted. "I'm glad that you're acquainted. Maggie, I have work to do. Please help Mr. Montoya with what he needs." The older woman excused herself and walked away.

"Gladly," Maggie replied to the woman as she left. "What can I help you with, Mr. Montoya?"

"It's still Rance, like it was on Sunday. Mr. Montoya is my grandfather." He smiled. "And your name is Maggie. We didn't quite finish exchanging names the other day."

Maggie extended her free hand. "Maggie Callahan. It's nice to officially meet you, Rance." A pleasant warm sensation worked its way up her arm as Rance's strong, dark hand closed over hers.

"The pleasure's mine," Rance replied.

"Well, now that we've been properly introduced, what can I help you with?" Maggie marveled that she could talk coherently, considering the way her heart was beating.

"Mrs. Larson said you could help me with some back issues of the *Pittsville Partner*."

"Sure. They're in the storage room in the back. We

have a deal with the *Partner* to archive their back issues. We keep their copies, and they give us a free subscription.''

''Sounds fair.''

Maggie turned away from Rance Montoya's compelling black eyes. ''The storage room is back this way. I hope you don't have any allergies to dust. We don't have much traffic in there, so it's pretty dirty.''

''I think I can handle it.''

''What year were you interested in?''

Rance told her.

A groan escaped before Maggie could catch it.

''I got the same reaction from Mrs. Larson. Is the filing system that difficult?''

Maggie laughed. ''If there were any sort of filing system, it would be an improvement. Basically, the papers are just stacked. If we're lucky, they'll still be in something that resembles chronological order.''

Maggie deposited the pile of magazines she had been holding on a cart and indicated a door at the back of the main room. ''In there.'' She produced a key from her pocket and unlocked the door.

Rance entered first and located the string that turned on the bare bulb above them. He gave it a yank, bathing the cluttered, dusty room in dim light.

''Ugh. Cobwebs,'' Maggie muttered as she skirted an overloaded worktable and brushed the sticky strands from her hair. ''I think I'll force myself to come in here with the vacuum after work.'' She wiped her hands on her skirt.

''Why don't you get the cleaning crew to do it?'' Rance asked as he scanned the stacked shelves.

''I am the crew. Or at least part of it. Our operating budget keeps shrinking, and luxuries like cleaning were among the first things to go. Now we all pitch in after work and do it.''

Rance nodded, seeming to accept the explanation.

"These stacks of newspapers are unlabeled. How do we go about finding the issues I need?" He wore a definitely discouraged expression.

Maggie chuckled. "Trial and error mostly. There is some method in our madness, though. The stuff closest to the door is the most recent. We just have to work our way back."

Maggie studied the shelves of stacked papers, then hurried to a section and tried to pull the stack down. "Let's see this one." He reached to help her, and his warm hands touched hers. Maggie jerked back as if he were fire.

"I'll get it," he grunted as he took down the papers and showed her the top one.

"This one's 1976," Maggie announced as they both glanced at the date on the masthead.

"We're not too far off." Rance moved several feet farther down the row.

"Why do you care about ancient local history, anyway?"

"Curiosity about the haunted Hightower house," Rance replied as he slid another pile of papers from the shelf.

"Oh. You've heard the stories."

"From everybody but the real-estate agent."

Maggie laughed. "Bill's financed three kids' college educations on the resale of that house."

"Well," Rance stated with surprising finality, "he's made his last penny off my house. The buck stops here." He glanced at the masthead of the paper he held. "Bull's-eye!" He sorted through the dusty stack of yellowed newspapers. "I'll start with the mid-sixties. Is there someplace I can spread this out?"

"We normally don't let people bring the papers out of the room, but it's too dark and dusty in here. I think it'll be all right if you bring what you need out into the reading area. The light's better."

Rance picked up the stack of papers, and Maggie followed him out into the lit room. "I can handle the rest from here, Maggie."

Rance Montoya's sudden dismissal startled Maggie. She'd thought that they were getting along well, but the sudden chill was hard to ignore.

Maggie shrugged mentally. She didn't have time for neighbors with split personalities, no matter how attractive they were. She still had plenty of other things to do. "Call me if you need any more help." She turned and went back to work.

Rance supposed he'd been a little abrupt with Maggie, the woman who'd struck a feeling in him he never expected to experience. He turned and watched her walk away.

Why couldn't he keep his mind on what he'd come here for? She was attractive and obviously intelligent, but he had to keep reminding himself that she was a married woman. God, she lives right across the road, Rance reminded himself. He hoped he would meet the missing husband soon. Maybe that would keep him from thinking about another man's wife.

His mind returned to his work. He knew his father had killed himself in 1966, but reasoned that the answers he sought would be found in the years before and after that time. He probably could have learned all he needed to know by asking almost anyone in Pitt County about what had happened. But he couldn't ask anyone about it without giving the secret of his identity away. He didn't want anyone to know who he was until he had all the answers. And the only way to find out was to read these musty old papers.

Rance found a spot at a vacant table, as far away from Maggie as possible, and sat down. He dusted off the sheaves of yellowed newsprint and set the stack to the left of his elbow.

Carefully he unfolded the first issue from the stack and spread it out in front of him. The paper was old and brittle, but the print was easy enough to make out. Half-afraid of what he would discover, Rance began to read.

The morning passed quickly. Maggie had more than enough to do to keep her thoughts occupied and away from her enigmatic neighbor. By noon she had nearly forgotten Mr. Rance Montoya.

"Hey, isn't that your new neighbor over there?" asked Tess as she shook the rain off her umbrella and propped it against the wall by the door. "He sure cleans up good."

Maggie felt her face warm, and she looked away. "Really? I hadn't noticed."

"In a pig's eye. You'd have to be blind not to notice," Tess all but shouted. "Besides, you're blushing to the roots of your hair. You never could lie."

Maggie looked down and hissed, "Tess, lower your voice. This *is* the library."

"Any resemblance our little collection of books has to a real library is strictly coincidental." But Tess lowered her voice. "What's he doing here?"

"He said he wanted to get the straight scoop about what happened at the Hightower place way back when."

"So you did notice." Tess presented Maggie with a know-it-all grin. "You sound skeptical," she added, tucking her purse under her arm and walking around to the back of the circulation desk, where Maggie was seated.

Maggie shrugged and glanced over to where Rance Montoya was still engrossed in dusty back issues of the local paper. "I guess I believe him. He certainly has been at those old copies of the *Partner* for long enough. But something just doesn't ring true."

"Like how?"

"I don't know. His explanation for wanting the information is certainly plausible. He said everybody in town

has told him that the place is supposed to be haunted."
Maggie shook her head slowly.

"Can you blame him for being curious? Now that you
mention it, I am."

Maggie arched a brow. "Why? You've heard the stories
all your life."

"Yeah, but there's one thing about it that has bothered
me lately. I really didn't think much about it until I helped
Tom with a report on ghosts last fall."

"It couldn't have been too important. That was almost
a year ago," Maggie commented dryly.

Tess paused, a pensive look on her face. "I didn't make
the connection till now. Everyone says the so-called ghost
of Hightower's Haven is Luther Hightower. But it doesn't
make sense. Ghosts usually haunt the place where they
died or have come to complete some unfinished business.
And he didn't die at home."

"Nor is he buried on the property," Maggie added.
"But you have to admit that he could have some unfinished business, with that land-deal situation and all."

"Maybe," Tess acknowledged. "But what if it isn't
Luther there at all? What if it's somebody else haunting
the place?"

"Oh, really, Tess. We don't know of any other unexplained deaths around here." Maggie shrugged. "By the
way, Mrs. Larson told me she asked him if he'd had any
'manifestations.'" Maggie chuckled. "He said he hadn't.
And you know what else?"

Tess raised a questioning brow.

"He was pleasant enough until he'd located what he was
looking for. Then he gave me the brush-off."

"Gave you the old cold shoulder, did he?"

"Colder than a penguin on an iceberg," Maggie replied
dryly.

"Maybe he was just preoccupied," Tess suggested.
"I'm going over and say hey while you get ready."

"Why do I need to get ready?" Maggie watched Tess go around the desk.

"We have a lunch date, remember?"

"Do we?"

"I can see that you definitely need a break. You never forget about lunch." Tess crossed the distance between the circulation desk and the table where Rance Montoya was reading.

Maggie watched as her gregarious older sister chatted with him. He looked friendly enough, from a distance. He smiled at Tess and seemed to respond to her as he had earlier. Before he turned so cold. Was it something that Maggie said that had turned him off? Or just her?

Tess grinned at Montoya and turned to leave, then turned back. Maggie couldn't hear what she said, but Rance smiled and shook his head. Tess waved and hurried back to Maggie. "Are you ready? I'm hungry enough to eat two lunches."

Maggie chuckled, found her purse and umbrella and followed Tess to the door. What was not so funny was that tall, slim Tess probably *could* eat two lunches and not gain an ounce. At the same time, Maggie counted every calorie just to maintain her size ten. She and Tess actually weighed within a pound or two of each other, but on Tess's five-foot-eight-inch frame, it looked better.

"I invited Rance to join us."

Maggie stared at Tess. "You didn't! Did he accept?"

"No. I think he's shy."

"He's not shy, Tess. He just doesn't want to get to know us."

"Maybe if you'd show him some southern hospitality, he'd warm up."

"Maybe you should mind your own business," Maggie answered amiably as she unfurled her umbrella and prepared to duck out into the rain.

Tess pulled her back. "You are my business, little sister.

Besides, he sounded plenty southern to me. Maybe not Alabama southern, but he's from somewhere south of the Mason-Dixon line. Maybe you could give him a refresher course.''

"I'll think about it," Maggie told Tess, just to divert her from the subject. Her stomach reminded her of the business at hand, and she dashed outside.

Rance relaxed the instant the Popwell sisters left the library. It had been difficult to concentrate with Maggie in the room, but he had forced himself to keep his eyes on the newspaper. He'd had to read everything twice to make any sense of it. Maybe now that she was gone, it would go faster.

So far, he'd been able to figure out that Luther Hightower's troubles began when word got around that Interstate 65 was going to cut through a corner of Hightower land. From what he'd been able to piece together, Luther had speculated on more land surrounding the intersection of the proposed highway and the road that ran in front of his property. He'd taken on some partners, and they had bought the other three parcels around the intersection.

Rance still wasn't any closer to finding all the details. Small-town papers being what they were, there was a lot missing, including the names of the other investors. Rance was certain that one of them had to be the mysterious Mr. Drake.

He read on.

The group composed of Luther Hightower and his investors had expected that a highway off-ramp would be placed at the intersection. They had planned to erect the usual off-ramp conveniences and make a fortune. That had been before the ramp was slated for Myrtle Ridge, about five miles closer to Pittsville. Luther and his partners had gambled and lost.

Rance sighed, long and deep. He rubbed his tired eyes

and propped his head on his hands. He'd gleaned as much as he could from the stack of papers. He carefully re-stacked the pile and got up. He'd been sitting in the same spot for two hours, and his cramped legs protested. His stomach rumbled, telling him that he should have accepted the invitation to join Tess and Maggie for lunch. But his hunger for knowledge overrode his physical need.

Rance picked up the stack of brittle newspapers and carried them back to the shelf in the storage room. His stomach complained again, and he turned to go. But some-thing made him turn back. The answer he sought was here in this room. All he had to do was find it. He couldn't let a grumbling stomach get in his way.

Next to the pile he'd just gone through was the stack for the next year. The answer might be there. He took the papers down.

The reading went more quickly this time. Rance had learned to ignore the local gossip, so he just read what he needed. And, of course, distracting neighbor Maggie was gone. He skimmed through the first six months without finding much. But as the summer unfolded, Rance sensed that he was closer to his answer.

Luther and his partners had tried to sell the three extra parcels of land. When no buyers appeared, thinking that he could use the land to expand his farming interests, Lu-ther had then borrowed the money to buy out the other investors. At the end of 1964, Luther had had all the land, and a huge debt to pay.

Rance didn't have to read any more to figure out what happened next. Luther had been unable to repay the loan, and the bank had foreclosed.

Rance considered this new scenario. Since his father had paid off the investors, he no longer suspected that Drake was one of them. Instead, he turned his attention to the bank officer who'd worked the deal. He still didn't know who the man was, but he would bet good money he was the one who'd taken the land. His nemesis, Drake.

He policed up his stack of papers and crossed the library again. He guessed the answer would be in the year Luther Hightower had ended his life. Rance shoved the pile he'd finished back into its niche on the shelf and grabbed the next year off its perch, displacing dust and cobwebs. He read through that stack, and went back for another.

The answer was in these papers, he just knew it. But Rance's stomach complained again as he hefted the stack of papers off the shelf, and he sighed. He'd collected enough information to digest for one day, and if he didn't do some other digesting, he would be a bear to be around. Reluctantly he hoisted the papers back to their position on the shelf. At least he would know where to look next time.

Chapter 3

"The nerve of that man," Maggie muttered as she gathered up her purse and umbrella. "Leaving without even waving goodbye. I'll show him."

"Did you say something, Maggie?" Mrs. Larson looked up from her work.

"No. Sorry, I was just thinking out loud. I'm going to go on home now. Unless you need me for anything."

"Just one quick thing, Maggie," Mrs. Larson replied.

Maggie sagged against the desk. Would it really be one quick thing? She'd just made up her mind to kill Mr. Rance Montoya with kindness—her attempt at southern hospitality—and she was afraid she would change her mind if she thought about it too long. "Sure. What do you need?"

Mrs. Larson held out the application form that Rance had filled out. Maggie had forgotten about it. "Would you pop this into the file on your way past? I didn't get to it."

Was that all? Maggie held her breath, waiting for the rest. When no more came, she sighed with relief. "Sure."

She could look at what he'd revealed on the way across to the file cabinet. And it wouldn't be snooping. Not really.

He'd filled in most of the blanks with routine stuff. There wasn't much she didn't know already. She didn't know what she'd expected to find, but it had been more than this. The only thing that surprised her was that he'd noted that he was born in Pittsville.

She had never heard of any Montoyas there before. In a small Alabama town like Pittsville, a name like Montoya would be remembered. Maggie made a mental note of his date of birth and filed the form under *M*. There were no other Montoyas filed in the *M* section, she noted as she closed the drawer.

Maggie hung her purse over her shoulder and pushed through the door. The rain had stopped, and the sun was beginning to clear a path through the clouds. Maggie viewed the change with dismay. How could she make her world-famous spaghetti if the sun heated the house trailer to two degrees short of a steam bath? Even with air-conditioning, it was too hot for anything but the quickest recipes in her superheated trailer kitchen in July.

She would just have to risk it. If she was going to kill Mr. Montoya—Rance—with kindness, she would have to go all the way. She might want to show him southern hospitality, but she was sure his arteries wouldn't appreciate southern-fried everything. She wanted to impress the man, and somehow she didn't think cold tuna salad would do the trick.

By the time she had stopped off at the Winn-Dixie for the basic ingredients and driven home, Maggie wasn't sure she'd had the right idea. She could still back out, but she remembered his about-face earlier. She wouldn't back out now.

Rance had known he would have to split the cord of oak eventually to hasten the drying process, but he had put it off. For some reason, today seemed like a good time to get started. Maybe the cloudy, damp day had suggested cooler temperatures. Or maybe he wanted to work off some of the frustration he felt. He had finally found some of the answers to the mystery, but now that he had, they weren't enough. Now he just had more questions. Would he ever know the whole truth?

Rance stood back and surveyed his afternoon's work. It was amazing what a little righteous indignation could accomplish; he'd split nearly half a cord of wood in three hours' time. And maybe he'd done about a quarter cord too much, he thought as he flexed his stiffening muscles.

He hadn't split wood since he was a teenager back in Texas. Though he'd found his old rhythm quickly enough, he'd used muscles he hadn't exercised in years. Muscles he'd forgotten he had. Military physical training was fine, as far as it went, but it did not take the place of hard physical labor. He was going to be sore in the morning.

Rance jammed the ax into the chopping block and headed for the house. He was tired and hungry and in need of a shower. Or a hot, soaking bath, if he could stand the temperature. Maybe if he soaked his muscles in a hot tub and had a couple of stiff drinks, he wouldn't be too sore tomorrow.

He laughed. Nobody could be that lucky. As he strode back to the house, Rance decided to forgo the stiff drinks. He popped a couple of aspirin instead, as he ran a tub as hot as he could stand. Then he lowered his already rebelling body into the steaming liquid. There was something to be said for these big, old-fashioned claw-footed porcelain tubs, he thought as the hot water began to do the trick; they offered plenty of room for soaking his legs.

The water comforted his work-fatigued body and soon lulled him to sleep. Rance woke an hour later to water that was rapidly cooling, in spite of the ninety degrees in the house. Rusty was barking. And someone was knocking on the door.

Rance submerged quickly into the tepid bath. He needed to clear his sleep-drugged head, and he knew the water would help force his hair into submission. He pulled the plug and surfaced as the water began to drain. Shaking like a huge, wet dog, he stepped from the tub.

"Keep your shirt on! I'm coming!" he shouted toward the front of the house as he hastily toweled himself dry.

Maggie stood at the door, flanked by her son, Buddy, and daughter, Jen, and waited for Rance to approach. In rural Mattison, Alabama, it was customary to yoo-hoo and walk on in, but Maggie didn't. She had a feeling that Rance Montoya would need training before he would accept that time-honored convention.

She'd heard him holler from somewhere in the back of the house, so she knew he was home. She would just wait at the screen door until he let them in. If he did.

The house hadn't looked frightening in the bright afternoon sun, as she came up the red dirt lane, shaded by a blooming crepe myrtle hedge. It looked shabby and neglected, but hardly intimidating. Yet, as she stood on the porch waiting for Rance, she felt the hairs on the back of her neck rise as she remembered her conversation with Tess. As an adult, she shouldn't believe in ghosts. Should she?

The wicker basket containing the dinner she'd prepared grew heavy in her arms, and Maggie shifted positions, trying to ease the burden. She'd brought enough for four, though she wasn't counting on Rance inviting them to share. There was more than enough left at home if he didn't. She had prepared for his rejection. After Rance's dismissal that morning, Maggie wasn't even certain that he would thank her for intruding.

The tone in which Rance had bellowed for them to wait

hadn't sounded encouraging, even to Maggie's world-traveled ears. That was why she'd brought the kids with her. For protection. Well, maybe not that, but she didn't think it would hurt to have some backup. There was safety in numbers, after all.

Jennifer fidgeted, and Buddy scowled.

"This is boring, Mom. Can't we just leave this on the porch and go home and eat?" It was just like Buddy to think of eating. At thirteen, and nearly six feet tall, he ate more than Maggie and Jennifer combined. Having grown more than six inches in the past year, he needed all the nutrition he could get.

And he needed more guidance than she was prepared to give him. If only Chet hadn't died. So there Maggie was, standing at the front door of her attractive but standoffish neighbor's house. She wasn't really sure why it was so important that she establish a friendly relationship with Rance Montoya. She tried to convince herself that it was for her son.

"Shush, Buddy. I know people didn't call on their neighbors like this back in Virginia, but this is the way we make new people welcome here. We'll be finished soon enough, and we can go home."

Buddy scowled again. He started to say something else, but stopped and stared through the screen door as Rance Montoya came into view.

Rance was barefoot, and moved slowly and deliberately, but still with the catlike grace that she had appreciated earlier in the day. He must have dressed hastily, donning jeans that were zipped but not buttoned. And he was almost wearing a shirt, which he had pulled on over a body still wet from a shower. It hung on his shoulders, open, and Maggie saw more of a healthy man than she had seen in a very long time.

His hair was damp and tousled, and he raked a long hand through it as he came to a stop in front of the door.

With only the wire screen separating them, Rance looked at Maggie and then the kids. "Yes?"

Rance's uncertain question, and his unexpected male sexuality, startled Maggie into forgetting her carefully planned speech. She stared at him for a moment, taking in the broad chest, covered with thick, dark hair that traveled down his lean torso. The opened closure of his jeans rested against his flat stomach and barely kept him decent. A shiver of excitement ran through her, and Maggie stopped herself from supplying the last detail of the imagined picture her mind was drawing. She shook herself to attention.

"I'm sorry. We've come at a bad time." Maggie blushed, not because of her inarticulate response, but because of what she had been thinking. "We're here to welcome you to our community." She held up the basket.

Montoya smiled a huge smile that creased his dark cheeks and painted laugh lines around his eyes. "Come in." He pushed the screen door outward.

Maggie stepped back, allowing the door to swing open, and followed her offspring inside. She couldn't help noticing the stiff way Montoya had moved, and the grimace he hadn't been able to hide as he reached for the door handle.

She gave him the basket. "I have everything here for a complete spaghetti dinner. I wasn't sure you'd be set up for cooking yet." She looked around at the room, which was newly furnished in a tasteful style that fit the character of the old house. What had she expected? Plastic furniture and a lava lamp?

Rance followed her eyes on their private inspection tour. "I'm still trying to get the place livable. The kitchen functions, but just barely. I'm afraid I'll have to completely rewire the house before I can modernize the kitchen. Man, I miss my microwave." He grinned, then grimaced again, as he hefted the basket. "Thanks for this."

"Mr. Montoya, is something wrong?" He had seemed

agile enough that morning. What could have happened in
the short time since she saw him last?

"It's Rance, remember? I thought we'd established
that." Then he laughed ruefully. "When I got back from
town, I decided to attack a cord of firewood. The wood
won. I've just rediscovered muscles I'd forgotten I had."

Rance looked at Maggie and her children, standing just
inside the front door. He guessed he should invite them to
join him in the feast Maggie had prepared. The sauce
smelled fantastic, and his afternoon had left him with a
hefty appetite, as well as complaining muscles. The burger
he'd gotten on the way back from town had long since
worn off.

He started toward the kitchen, but the little group didn't
budge from their posts by the door. The boy, as tall and
skinny as Rance remembered being at that age, wore a
wary expression. He looked tense, and ready for fight or
flight. The girl, a preteen version of her mother, looked
downright scared. Only Maggie looked calm.

What were they afraid of? Then Rance remembered. Of
course! They had heard tales of the horrible, haunted Hightower's Haven. He'd even mentioned it himself that morning. Did the kids actually believe the tales? He grinned.
"I guess you've heard about the ghost."

The boy affected a fearless pose. "Yeah. But I'm sure
it's just a story." His voice sounded brave, but his eyes
said something else.

The girl made no attempt to disguise her discomfort.
"Do you really have a ghost?" she asked timidly.

"I haven't seen one since I've been here," Rance answered carefully.

"Some people hear night sounds and think they're
ghosts," Maggie explained.

The boy uttered a disgusted snort. "You won't see me

making up ghosts that aren't there to be afraid of," he said bravely.

"Well, I've got something that you'll find more interesting and friendlier than any ghosts. Why don't you come with me?"

Both kids looked at their mother.

"Sure, go ahead. I bet I know what it is. Remember the other day when Rance said his dog was having puppies? Well, he told me today that they had been born."

"Is that true?" the little girl asked, interest filling her carbon-copy blue-green eyes.

"Four of them," Rance announced heartily. "They're in a box in the kitchen."

Rance shifted the basket to one hand and moved his arm stiffly to point the way. He grimaced again. It would be several days before he was up to much hard labor.

"Buddy, why don't you take the basket and carry it to the kitchen for Mr. Montoya?" Maggie suggested.

The boy took the basket and puffed up with pride at being able to do the simple task. Rance was grateful to be free of the burden. He glanced at the girl and wondered what she was called.

Maggie seemed to be reading his mind. "I'm sorry. I should have introduced my children." She placed a hand on Buddy's shoulder and one around the girl's waist. "This is Buddy," she said, indicating the boy. Then she turned to the girl. "And this is Jennifer."

Jennifer offered her hand. "Pleased to meet you, Mr. Montoya. Now can we see the puppies?"

Rance had to laugh. He'd nearly forgotten about Rusty's litter after looking into Maggie's sea green eyes; obviously, Jennifer hadn't. He led the way into the kitchen.

Jennifer spotted the battered cardboard box and scooted over to it without waiting to be shown. She squatted down and watched, wide-eyed, as four squirming balls of fuzz jostled for the best spot at their mother's side.

Buddy deposited the basket on the table and followed his sister. He stood, trying to appear unimpressed as he looked down at the nursing pups. "What are their names?" he asked gruffly.

Rance remembered what it was like to be almost a man and yet not. Buddy was trying so hard to act mature, but Rance could see the boyish delight in Buddy's eyes.

"Well, the mama's name is Rusty. I haven't named the puppies yet. I thought I'd wait until they're bigger. I'm going to have to find homes for them, and their new owners may want to name them themselves."

Jennifer looked at Rance with wide turquoise eyes. "Can I have one of them?"

Buddy echoed his sister. "Yeah. Can we have one?"

Maggie sighed wearily. Another mouth to feed was all she needed. Her small home might hold one small puppy, but Rusty was a big dog. The puppies would be, too. What would they do when the puppy grew?

"I think it's a little soon to be asking to have a puppy. They can't leave their mother just yet" was all Maggie could manage. It was only a stall to avoid saying yes. Or no.

She looked away from her children and encountered Rance's midnight-black eyes. He looked at her, as if he understood her predicament, and nodded slightly. Maggie looked away just as quickly and busied herself unpacking the basket of food she'd prepared.

Rance crossed back to Maggie and leaned over, his breath brushing her neck as he apologized in a low tone, not intended for the kids to hear. "I didn't mean to get you into a jam with the kids."

Maggie's heart fluttered, and she drew in deep breaths of air as she tried to decide what to say. "You've seen where I live," Maggie explained quietly, grateful that Rance did understand. His warm breath on her skin was more than distracting and sent chills down her spine. Chills that couldn't be explained by the temperature in the room. "We might have room for a puppy now, but they grow," she explained, moving away.

"I know. But what if I let them adopt one and keep it over here?"

That was an alternative, but Maggie still had doubts. She hadn't forgotten the Jekyll-and-Hyde act that he had treated her to that morning. Would he turn on her kids the same way? She couldn't risk it. "I'll think about it."

Rance seemed to accept Maggie's answer. He lifted the lid of one of the pots. "This sauce smells great. How did an Alabama girl learn to cook Italian?" Rance set the pot on the old gas range and struck a match.

Maggie smiled. "Twelve years as an air-force wife allowed me to see more of the world than Alabama. I learned to cook Italian when we were stationed in Japan."

Maggie grinned at Rance's surprised expression.

"And I suppose you learned to cook Japanese in Germany?"

"Something like that. Actually, I was in Washington State. I never got to Germany. But I learned to cook German in Virginia." Maggie looked around. "Where are your dishes?"

Maggie's breath caught in her throat as Rance leaned toward her and snaked his arm around her shoulder. "They're in the cabinet here."

She turned as Rance pulled the cabinet door open, wincing as he reached for the stack of plates. His close and intensely masculine presence was strangely unnerving. And Maggie wished he would button his shirt.

"I think I owe you an apology about this morning," Rance said quietly as Maggie set a pot of water on the stove to boil the noodles.

She looked up, puzzled. It was the last thing she'd expected to hear.

"You had been very helpful, and I was rude. I had something else on my mind. And I had to get back here and attack the wood." He flexed his shoulder, wincing as he did. "I'm beginning to regret that decision."

The expression on Rance's face was sincere, and some of Maggie's doubts about him disappeared. Maybe the dog plan wouldn't be such a bad idea, after all. But she wasn't going to decide just yet.

Rance's voice interrupted Maggie's thoughts. "I haven't made a great impression since I showed up here. After the Fourth of July incident..." He shrugged. "And my rudeness today."

The apology didn't seem to require a response, so Maggie made none. She bustled about Rance's old-fashioned kitchen, quietly putting the final touches on the meal. She had never been good at idle conversation and had nothing else to say. Besides, being so close to him made her very uncomfortable. She shook her head at the notion that was forming. She had no business thinking about that stuff, anyway.

Rance drifted back over to the carton of puppies and chatted with the kids. Maggie felt vaguely disappointed that he had abandoned her so quickly, but she was relieved at the same time. She smiled as she watched him with the children. Rance had even managed to draw Buddy out of his shell.

Even more surprising than Rance's easy rapport with the kids was Maggie's growing attraction to the man. What business did a woman her age have panting after the first good-looking man she'd met in ages? She glanced away from where he crouched, joking and laughing with her children. Then, as if drawn, she looked back.

She studied the lean angle of his jaw and the straight, dark hair that fell unheeded into his obsidian eyes. So different from Chet Callahan, yet so familiar in the way he had fallen into an easy camaraderie with Buddy and Jen.

* * *

Rance had felt her eyes like cool daggers in his back. Though he had known she was watching him for some time, he had resisted the urge to turn and look back. There was that air-force husband of hers to consider. He'd served twenty years in the air force himself; there was no way he would cut in on a fellow serviceman's territory.

Finally, he could stand it no more. He looked up and found himself falling into Maggie's eyes. She lowered them quickly as they met his, and color rose into her creamy complexion. Rance watched, amused, as she fanned her glowing cheeks and muttered something about the heat in the kitchen.

He levered himself to an upright position and flexed his protesting muscles. Even his legs were sore. He sauntered over to the stove. "I hope it's ready," Rance announced. "The smell is too good to resist much longer."

Maggie flashed a smile that could have lit the darkest night. "All done." She handed Rance a platter laden with sauce-covered noodles. "Would you take this to the table while I straighten up here?"

Relieved to have something to do, Rance carried the platter to the table. He didn't know how much longer he could have resisted the urge to run his fingers through her fiery hair. He focused on the steamy spaghetti.

It tasted even better than it smelled, he discovered a few minutes later. Rance wasted little time with small talk, but ate ravenously. He had tried to temper his appetite and eat slowly, and almost succeeded.

Rance pushed his plate away and leaned back in his chair, feeling comfortable and satisfied. "That was the best pasta I've had in years," he announced. "Next time I'll have to fix dinner for you." And the mysterious missing husband, he supposed with regret, feeling guilty about lusting after a fellow airman's wife. Where was he, anyway?

Maybe he was on an unaccompanied overseas tour. "I'm a pretty fair Mexican cook."

Maggie smiled. "And you learned to cook that kind of food in New York City, I suppose," she responded dryly.

Rance laughed. Damn, she had a pretty smile. "No, I came to it naturally. I learned how to cook from my grandfather. He owned a small Mexican restaurant in San Antonio."

"And you didn't go into the family business?"

"No. Grandfather died when I was nineteen. I was in college, and I had no interest in keeping the restaurant. I wanted to be a farmer like my father, and I was studying agriculture at Texas A & M. When *Abuelo* died, I couldn't afford to finish, so I joined the air force. The rest, as they say, is history."

Rance realized that he had probably revealed more about his past than he should, but Maggie was so easy to talk to. And she couldn't possibly connect a boy from Texas with this place.

She looked puzzled. "The air force is a rather round-about route to being a farmer."

"I was a nineteen-year-old kid from San Antonio. I had no family and no money. I had to get the money to buy a farm first. The air force seemed as good a way as any to go forward." He laughed. "I finished my degree at night school. But the money took twenty years."

"So you joined for the money. What about your parents?"

"They died when I was a kid." It wasn't the entire truth, but for all he knew, his mother was dead. Surely she would have come back for him if she was still alive.

"I'm sorry."

Rance murmured a polite response, as embarrassed as Maggie probably was. He smiled sheepishly. "I read every book on farming I could find, but I've still got a lot to learn."

"If there's anything we can do to help you, let us know. My dad was in the same position about twenty-five years ago. I'm sure he'll be glad to help."

No wonder there had been no mention of the Popwell name when he was reading all those old newspapers! They hadn't even been here at the time, Rance realized with relief. Mr. Popwell must have bought his acreage after the bank foreclosed on Luther Hightower.

"Speaking of help, I could use some around here, getting the yard and peach orchard cleaned up. How about it, Buddy? I'll pay."

Buddy looked up from his third helping of spaghetti at the mention of his name. "Can I, Mom?"

"That is, if your husband doesn't need him to work for him," Rance added.

Jennifer glanced up from the design she was drawing in a puddle of sauce on her plate. "He won't mind. He's dead."

Chapter 4

"I tell you, Tess. I could have died right then and there."

"Oh, Maggie. What did you do?" Tess managed to ask between giggles.

Maggie took a long, cool swig from her glass of iced tea before she answered. "What could I do? I was mortified, but it was the truth. And Buddy, bless his heart, didn't blink an eye. Just kept scarfing down his spaghetti." It seemed funny now, two days later, sitting in the Pittsville Dinner Belle Diner. But Jennifer's blunt statement about Chet had seemed very callous and cold at the time.

Tess shook her head in amazement. "Well, the little darlin' did you a favor."

"You call embarrassing me in front of Rance Montoya doing me a favor?" Maggie looked longingly across the table at Tess's French fries as she played with her low-fat meal.

"She let Mr. Rance Good-lookin' Montoya know that you are available, in her own inimitably crass way," Tess clarified, brandishing a ketchup-covered French fry.

"But I'm not available," Maggie insisted, then shoved a forkful of tuna salad into her mouth. She chewed energetically to forestall any more conversation. She should have known better.

Tess took Maggie's otherwise-occupied silence as an invitation to continue. "I know you're interested, or you wouldn't have gone over there with picnic basket in hand."

Maggie swallowed. "I was just trying to show him some of that southern hospitality you were harping on the other day," she protested.

"And you wasted no time, sister dear. How long was it? Twenty minutes?"

"Good grief, Tess. It was more like five hours. And I'm not interested. He's a perfect stranger."

"Perfect is right. Stranger? No. After all, you've shared a meal with him and read his library application. You know everything there is to know about the man."

"Hardly." Maggie scooped up a forkful of fat-free cottage cheese. "And now I'm even paying for my good deed."

"I guess we'll just have to have Eula Larson amend the application form. Apparently, there are a few questions she forgot to ask."

Maggie had to smile. It was no secret that half the questions on the Pittsville Library application were for Mrs. Larson's curious eyes only, and had no business being on the form. Maggie sobered. "I can't help wondering if there's more about Rance Montoya than we know."

"You're not still hung up on that ax-murderer business, are you?"

"No. But Rance Montoya is not telling us everything. He's been pretty friendly since we saw him in the library, but I don't think he's being entirely forthcoming."

"You mean he's lying?" Tess's blue eyes grew wide.

Maggie sighed. "No. Just more like he's leaving things out."

"Like what?"

"Tess!" Maggie rolled her eyes. "He left it out. How should I know?"

"I guess you're going to have to do some investigating on your own."

"Of course." Maggie slapped her forehead and rolled her eyes. "I forgot. I'll just brew up a batch of iced tea. Then I'll lace it with truth serum and interrogate him until I get the answers."

Tess shrugged and gave Maggie one of her irritating big-sister grins.

Maggie shook her head and looked at her watch. "I have to get back to the library," she said as she plucked her napkin from her lap and tossed in on top of her emptied tuna platter.

"Yes, you do have to go back to the library," Tess commented knowingly as Maggie applied a fresh coat of lipstick.

"What's that supposed to mean?"

"He's not the only one who can use the library for research."

"Don't be ridiculous, Tess. I'm not going to spy on the man."

"You wouldn't be spying. The *Pittsville Partner* is public record." Tess raised her eyebrows in an unspoken challenge. "Besides, Mata Hari Larson might know something else."

Maggie slid out of the booth and adjusted her skirt. "Is that a dare?"

Tess shrugged. "I think we're a little old for dares. Just call it a suggestion."

"I'll think about it." Maggie tossed the words over her shoulder as she crossed over to the register and paid her check.

And she did think about it as she crossed the street and walked back to the library. But she didn't do anything.

It didn't look as if there was much in the peach orchard that could be saved, Rance finally forced himself to admit as he lowered himself to sit in the shade of a gnarled old tree. Most of the trees were dead, or nearly so. Only one or two showed evidence of having borne fruit recently. Rance sighed. He had hoped to bring the orchard back to fruition, but it was just too far gone.

He grabbed a match from his pocket and chewed on it as he swiped an arm across his brow to catch a trickle of sweat that threatened his eye. Managing only to smear the wetness around, he peeled out of his T-shirt and used it to mop his forehead. Damn, it was hot.

Buddy loped over, sank to the ground beside Rance and reached for the five-gallon insulated water jug that sat between them. He grimaced when only a trickle of water came out. The boy looked as sweaty and tired as Rance felt.

The kid had worked like a Trojan, hauling out the deadwood that he'd cut. For a scrawny kid, he had stamina. Rance had studied the boy as he worked, searching for any resemblance to Maggie. He'd found none, and assumed that Buddy must take after his father. The avid way the kid hung on his every word showed how starved he was for male guidance. And maybe it wasn't his place, but Rance was happy to give it.

Rance wiped the sweat from his eyes and sighed. He was sorry that the kid had to grow up without a father, but more than relieved that it meant his mother was available. That Buddy was hungry for male companionship had been evident from the way the kid had hung on his every word. Hell, he'd even enjoyed the fatherly talk he found himself having with Buddy during one of their longer rest breaks.

They'd spent the better part of the day clearing out the

scrubby pines that had taken over the neglected orchard. Rance wondered idly what he was going to do with all that cut pine; it was too small to use for lumber. And too tarry to use as firewood.

"Look. Somebody's coming."

Rance followed the boy's pointing hand to a plume of dust headed their way.

"Let's go see who it is." Rance hoisted himself up out of the meager shade of the tree and headed for the lane. He debated whether to put his shirt back on, and discarded the notion. It was soaked through with perspiration, and it would just make him more uncomfortable than he already was.

He looked up and realized that the ninety-degree-plus heat had changed the blue sky to a milky white and the air was thick with moisture. Skies like this could brew up a thunderstorm in no time at all, and the white overcast was already starting to turn gray.

Rance turned to Buddy, who was scrambling up behind him. "Go back and get our stuff. I think it's time we called it a day."

Buddy trotted back to the tree where the water jug and the chain saw were, and Rance went on to greet the visitor. He reached the spot where he'd left his truck just as a dusty gray minivan pulled up.

Rance wished he'd gone ahead and put his shirt back on when he saw Maggie come around the van, but it was too late now. Besides, she was hardly unfamiliar with male anatomy, having been married. He took the match out of his mouth, broke it, tossed it away and waved.

"You look like you've put in a good day's work," Maggie called. "I thought you might appreciate this about now." She looked like an angel, carrying a sweating plastic jug and a stack of tumblers.

Rance grinned. "Thanks. We just emptied ours. How did you know?"

"It goes fast on hot, muggy days like this." Maggie undid the top of the jug and poured a tumblerful of cool liquid. She handed it to Rance as she looked over his shoulder for her son. "As I was driving over, I heard over the radio that we're under a severe-weather watch. Are you about finished?"

"I think so. We'd run out of water, and I didn't much like the looks of this sky." Rance glanced skyward as he reached for the tumbler, carefully avoiding touching Maggie with his grimy, sweaty hands. Was that the only reason he was trying not to touch her?

"I'm glad you made the weather decision. I was afraid I'd be accused of being an overprotective mother if I came over and told Buddy he had to come in out of the rain."

Rance laughed at that. He ran the cool, sweating tumbler of liquid across his heated brow. Then he took it to his lips to drink. It was lemonade, he realized after he had tossed the whole thing down in one gulp. He sighed contentedly. "This is good."

"Daddy always likes lemonade when he's out in the hot sun. He says it quenches better than water."

"Yeah. I suppose it does." Damn, she looked good. Even with her red hair plastered damply to her head. Her blouse clung to her, moist with perspiration, and revealed all the curves it was meant to hide.

Buddy crashed through the underbrush, carrying the jug and the chain saw, giving Rance another topic of conversation. "Your son did a good day of work for me," Rance told Maggie as Buddy deposited his load in the bed of the pickup.

"That's a surprise." Maggie laughed. "I can never get him to clean up his room." She poured her son some lemonade.

"Aw, Mom. That's women's work."

Rance looked at Buddy as the boy reached for the glass.

"Remember what we talked about earlier. Sometimes men have to shoulder responsibilities they don't want."

Rance didn't know who looked more surprised at his statement, Maggie or Buddy. But Maggie recovered first. She wore a very grateful expression, but had the grace not to rub it in.

"Get your stuff together. I'll drive you home," Maggie said to her son.

The boy looked as if he was going to protest, but Rance fired him a stern look. Reluctantly Buddy went to his mother's van.

Maggie looked up into Rance's eyes, her own eyes seeming to draw him into their cool green depths. "Thank you," she said softly. "He really does need a man's influence. I try, but I don't seem to make the grade." She turned and climbed into her van.

Rance watched as she backed to a wide spot in the dirt track and turned around. With a jaunty wave, she gunned the engine and left him standing in a cloud of dust.

He didn't know why Maggie felt she didn't make the grade. She was A-plus in his book. And one day he was going to tell her so. And now that he knew she was available, he had plenty of time to plan his course of action.

The air seemed to press down on her as the white haze grew into thick, dark clouds. Nervously Maggie scanned the sky to the southwest as she plucked clothespins and T-shirts off the line. It was a little late in the summer for tornadoes, but you never could tell. Any summer storm could produce severe winds, if not a twister. A gust of wind blew in the smell of rain, and thunder rumbled ominously. She hurried to finish taking in her washing.

The impending storm kept Maggie from reflecting much on her brief exchange with Rance Montoya earlier in the day, but then the thought of Buddy brought it all back. It wasn't so much what her teenage son said as what he did.

Or didn't do. Buddy hadn't exactly volunteered to help with supper, but he hadn't argued about it, either. Perhaps he was just too worn out from his day's work, or maybe Rance's words had hit home. Whatever the cause, Maggie appreciated the change. Even Jennifer seemed to notice the difference.

They sat down to eat a quick dinner of sliced, cold ham and salads just as the first wave of the storm reached them. Wet drops of rain began to pelt the windows. Maggie held her breath as the lights flickered. They stayed lit, but she jumped up to locate a flashlight, matches and candles, just in case. She had always enjoyed a good thunderstorm, but Jennifer had never liked them. And it didn't hurt to be prepared.

Jennifer reached for a serving of potato salad just as the lights winked again. This time they flickered and went out.

"Mom." Jennifer's voice was panicky. A flicker of lightning showed the child's hand still poised in midair, holding the scoop of potato salad.

"It's okay, Jen." Maggie switched on the flashlight and propped it on the table. She struck a match and lit the two candles she'd arranged in the center of the table.

"See, Jen. Dinner by candlelight." Was that really Buddy's voice? Yesterday he would have teased Jennifer about being afraid of the dark.

What had Rance said to her son? He must have done something she hadn't thought of. Whatever it was, Maggie liked it.

It was early enough that it still should be light outside, but the storm had made it as dark as midnight. The thick clouds and driving rain made it impossible to see outside, and the sound of thunder and rain lashing against the aluminum siding of the double-wide made conversation impossible. They finished the meal quickly and without speaking.

Normally the kids disappeared immediately after a meal,

each attending to his or her own agenda. But tonight neither of them moved, both of them more than willing to remain in their little island of light and their mother's protection.

The storm dissipated as quickly as it had built. In less than an hour, the sky had begun to clear, rinsed free of the heat and humidity. It showed off with a rainbow and then the glorious beauty of the setting sun.

As soon as it was safe, Maggie and the kids piled outside to appreciate the grand finale. Maggie toweled off the wooden glider swing that sat in the shade of the mimosa tree in the yard. She and Jennifer took a seat there and swung gently as Mother Nature did her best to impress them.

Buddy lounged on the front stoop, less impressed by the colorful show. He scanned the grounds and the trees and the road. "Mom, Rance is going somewhere."

Maggie looked down the road to the narrow lane that led to Hightower's Haven. The red pickup was turning out onto the road and heading their way. She couldn't help wondering where he was going at this time of day.

She didn't wonder long. The little red pickup truck, glistening with raindrops, turned into her lane. Maggie rose to greet him, suddenly all too aware of the dampness soaking into her skirt from sitting on the saturated wooden swing.

"Hi. How'd you weather the storm?" Maggie called as Rance swung his strong, lean body out of the truck. He'd changed clothes and was wearing an appropriately buttoned shirt, she noticed with relief. Or was it regret?

"You stole my line. That's what I came to see you about." He crossed the yard and took a spot on the stoop next to Buddy.

"We're snug as bugs. How about you?" Maggie asked. "I'd have thought your old house would be full of leaks and drips."

"Only from the bathroom window I forgot to close."

Rance laughed. "That house was built to last, and all the previous owners tried to keep it watertight. The roof is nearly new." He looked down toward the spot where the tower to Hightower's Haven showed among the trees.

"I guess folks always made sure they had a solid roof to live under before old Luther's ghost ran them off." Maggie was unprepared for the look of…what?…that came over Rance's face. What she meant to be a joke had apparently struck Rance deeply. "I'm sorry, I suppose that was tacky of me." Then she remembered what Tess had mentioned the other day in the library. Could there be another ghost at play in Hightower's Haven?

Rance said nothing in response to Maggie's apology. He just dug in his pockets and came up with a match. Maggie watched as he stuck it in his mouth and gnawed on the end, then rolled the wooden stick from one corner of his mouth to the other. Finally he removed the match and sighed.

"I think my…Mr. Hightower has had a bum rap for all these years," Rance said as he broke the stick in two and pushed himself upright. "I haven't seen any sign of him at all." He tossed the pieces of stick into the wet grass.

The momentary slip of the tongue almost passed Maggie by unnoticed. But she had caught his hesitation. Suddenly the curiosity she'd claimed not to have was up and running. The stricken look on Rance's face had to come from deeper than just a reference to his resident ghost.

"You know, I certainly felt nothing unusual about the house when we were over there the other day." Not like the time she'd tried to camp there and been frightened away, she thought but didn't say. "In fact, I felt quite welcome."

Rance grinned. "You sure it wasn't my wonderful hospitality?"

"It could have been."

Rance started for his truck.

Buddy asked the question that Maggie had wanted to voice. "Do you have to go?"

"Yeah. I just came over to see how you were."

"Thanks. We're fine," Maggie murmured as she watched him cross the tiny yard and climb into his truck. "Don't be a stranger," she called as he switched on the engine.

And she vowed that he wouldn't be, if she had to pester him herself. He'd done more with Buddy in one day than she'd been able to in two years. Rance seemed to care about her. Them.

But he was obviously hiding a secret. And now that it was plain to her, Maggie Callahan was determined to find out what it was.

The truck's headlights caught something in their high beams. Curious, Rance slowed the truck to a crawl and inched down past the entrance to Hightower's Haven. He was nearing the narrow, low bridge that spanned Beaver Creek.

Was it his imagination, or did the water seem to be unusually high? The little stream usually meandered lazily through his property and passed under the bridge. Then it wandered just as sluggishly through Joe Popwell's place. Maybe it was normal for the creek to run high after such a heavy downpour. Rance had only been around for a little over a week, hardly enough time to get to know the normal fluctuations of the stream.

He stopped the truck and climbed out, leaving the lights on. He followed the headlights' beams down to the bridge and took a careful look. The bridge seemed sound enough, and there was no evidence that the water had undermined the structure. But the water level was definitely higher than Rance had seen it before.

He took another long look, then returned to the truck.

Everything seemed all right for now, but first thing in the morning he would go out and check again just to be sure.

The sun was awfully bright for this time of morning, Maggie thought as she rubbed her eyes and blinked herself awake. She looked at the clock. No wonder it was so bright. She'd overslept!

Its red digital display blinking, the bedside alarm clock reminded her of what she'd forgotten to do the night before. The power had still not returned when Maggie went to bed, and she'd forgotten to set the windup backup alarm. She groped for her watch on the bedside table. Eight o'clock. And she had to be at the library by nine.

"That's one of the joys of country living I had conveniently forgotten," Maggie muttered as she flung herself out of bed. Grabbing her robe, she headed for the bathroom and her wake-up shower. She banged on the kids' doors as she passed.

Ten minutes later, she emerged from a cloud of steam, refreshed and awake. Dripping from her shower, Maggie peered through the clouded mirror, but she couldn't see well enough to put on her makeup.

"I wonder if I'd scare too many people if I went in without my face on, just this once?" Maggie muttered, squeezing toothpaste onto her brush. She brushed her teeth without being able to see her reflection in the mirror. Too bad she couldn't do her makeup by the Braille method as well.

Hoping she would have time to do her face when the mirror cleared, Maggie tugged her robe over her damp body. Still tying the sash, she headed back for her bedroom.

The kids' doors were still closed, and Maggie sighed. "I don't have time for this," she muttered as she banged on their doors again. Two sleepy voices answered, assuring

Maggie that they were awake. Relieved, she headed for her room to dress.

Just as she reached her bedroom door, she heard a loud banging at the front of the house. She turned back down the hall.

"Kids, are you making that noise?"

Buddy stumbled out of his room, rubbing his eyes. "Not me."

The sound came again. Someone was at the front door. Maggie hurried to answer it.

It wasn't usual for people to come calling this early, even in rural Mattison. Taking the side of caution, Maggie peered through the drawn drapes to see who was there.

Rance Montoya, dressed in running shorts, his bare chest glistening with sweat, stood outside. Maggie wanted to take her time examining his rock-hard, tanned body, but she let the curtain fall back into place.

"Damn. And here I am with no face, no clothes, and no time." Maggie tugged her robe tightly around her and reached for the doorknob.

Chapter 5

How long could it take to get from one end of the tiny house to the other? Rance fretted impatiently as he waited, still breathing hard from his record-breaking dash up the hill from the bridge. A movement of the curtains at the window showed him that someone was up.

The sight of Maggie in a damp cotton robe nearly made Rance forget what he'd come for, and shot his almost-normal-again pulse rate back into the danger zone. The clingy fabric left very little of Maggie to his well-tuned imagination. And he liked what he saw.

"I'm sorry to get you up this early, but I need to use your phone. Mine's not in yet."

Maggie pointed him in the direction of the phone on the wall.

"The creek's overflowed. The bridge is under water." Rance snatched the phone off its cradle, then realized he didn't know who to call. He turned to Maggie and tried to ignore the inviting view as he explained. "I'm sure I should notify somebody about this, but who?" Rance stared, mesmerized as a tiny trickle of water made its way from Maggie's damp russet curls, down her cheek, to the corner of her mouth. She caught it with the tip of her tongue and nearly drove him wild.

Maggie took the phone from him, brushing his heated fingers with her cool ones. "I don't know, either, but surely Daddy will." She punched in a number.

Rance took the opportunity to look around the tiny home. Anything to keep from looking at Maggie in her delicious state of undress. In spite of its small proportions, Maggie had arranged the room well, making the best of the cramped space. It was obvious that he wasn't looking at standard-issue trailer furnishings. He wondered why she would leave a much wealthier lifestyle to come way out here.

Maggie put down the phone. "Daddy says he'll call the county road commissioner. They'll have to check out the bridge. In the meantime, he says that he'll have to see if he can find out where the stream is blocked. I imagine a tree or some other debris from the storm has fallen and dammed the creek. If the bridge is flooded, the obstruction must be on our side of the road. Will you be able to give him a hand?"

"Yeah. No problem. I guess I should have told somebody last night. I saw that the water was high, but I figured it was normal after a storm."

As much as Rance enjoyed looking at Maggie in her almost-undressed state, he wished she would put her clothes on. It was too much for his heart to take so early in the morning. And the tightening he was feeling in his groin was going to be damned hard to hide in these nylon running trunks.

"Go on and finish dressing. I'll go home and change into work clothes. Tell your dad I'll be back to help," he told her as he reluctantly turned to leave.

An expression that could only have been described as

dismay came over Maggie's face, and Rance hoped it meant she was sorry he was going. "Oh, no," she wailed. "If the bridge is out, I'll have to drive to Pittsville by way of Mattison. And I'm already late."

So much for that idea, Rance thought as he heard the reason for Maggie's distress. She turned abruptly and headed for the back of the house. Rance chuckled as he watched her well-shaped backside disappear down the hall.

The obstruction that had dammed the creek was easy enough to find. Rance, Joe Popwell and Buddy just followed the edge of the ever-widening stream until they found the dam. It was barely a half mile away from the point where the road crossed the creek.

Rance stood with his hands on his hips and surveyed the small logjam. It was amazing to him that a few logs and branches could stop a creek so quickly. He reached for a match and discovered he'd forgotten them. Taking a sprig of grass, he turned to look at the dry side of the dam, where Buddy was picking his way across the muddy stream bed, using rocks and stones that had not felt the touch of air in a long time. The rocks and mud floor of Beaver Creek showed through clearly, where once water had been.

Before doing anything about the logjam, Joe Popwell surprised Rance by saying, "I heard there's supposed to be a deep pool down yonder somewheres that's probably a good fishin' spot. I never looked before, 'cause I just couldn't get down to it, with the trees and all. Reckon I'll just stroll on down and take me a look."

The older man set off down the stream, picking his way over slippery rocks. He was surprisingly agile for a man of his age, and moved fast. Rance watched him as he went and realized that Maggie must have gotten her Irish coloring from her father. His hair was that muddy kind of gray that redheads always faded to, and his rough, work-

worn hands were covered with freckles. Rance laughed.
Tess must look like her mother.

Joe was almost out of sight when Rance heard an excited yell. A list of possible reasons for Joe to shout ran
through Rance's head, most of them bad. He sprinted, slip-
ping in the mud and the puddled water in his haste. Buddy
brought up the rear. When Rance arrived at the spot where
Joe was standing, he saw the reason for Joe's excitement.

The man was staring into a deep pool, clearly visible
now that the creek level was lowered. "What do you make
of that?" Popwell asked, and pointed to a large, rusty form
barely visible in the murky water, still cloudy from the
storm.

Rance stared at the hulk, and chills ran down his spine,
in spite of the July humidity. The submerged object was
a car.

"How you reckon it got there?" Joe asked.

Buddy looked in and provided his opinion. "It's a car,
isn't it?"

"Yeah, an old Chevrolet, I'd say." How he knew that,
he didn't know, but he was positive of the make, if not
the model. Another chill raced through him. Rance surveyed the close growth of forest around them. "But how
the hell did it get through here?"

Judging from the tangled underbrush that surrounded
them and the rounded styling of the car's roof, Rance figured the car had been there for a very long time. The length
of time was of less concern to him than the reason. It
would have taken a lot of work to get a car to the pool
through the woods and the trees that far from the road.
Nobody would do it just for fun.

Was foul play involved? There was no way that car
could have gotten into that water by accident. It had to
have been put there intentionally. Another set of chills
overtook him. Could there be a body in there?

Joe Popwell had apparently been thinking along similar

lines. "I druther just pull out a few of them logs back yonder and get the water running again, but I think we ought to call in the sheriff. He'll want to take a look while the water's down."

"I think you're right." Rance stared down into the murky water, at the barely visible hulk. He didn't know why he was so certain, but he had a terrible feeling he knew whose car that was.

ROSIE H. Why had that image popped into his mind? Rance shook his head. He would just have a little while longer to wait.

The car tags would prove it beyond all doubt.

But he hoped he was wrong.

The news that her father had found a car submerged in a pool in the creek found its way to Maggie in the library by the usual small-town grapevine. By the time she took her lunch break, it was all over Pittsville. By the time she got home, it was almost all over.

Maggie pulled her minivan into her lane at about four o'clock, having driven the long way, via Mattison, just in case. By the time she'd changed into jeans and walking boots and smeared on sunscreen and mosquito repellent, the sheriff's department was almost finished. The diver had concluded his underwater search and was preparing to hook a towline to the car.

Maggie edged into the crowd of onlookers who had found their way to the site by way of the newly cleared track through the pines. For a small town, there were an awful lot of gawkers hanging around.

She looked for her family among the jam of people. Her dad was easy enough to find; he was leaning against a tree, operating on a piece of wood with his pocketknife. A moment later, she spotted her daughter. Why wasn't she at Mom's? That question was answered a second later, when Maggie caught sight of Daisy Popwell's silver cap of hair.

Buddy was standing to one side looking important and smug. Then Maggie realized why. Her son was being interviewed, or so it appeared, by Harper Clodfelter, the reporter for the *Pittsville Partner.* Maggie chuckled. That would certainly give Buddy's adolescent ego a boost. *If* the story made it into print with his name in it.

She didn't see the one person she really wanted to see. Maggie scanned the crowd again, looking for Rance Montoya.

He was propped against a tree, intently watching the goings-on from his vantage point, well out of the way. Maggie's heart leaped. He looked so handsome, with his woven cowboy hat, and jeans that hugged his narrow hips and powerful thighs almost indecently. He looked more like a cowboy than a farmer, but instead of cowboy boots he wore laced tan leather work boots, and a red T-shirt stretched tightly across his broad, muscular chest.

A brief vision of white skin against tan flashed into Maggie's mind. Blushing, she shook it away.

The object of her attention plucked a piece of straw from his mouth and tossed it lazily to the ground. He must have felt Maggie's hungry eyes on him, for he looked directly at her and smiled. His smoldering eyes seemed to bore right into Maggie's soul. She looked away, embarrassed by the color that rose, unbidden, to her cheeks. When she looked for him again, he was gone. Disappointed that she'd scared him away, Maggie turned her attention back to the salvage operation.

"I guess this is more excitement than you've seen in a long time," said a familiar masculine voice from a spot just behind her.

Maggie spun around, startled. How had he gotten to her so fast? And so quietly? She took a deep breath and tried to still her racing heart.

Finally Maggie felt calm enough to trust her voice. She drew in a deep breath. "Do they know anything yet?"

Rance slid his arm around Maggie's waist, making her heart turn flips as he propelled her toward a secluded spot in the shade. "Not much. The diver didn't come up with anything. Not even car tags." A pained expression crossed his face fleetingly.

Odd, Maggie thought. He seemed really bothered by the car. Especially the missing tags. "Is there…?"

"A body? No." Rance had a disconcerting habit of finishing her sentences.

Maggie looked up into Rance's dark eyes. He was smiling, but his eyes were clouded. Was it her imagination, or had the lights that had shone from within dimmed? Why was he always so confusing? Maggie renewed her vow to find out more about Rance Montoya.

Or am I just confused? Maggie asked herself. It had been a very long time since she had any practice dealing with men who were not family. Could she be that rusty, that the unfamiliar about someone new became something to distrust? Maggie wasn't certain what to think. She wanted to trust him, but he seemed to be keeping something inside. Would he ever open up?

"Maggie?" The sound of Rance Montoya's rich voice speaking her name penetrated her muddled thoughts.

"I'm sorry. I was…" She couldn't tell him that she'd been wool-gathering about him. "I was wondering about the car," she said lamely.

"Me, too" was all Rance said.

The growling whine of the electric winch of the truck with Ted's Toe Truck painted on the side interrupted the silence. Maggie and Rance both turned in response to the sound.

The slime-covered, rusty hulk rose slowly from its watery grave until it strained against the surface. The tow truck quivered and shook with the waterlogged weight and tugged on. The car seemed to hang suspended, half in and half out of the water. Then, with a jerk, it lurched over the bank and onto dry land.

The terrain was rough, covered with rock, scrub and debris from the hasty clearing job that had been done to provide access to the fishing hole. Ted pulled the car away toward the main road to Pittsville and the sheriff's impound lot. As the truck and the car reached a position parallel to where Maggie and Rance stood, the car hit a concealed log. The force of the impact popped the passenger door open, sending a cascade of water and debris to the ground.

Rance made a cursory search of the ground for a small, misshapen object that had fallen from the car, but he couldn't find it. Why it was important for him to see it, to touch it, he didn't know. Yes, he did. Rance knew he had seen it before. Though he had only seen the object for an instant amid the debris, it had reminded him of something—something that, by all that was right, should not be here.

He had just started to make a more thorough search when he remembered the redhead at his side. How could he forget her? Her snug jeans and the tight tank top that stretched across her curves should have distracted him from anything. But for a moment he had forgotten. Damn. He wished this mystery would come to a conclusion. Would he ever learn the truth about his past, so he could get on with his future?

Turning back to Maggie, Rance forced the questions from his mind. "Look, I'd like to walk you home, but I promised Joe I'd stay to help clear the logjam when the sheriff gets done."

Maggie looked up at him expectantly, and Rance felt as if he would drown in her deep turquoise eyes. Why did she always make him feel so tongue-tied?

"I don't know when I'll be done tonight, but how about

dinner at my place tomorrow? I haven't forgotten my promise to fix you an authentic Mexican meal. The kids, too,'' Rance added.

That had been easy enough. Had he just asked Maggie for a date? Yes, he had. And he'd invited two chaperons. Damn.

"Sounds good. What time?"

Maggie's practical question brought him back down to earth. He thought a minute. "How about six? I have to mow the orchard and the area around the house. But I should be done early."

"Perfect. I'll make dessert." Maggie turned, but she stopped short and uttered a cry of pain.

"What is it?" His first thought was a snake, and he scanned the ground for signs of one.

"My hair," she muttered, reaching up behind her.

Rance saw that Maggie's riotous red hair was caught in the thick tangle of blackberry vines behind her. "Don't struggle. It'll just make it worse. I'll do it," he said as he reached behind her.

Maggie drew in a sharp breath, and Rance wondered if he'd hurt her as he tried to pull her free. But the rapid rise and fall of her chest seemed far out of proportion to the inconvenience of being caught in a bramble bush. He glanced at her face just in time to see her drop her gaze and the color rise in her face. It wasn't the stickers.

He willed himself to concentrate on the task at hand while a less controllable part of his body had other ideas. He tried to ignore the tingling in his groin, and almost succeeded. Almost. Then he loosened the captive strand with a gentle tug. "There, you're loose," he announced.

Free, Maggie stepped forward and stumbled on a tree root, falling right into his arms. Her soft body against his undid all his good intentions, and he stared down into her blue-green eyes.

"Rance, I..." Maggie pushed herself gently away, but, to her credit, she didn't avert her eyes. "Thank you."

"Don't talk," he whispered. "And I can think of a much better way for you to thank me." He looked down into her blue-green eyes with an unasked question in his own. Her forthright gaze seemed to answer yes. He drew in a long breath. "Let's just go with the moment." He lowered his head toward her, and she closed her eyes in quiet acceptance of his intent.

"*Mo*-om, Grandma wants to know if you want to eat supper at her house," a young voice called from behind them.

Rance groaned and stepped back, creating too much distance between them while Maggie ran her hand self-consciously through her hair. Jennifer's intrusion had dampened his heated feelings, so at least he could face the child and give Maggie a moment to compose herself. He turned and presented the girl with a crooked smile.

"Whatcha doin'?" Jennifer's innocent question had anything but an innocent answer.

"Mr. Montoya was helping me untangle my hair from these sticker bushes," Maggie replied as she stepped out from behind him. She pointed to a tuft of red fluff still caught in the briars.

Jennifer made a face. "Ooh... That must've hurt."

Not as much as being interrupted by you, Rance thought, but didn't voice.

"It wasn't too bad, but it was scary being caught so tight," Maggie explained, her voice still too breathy. She cast an apologetic look over her shoulder as she looped her arm over her daughter's shoulder and headed toward the trail.

With a wave of her hand, she left. He tried to follow her progress, but she quickly disappeared into the crowd of dispersing bystanders. Maybe it was just as well. It was much too soon for him to be thinking about her as a lover.

He knew he could handle it, but he wasn't so sure about Maggie.

Rance turned to look for Joe. "She didn't need to bring dessert," he mumbled as he strode across the clearing. *She was dessert!*

If only he could figure a way to get her to his home without the kids.

The invitation, and the strange expression she'd seen in Rance's eyes, worried Maggie throughout the evening. Not to mention the kiss that wasn't. It hadn't been enough to ruin her sleep, but she'd had an unsettled feeling that wouldn't go away. Though she looked forward to dinner with Rance Montoya, she still worried that he wasn't who he appeared to be.

When her doubts were still with her the next morning, Maggie decided to investigate. Anybody else would have just asked the neighbors about the story. Yet Rance had all but acted as if he had something to hide. If Rance wouldn't open up to her, then she would just have to find out on her own. After all, she had all the resources of the Pittsville Library at her disposal. And she already knew where to look.

The only problem was, she didn't know what she was looking for.

Maggie arrived at the library early on Saturday morning. She had allowed time to take the long way around in case the bridge was still flooded. But Beaver Creek had rambled lazily under the bridge, staying politely between its banks. The bridge seemed none the worse for wear, and Maggie arrived at work a full twenty minutes early.

She pulled out her key to let herself in, but the door was already open. Drat. Now she would have to explain why she was researching her new next-door neighbor. Mrs. Eula Larson would never let that get by without comment.

Composing a logical reason for wanting to know about

Rance's connection to the Hightowers, Maggie approached Mrs. Larson, who was working busily at her desk. "Good morning, Mrs. L. Do you have anything pressing that needs to be done?" Maggie crossed her fingers as she waited for the librarian's response.

Mrs. Larson looked up, a baffled look on her face. "No, hon. Why?"

Maggie glanced at the clock. "Since I'm here early, I thought I'd use the time for some personal research. If you don't need me."

"We're not officially open yet. Go ahead."

Maggie thought she had managed to avoid Mrs. Larson's inquisition. But she congratulated herself too soon.

"What are you looking up?"

Sighing with resignation, Maggie stopped and turned back to Mrs. Larson. "Rance got me curious about my ghostly neighbor. I thought I'd look him up."

"Didn't he tell you what he found?" Mrs. Larson asked absently as she sorted through a stack of cards.

"No. Frankly, it didn't occur to me to ask at the time. We were busy with the submerged car." Maggie resumed her course for the newspaper storage room, then stopped.

"Mrs. Larson, were you living in Pittsville when Luther Hightower died?" Why not use her nosy boss to advantage? There wasn't much that happened in Pitts County that Eula Larson didn't know about.

"Why, yes. I'd just married my Ray. Let's see, we married in 1965. Luther Hightower killed himself the next year." Mrs. Larson proceeded to describe her first years of married bliss, but Maggie tuned it out. She'd heard it all before.

"Do you remember what time of year it was?" Maggie asked when Mrs. Larson paused for breath.

"Certainly. It was right before Christmas. It was so sad. Him leaving that pretty young wife and his little boy like

that. And at Christmastime, too.'' Mrs. Larson tut-tutted
and shook her head.

''Do you know why?''

''Oh, yes. It was quite a scandal. He had lost the family
farm after a business failure. He shot himself after the bank
foreclosed on the property.

''His widow got the insurance money, but it wasn't
enough to buy the place back. In fact, I think most of it
went to the bank, but still didn't clear the debt. She took
the little boy and went to live with her folks. No one's
heard from them since.''

''Well, thanks.'' Maggie turned toward the storage
room.

''Oh, did I tell you?'' Mrs. Larson looked as if she had
the latest juicy gossip, and Maggie sighed. ''Somebody's
been putting flowers on Luther Hightower's grave.''

''So?''

''The last time that happened was right after the bank
sold the house.''

''Hmm…'' It didn't seem significant, but maybe Maggie
would have to think on it some more. ''I'm sure there's a
logical explanation. Maybe it was some distant relative,
just passing through.''

''I suppose,'' Mrs. Larson agreed reluctantly. Maggie
had a feeling the older woman had wanted to make a mystery out of it.

''Well, let me get to my research before we get inun-
dated by customers.''

''All right. You go on.''

Relieved, Maggie hurried away. She wasn't sure how
much of what Mrs. Larson had told her was of any help.
But she'd at least narrowed down the time of death to
about two months in 1966. She didn't know why, but Luther Hightower's obituary seemed to be the key to everything.

It didn't take Maggie long to find the issues of the *Pitts-*

ville Partner she wanted; Rance Montoya had already cleared the way. She leafed through the November issues. Nothing. Then, in the December 6, 1966 issue, she hit paydirt.

"Hightower Found Shot. Suicide Suspected," screamed the headline.

Maggie skimmed the story. The details were sketchy, pending a police investigation.

She moved on to the next issue. The story had been relegated to a corner of the front page, already displaced by a fire at the local grocery store. The article confirmed that Hightower's death was suicide and referred the reader to the obituary section.

Maggie flipped to the obituaries at the back of the paper. It was amazing how little the paper's format had changed in thirty years. She knew right where to look.

There were three death notices that week. Luther Hightower's was the shortest. He hadn't lived as long as the two other occupants of the section. Maggie was saddened by that, reminded of her own loss of Chet, who had also died before his time.

She skimmed the obituary, then read it again. The paper listed Hightower's survivors. There were only two. He was survived by his wife, Rose Montoya Hightower, and a son. She shrugged, ready to turn the page when she saw it. *Rance.* The boy's name was Rance! Rance Hightower. Rance *Montoya* Hightower?

Rance and Montoya were not common names, at least not around Pittsville, Alabama. A chill shuddered through her. It couldn't be a coincidence that thirty years after Luther Hightower's death, a man named Rance Montoya had bought his place. His age was even about right.

That probably explained the recent flowers on Luther Hightower's grave, but why hadn't he admitted it when Mrs. Larson brought it up the other day? And what about those other flowers that had been found, thirty years ago?

* * *

It had taken Rance longer to mow the tall grass and brush in the peach orchard than he had expected. So he was getting a late start on the overgrown front yard. He'd hoped to have time to search for the object he was sure had fallen from the car they'd found yesterday.

He parked the used light-duty tractor in the shade of one of the towering pecan trees by the house. He'd purchased the tractor with the remainder of his life savings, and he couldn't afford to make any undue repairs right now. The engine needed to cool, and so did he.

Rance went into the house for something to drink while the tractor cooled. A slight breeze blew through an open window as he sat at the kitchen table, nursing a tall glass of iced tea. He smiled.

In just a few hours, Maggie would be sitting at this table. Already he felt that she belonged here as much as he did.

He checked to see whether the meat was thawing properly in the aged refrigerator. Satisfied that it was, Rance downed the rest of his tea and went to finish the job.

The gas in the tractor was low, so Rance filled the tank before starting the machine. He guessed he should have gone over the yard to check for obstacles, but it was late; Maggie would soon be here. He'd walked the yard a couple of times before and not seen anything that looked dangerous. It would be okay.

Rance switched on the engine and smiled as the old tractor grumbled to a start. Some people got off on the sound of a shiny new car purring to life; he loved the throaty growl of this lumbering machine.

It didn't take long to lop off the tall grass and brambles that had overtaken the once-spacious yard, and he entertained himself during the mindless task with thoughts of Maggie and that kiss that hadn't quite happened, but that he hoped to get another shot at soon. The crude mowing job had made the yard look even bigger, but he decided to make one more pass around the edge by the pines before he quit.

Rance wheeled the big machine into position and lowered the cutting blades. In just a couple of minutes, he would be done.

At the end of his final sweep, he turned the wheel abruptly, eager to get the tractor into the shed.

He wasn't sure what happened next, but Rance felt a sudden jolt as he rounded the corner of the house and turned down the gentle slope that led to the equipment shed. One minute he was riding, the next the tractor was toppling over. Even though he seemed to fall in slow motion, Rance had no time to save himself.

He uttered a series of curses as he realized what had happened. A half ton of metal and growling engine lay on its side on top of him, trapping him underneath. By some miracle he had landed in a gap created by the huge tractor tire. It kept the full weight of the machine from crushing him, but didn't leave enough room for him to escape. He didn't think he was hurt, but he couldn't pull himself out from under the machine.

Damn. He couldn't move. He was pinned beneath a still-running engine with a full tank. The gravity of the situation hit him with a wallop as the odor of leaking gas reached his nose.

Stretching his arm as far as he could, Rance reached for the ignition. If he could just turn off the engine, it might not catch fire—as long as the spilled gasoline didn't make contact with the hot engine. His straining fingers found the key. He turned it.

Switching off the machine was just enough motion to cause the tractor to shift. Rance was still trapped, but now more of the weight of the tractor pressed down on him. After each attempt to free himself, Rance only felt wedged tighter. Finally, he gave up and lay still.

Rance flexed his fingers, then systematically tested the

rest of his extremities. He hurt like hell, but he could still move everything, so he guessed nothing was broken. And he didn't think he was in any danger of losing consciousness, though a nap would sure help pass the time.

Rance closed his eyes and forced himself to relax. He cursed his stupidity and set his mind for a long wait.

He hoped Maggie would be on time.

Or early.

Chapter 6

The old-fashioned ice-cream maker made a comfortable sound as it chugged and turned. Cranking the machine was one of the few chores the kids didn't complain about. In fact, they even patiently took turns. There was definitely something to be said about the positive reinforcement of homemade cherry-chocolate-chip ice cream, when it came to doing chores.

Maggie finished freshening her makeup and fluffed her hair. When she surveyed her appearance in the mirror, she was well pleased with the result. "Definitely okay for an old widow woman with kids," she told her reflection.

In just a few more minutes, they would be off to Rance's for dinner. She knew it wasn't really a date, but maybe they would get a chance to finish what they'd started yesterday. A thrill of anticipation ran down her spine as she remembered the way his hooded eyes had seemed to simmer as he lowered his head toward her. She was definitely looking forward to the date.

Then she glanced toward her children, still working with

the ice-cream machine. You couldn't call a dinner with two young chaperons a date, but it was close enough. And this was the first time since Chet died that she'd even had half an interest in someone of the opposite sex. Maggie smiled and headed for the kitchen. Maybe Tess had been right, after all. Maybe she did need a man.

"Mom, can we have some ice cream now?" Jennifer asked. She never could wait until after a meal for dessert.

Laughing, Maggie said the same thing she told her daughter time after time after time. "Dessert is for after you eat, not a warm-up."

Jen looked up as Maggie crossed into the living room. She grinned. "Just once, I wish you'd say yes."

Maggie grinned back. "Maybe just once I will. But not today. I promised Mr. Montoya we'd bring dessert. How would it look if half of it was gone before we got there?"

"It would look like it was real good ice cream," Buddy said as he looked up from his cranking duties.

Maggie laughed. "I bet it would." She bent over to check what Buddy had done. "A couple more cranks and it'll be perfect," she said when she'd straightened up again.

Buddy made two fast turns with the crank and stood. "Done," he announced with finality. "Let's go."

"I'm ready. How about you two?"

As the kids scurried off to wash up and comb their hair, Maggie finished getting the ice cream ready, scraping the frozen confection from the big wooden paddles and covering the drum. In a moment, the kids reappeared with clean faces. Buddy dripped with water from freshly combed hair, and Jennifer had fluffed her carrot red bangs.

"Last one in the car's a rotten egg," Maggie said challengingly, knowing she would be last. She smiled and looked at the clock as she left the house. They would be a couple of minutes early. She hoped Rance wouldn't mind.

* * *

The sun had sunk low enough in the trees that it was
no longer shining in his eyes. Rance couldn't see his
watch, because of the way his right arm was pinned beneath him, so he didn't know how long he'd been lying
there, but it had definitely been a long time. He squinted,
trying to gauge the time by the position of the sun in the
afternoon sky. He guessed it was getting close to time for
Maggie and her children to arrive. The two hours he es-
timated he'd waited had stretched out like two eternities.
Please don't let her be late, he prayed.

A sound came from the road beyond the trees, and hope
soared. It was a car, but it kept going. Rance grunted a
curse when he realized that his wait was not yet over, then
grimaced in pain. Damn. He must be hurt a lot worse than
he'd thought.

Rance twisted his head at another sound. Rusty had
wandered over from somewhere. Where had she been all
this time? Even if the dog couldn't do anything to help, it
was reassuring to feel her wet nose nuzzling his cheek. He
reached out to pet her.

"I can't feed you right now, Rusty girl. But it sure is
good to have you here to keep me company."

Rusty whimpered soft and low and curled up protec-
tively beside him.

Rance closed his eyes, grateful for Rusty's comforting
presence. It couldn't be much longer now.

Another sound brought his eyes wide open, and Rusty
leaped to her feet. Another car. And, judging from the
sound of it, this one had turned into the myrtle-shaded
lane. Rance breathed another sigh, remembering to keep it
shallow, because his ribs hurt like hell.

Maggie heard Rusty's agitated barking before she saw
the tractor lying on its side. Then it took her a long moment to recognize the significance of what she saw. She

looked cautiously around but didn't see anybody, and she hoped that was a good sign.

She slammed the car to a stop and simultaneously cut off the engine. Then she flung open the door. Praying Rance was inside the house, she called to him.

A voice answered her from the vicinity of the tractor, and Maggie knew her prayer had not been answered. Concern rushed through her, replaced quickly by relief. Rance was alive. But how badly was he hurt? She raced to the source of the voice.

"I thought you'd never get here," Rance said calmly when Maggie came to a halt and looked down at him. Her hand flew to her mouth too slowly to stifle her gasp of dismay.

"I don't think I'm hurt too bad. Just pinned." Rance shifted his body and winced as the tractor settled on him.

"You are hurt." Maggie knelt beside him and, for lack of anything else to do, felt his forehead. It was as cool as could be expected, considering it was the middle of July and he had been lying outside for who knew how long in the afternoon heat.

Rance grasped her fingers with his one free hand. "I'll be all right," he said calmly, taking shallow breaths. "You and Buddy have to find a fence post or something to use to pry this thing off me."

Of course. Archimedes. Long-forgotten principles of physics came back to her as Maggie scanned the grounds for something to lever the heavy tractor off Rance.

Buddy and Jennifer appeared at Maggie's side, and their appearance spurred Maggie into action. "Jen, run home and call Grandpa and tell him what's happened."

The girl raced back toward the road.

"Buddy, do you know where you can find some rails or pipe or something to use to lift this off?"

"I think so." Buddy dashed off toward the shed.

"I need something to use as a fulcrum," Maggie muttered as she searched the yard for a rock or something that would work.

"There's a heavy metal tool chest in the shed," Rance said, his breath raspy. It was obvious to Maggie that he was trying mightily to hide his discomfort.

"I'll get it." Maggie raced for the outbuilding.

It took only a moment to locate the toolbox. Longer to get it to the tractor. It was too heavy for Maggie to lift, and she kicked it in frustration. The contents rattled inside, suggesting to her that she empty out all the heavy tools.

It took two more minutes to toss out the contents and close it up. Straining with its empty weight, Maggie reached the tractor just as Buddy appeared, dragging a length of cut pine tree.

"I knew I'd find a use for that trash wood eventually," Rance murmured with a weak grin.

Was he getting weaker? The shallow, breathy quality of Rance's voice worried Maggie, urging her on.

Frantically trying to remember her long-forgotten physics lessons, she told Buddy what to do. Soon they had the toolbox and the log in position.

But would it work? There was only one way to find out.

"Rance, I don't know whether I'll be able to right this thing. Do you think you could push yourself out if Buddy and I just lift it a little bit?"

"Yeah," Rance grunted. "All I need is for you to raise it a couple of inches. Then I think I can slide free."

Maggie tried to calm herself. Her racing heart was tiring fast. She took a deep breath. "Okay, Buddy. On three."

She counted. They pushed. Nothing happened.

Calm down, Maggie ordered herself desperately. "We can do this. Archimedes said he could move the world. All we need to do is move one crummy tractor." She pushed the toolbox closer to the giant wheel and repositioned the log.

Maggie took several deep breaths. "Again on three," she said, her voice raspy. Again she counted.

This time adrenaline surged through her veins and into her straining muscles. She could feel the tractor give. "Push, Buddy, push!" she shouted as she put all her weight on the straining tree trunk.

"Just a little more," came Rance's calming voice.

Tears filled Maggie's eyes. Where would she find the strength?

"Push, Mom." Buddy's face was red from exertion.

"Hold it there. I think I can slide out now."

Maggie held her breath as she watched Rance ease himself carefully from beneath the heavy machine and roll over onto his stomach. He grunted with pain, but Maggie couldn't go to his aid.

They had to lower the tractor slowly, so that it wouldn't bounce back onto Rance's prone body. Muscles screamed in agony as Maggie and Buddy lowered the tractor to the ground.

Weak with exhaustion and relief, Maggie sank to the dirt beside Rance. She couldn't have held on to that log another second, and she knew her legs wouldn't hold her up now.

"Thank God we got you out." Maggie closed her eyes and leaned her head against the huge black tractor tire that had so recently been Rance's prison.

"No. Thank you," Rance whispered softly.

Of course, it had been unrealistic to expect he would be able to get up and walk away, but Rance was unprepared for the weakness he felt. He flexed his muscles, systematically testing his body parts again, now that he was freed of the weight of the tractor. Good. Everything still worked.

Nothing major appeared to be broken, but he was afraid that his ribs needed attention. Breathing still hurt, in spite of his release from the crushing pressure of the heavy machine, and that was not good. Rance took a deep, slow breath, gradually testing his limits. It was easier to breathe now that the weight was gone, but still painful.

"Damn!"

Maggie opened her eyes and turned slowly toward him. "Did you say something?"

Rance looked at Maggie long and hard. Even with sweat beading her brow and her face grim with fatigue, she was beautiful. He hadn't realized he had spoken the curse out loud.

"I think I'm going to have to get my ribs checked out." Rance grimaced as the effort to talk increased the pain. "I think I may have broken one or two." A sound distracted him, making him turn painfully around. He pushed himself to his side and winced from the sudden movement as he recognized Joe Popwell's battered fishing truck. "And I guess this means we'll have to postpone our dinner."

Maggie scrambled to her feet without acknowledging his remark, and Rance felt vaguely disappointed that she hadn't acted a little upset that the date had fallen through. "It's Daddy." She waved and looked back down at Rance. "He had medical training in the army. Maybe he should check you out."

"Couldn't hurt," Rance muttered. Talking was definitely not helping.

Buddy rolled over from where he lay on the ground and clambered to his feet. He hurried away. In a moment, Rance heard him filling in the old man on what they'd done.

Rance tried to push himself upright, but fell back quickly. Even that slight effort had left him panting and bathed in sweat. Damn, he hated feeling helpless like this.

Popwell sauntered over and squatted down beside him. "Hell, boy. Didn't nobody ever tell you not to drive one of these things down a hill slantwise?" His wrinkled face settled into a frown as he peered down at Rance. "Can you move, son?"

"Yeah," Rance grunted. "I hurt like hell, though."

"I'd be more worried if you couldn't feel nothin'," Joe commented as he began a systematic examination of Rance's extremities.

It was okay until the old man started poking around his ribs. Rance thought he would pass out. Though cold sweat oozed from every pore, he managed to remain conscious. "Careful." He ground out the word. "I think they're broken."

"You prob'ly right." Joe shoved himself to his feet. "It'll take as long to get an ambulance out here as it would to take you to town. You up to it?"

"Do I have a choice?"

"Not much of one," Maggie said, from a position somewhere near her father's elbow. "Let's get you into my van. With the seat reclined, you shouldn't be too uncomfortable."

"Okay. Let's do it." Rance tried to push himself to his feet.

Then everything went black.

How she managed to make the drive to Pittsville without major traffic violations, Maggie didn't know. She probably had broken more than one speed law, but nobody had caught her, and nobody had stopped her. As far as she was concerned, that was all that mattered. She forced herself to slow the van as she approached the Pittsville city limits.

Just a few more minutes, and she would be there. Maggie glanced at Rance, and saw that his face was pale beneath his tan. She drummed her fingers against the steering wheel as she waited for a light to change. He had regained consciousness shortly after they got him into the van, but he hadn't spoken for miles. Maggie looked again. His chest moved slightly. At least he was still breathing.

Maggie steered carefully around a corner, and the twelve-bed Pittsville Community Hospital came into sight. Hospital zone be damned, Maggie thought. She pulled into the driveway in front of the emergency entrance and leaned on the horn. She would gladly pay the fine.

Two white-clad orderlies and a man in surgical scrubs burst through the door in response to Maggie's desperate honking. Maggie punched the button and sent Rance's window down as one of the orderlies approached.

"He's been in a tractor accident! Possible broken ribs!" she shouted.

One of the men tugged open the van door, while the other ran back inside. The man in scrubs looked Rance over. He looked at Maggie. "We were told to expect you."

The second orderly reappeared, pushing a gurney. The two orderlies quickly and efficiently removed Rance from the van and lowered him to the gurney. The next moment, they hurried him inside, followed by the scrub-clad doctor.

Maggie sat all alone in the van in the driveway.

"Maggie. Maggie?" Rance mumbled, fading in and out of consciousness.

"Your wife is fine, Mr. Montoya. She's in the waiting room."

She was waiting for him. Rance liked the sound of that. It had a sort of warm, fuzzy feeling. But there was something wrong with what the doctor had said, he knew. He tried to shake the fog from his mind, but couldn't get the haze to clear. And the last thought he had before he succumbed to darkness was that he didn't want the warm, fuzzy feeling to end.

A man in a lab coat pushed through a set of swinging doors at the end of the waiting room. He peeled out of his gloves and scanned until his eyes fell on Maggie, curled in a hard plastic chair. He quickly crossed the room.

"Mrs. Montoya? I'm Dr. McDaniel."

"I'm not Mrs. Montoya, but I'm the one you're looking for." Maggie scrambled to her feet. "Is Rance all right?"

"Excuse me. I just assumed…"

"It's okay." Being married to Rance wasn't the worst thing she could imagine. And it was a pleasant enough notion, one she hadn't considered before. "How is Rance?"

"He was very lucky. He's got a couple of cracked ribs and lots of contusions. His excellent physical condition made a big difference."

Maggie closed her eyes and sighed. "Can he go home?"

"I'd like to keep him overnight, but he won't have anything to do with the idea. I was hoping you could convince him to stay."

"I'll try."

McDaniel led the way back through the swinging doors.

Judging from Rance's position, nothing Maggie could say would convince him to stay the night in the hospital. He was on his feet, face white with pain, hugging his taped ribs with one hand and trying to tug on the remains of his shirt with the other.

Rance looked up as Maggie and the doctor entered the examining cubicle. "The doc says I can go home if I have somebody to stay with me," he announced through clenched teeth.

"That's not what he told me," Maggie countered, alarmed. "You should stay here, where people know what they're doing." Already, one side of Rance's body, visible above the tape around his chest, was purpling with bruised tissue.

"It's just a precaution. They can't make me stay." Rance grimaced as he tried to tuck in his shirt. "I want to go home."

Maggie shot a panicked look at the doctor. "Would it be dangerous if he went home?"

"It could be. But I can't force him to stay."

"If you're worried about malpractice, I'll sign a release," Rance argued. "Anything. Just let me go. Maggie can stay with me."

"But I'm not a nurse." *I'm not even his wife. What business do I have taking care of him?* Maggie looked over at Rance. He shouldn't be able to stand, yet he did.

"Are you going to drive me home? Or do I call a cab?"

The thought of Rance riding all the way home in a cab made up Maggie's mind for her. She would take him back. She'd sat up with sick kids; she guessed she could sit up with him.

"I guess I have no choice." Maggie looked at Rance, and then back to the doctor. "Tell me what I have to do."

Dr. McDaniel briefed her about what to look for and what to expect. Maggie listened carefully. She rather liked the idea that the strong, handsome Rance Montoya needed her.

There were a few moments on the bumpy ride home when Rance actually regretted his decision to leave the hospital. But when Maggie steered her minivan into his lane and up the drive to his house, he knew he'd made the right choice. He couldn't have explained why it was important that he stay under the Hightower roof, but it was. After so many years dreaming of a home, he didn't want to spend even one night away from it.

The headlights flashed against a ghostly figure sitting on the steps. A chill raced through him. Could this be the ghost he'd heard about? Rance shook his head to clear it and looked again, more closely this time. He was surprised to see Buddy perched on the top step, one arm hugging his knees, another skinny arm wrapped around the rusty-haired dog. What was he doing there?

"I called the folks and told them I was bringing you home. We thought I might need some help getting you settled," Maggie told Rance, as if she'd read his puzzled expression. "When you're squared away, Buddy will go on over to my folks' house. He and Jen will spend the night with them."

Rance nodded in silent agreement with Maggie's sensible statement. Then he looked to the house again.

The steps leading up to the porch loomed like Mount Everest. "Good thinking. I don't know whether I'm up to mountain climbing tonight." Rance tried to flash a grin, but it was anemic at best.

Rusty barked a greeting as Buddy loped down the steps and jerked the van door open. The dog seemed to sense that something was wrong, for she stayed away and watched with interested eyes.

"Wait, kiddo. We're going to have to handle Mr. Montoya with kid gloves. He's pretty much one big bruise."

Maggie hopped out of the van and hurried around to the passenger side, where Buddy stood. While he waited, Rance looked down. Even the short distance from his position to the ground looked farther than that from the door of an airborne C-130 transport while you were waiting for the green light to jump. And now he didn't have a parachute.

Rance gingerly levered his feet around. So far, so good. But that twelve-inch gap between him and terra firma might as well have been a mile. A night in the hospital was looking better all the time.

"Rance, this is going to hurt, no matter what we do," Maggie pointed out, echoing the exact thoughts that had been running through his head.

"Don't remind me. How about I just sleep here?"

"Fine with me. I'm sure the mosquitoes will enjoy it," Maggie stated, swatting at her arm. "Inside, you'll have a whole screen between you and the thirsty little buggers. Not to mention a nice soft bed."

"That damned hospital bed is looking really good about

now,'' he grunted as he shifted his weight forward. When would that pain medication begin to kick in? It felt as if somebody were jabbing his chest with a red-hot poker every time he moved.

Rance worked his legs around until they were dangling a foot above the ground. He closed his eyes so that he wouldn't see the distance he had to go. Then he took a deep breath and stepped down.

He should have warned them about what he was going to do, Rance thought as his feet touched the ground and his knees buckled. But if he had stopped to think about it, he might still be sitting in the van.

And if he'd thought about it too long, Maggie's arms wouldn't be around him now.

Chapter 7

Maggie glanced around the bedroom while she waited for Buddy to help Rance into bed. The more she saw of this house, the more she liked it. The room hadn't originally been intended for sleeping, but it seemed an ideal choice. The real bedrooms were all on the second floor, and in the nearly tropical summer heat of Alabama they would be stifling. So Rance's choice of the old library on the first floor was a good one.

The room was paneled in knotty pine, not the plastic imitation paneling in her prefab home, but the genuine article. Maggie ran her fingers over the smooth, varnished surface and admired the warm patina that age had given the wood. The east and south walls each held two floor-to-ceiling windows; the ones that faced the front were really windowed doors that opened out onto the porch.

There was no doubt in Maggie's mind why Rance had chosen this room for sleeping; it was probably the coolest room in the house. And with the big stone fireplace that

stood between the two south-facing windows, the room
would be cozy and warm in the winter.

Two of the walls were covered with shelves, and Maggie was surprised at the titles they displayed. The library
contained everything from the classics to the latest on
farming techniques, as well as a large collection of paperback novels.

Rance had told her that he'd finished college at night
and read all kinds of farming books, but the extent of his
self-education surprised her. If heh ad actually read all the
books on the shelves, Rance was certainly better educated
than the average Alabama farmer.

She tried to ignore the bed that stood between the two
front-facing windows. It was large and inviting, with a
light corded spread of royal blue. Maggie's mind dredged
up an image of the two of them in tangled sheets, and she
suppressed a tingle of excitement as she turned down the
covers. But before her mind could fill in the details, Buddy
called from the hall.

"Turn down the bed, Mom. We're coming in."

More than once in the past hour, Maggie had thanked
her lucky stars she'd had the presence of mind to have
Buddy waiting. The two of them had barely been able to
get Rance into the house in one piece after he skydived
out of the van. What had gotten into the man? Leaping off
the seat like that. You would think he had a death wish!

Maggie frowned and shook her head as she turned down
the covers on Rance's queen-size bed. She smoothed out
the sheets, self-conscious about performing so intimate a
task for a man she barely knew. She frowned again.

"What's with the nasty look, pretty lady?" Rance
asked, his voice slurred. The pain pills must finally have
kicked in.

Rance had complained of feeling gamy and insisted on
washing up. Thank goodness Buddy had been there; Mag-

gie wasn't sure she knew Rance well enough for that kind of intimacy. Yet. If she ever would...

He stood poised in the doorway, half leaning on the door frame, half leaning on Buddy. Rance's head lolled like that of a man on a two-day drunk, but at least some of his color had returned. He was modestly dressed in a pair of nylon running shorts—a concession to her presence, Maggie supposed. She had a very strong feeling that Rance Montoya normally slept in much less. Like nothing.

"He's cleaned up and ready for bed, Mom."

Rance raised an arm and executed a floppy salute. "All clean and ready for duty, Mom." He grinned a sloppy grin and tried to step forward. Instead, he sagged against Buddy.

"I'm still not thrilled about your pigheaded decision to come home tonight. Are you sure you wouldn't like to go jogging before you turn in?" Maggie asked to mask the real concern she had about his condition.

"'S only way I could think to get you into my bedroom," Rance muttered, still wearing a foolish grin.

Buddy scowled.

Maggie rolled her eyes, though the notion appealed to her more each time she looked at Rance's well-toned body. Even as bruised and as bandaged as he was, he was magnificent. "Then you've wasted your time. I'll be over there." She indicated a battered recliner that sat catty-corner to the bed. "One of us has to stay awake."

"Too bad," Rance murmured as Buddy lowered him to the mattress. He didn't resist as Buddy, probably still remembering the suggestive remark, picked up his legs and positioned them, none too gently, parallel to the edge.

"Yeah. Right." Maggie shooed Buddy away and adjusted the pillows and pulled the sheet up over her patient. Even when he was weak and in pain and with his ribs swaddled in bandages, Rance's muscled body was distract-

ing. Given some other night and two able bodies, there
was no telling what could happen.

Maggie felt her face warm and thanked providence for
the dim light in the room. It had been a long time since
she had been with a man, but this fantasy was ridiculous.
She shocked herself with the image she was painting in
her mind's eye. Thank goodness, Rance was not able-
bodied, at least not tonight. She couldn't believe her tired
mind was actually considering the drug-induced suggestion
he had made. A slight shiver, not unpleasant, ran through
her. Her face heated more. Even her body was responding.

She glanced over to Buddy, whose young face showed
an emotion that hovered somewhere between anger and
confusion. Thirteen-year-olds didn't happen to hear their
mothers get propositioned every day, even by the walking
wounded. "It's okay, Buddy. It's the pills talking. He'll
be asleep in a minute. I can handle things from here on.

"Why don't you go home? It's late, and I'm sure your
grandparents would like to know what's going on." Maggie winked at her son conspiratorially. "We won't mention
Mr. Montoya's silly proposition."

"You sure, Mom? I can stay."

Maggie patted Buddy's cheek, then folded his gawky
teenage body into a huge bear hug. "You've been a big
help, but thanks to the pills the doctor gave him, I think
Rance will sleep through the rest of the night just fine. I'll
be all right."

As if to punctuate Maggie's statement, Rance sighed
and nuzzled his head into his pillows. "See. He's asleep.
We'll be fine."

Rance!

Something brought Rance wide awake with a start, and
the slight jerk sent waves of shocking pain through him.
He gingerly cocked his head and looked around. He was
sure he had heard somebody calling to him. He looked

toward Maggie, who was sitting in the recliner, thumbing through a copy of *The Farm Journal*. How could anyone reading a farming magazine look like an angel?

When she didn't look up, he spoke. "Did you call me?" He was mildly surprised at the way his voice sounded, gravelly and rough.

Maggie looked up and smiled one of those reassuring it'll-be-all-right smiles. Then she dropped the magazine, got up and crossed over to him. "Are you in pain?" She felt his head. "It's too soon to take another pill."

It was the second time she had brushed his forehead with her cool, soft hand, and the tender gesture nearly set him on fire. How could one woman affect him so? And when he was in no position to do anything about it. He willed his body to behave in an appropriate, patientlike manner, but his mind had no control over the matter. Fortunately for both of them, the light was dim and the sheets were bunched up where it counted. He cleared his throat and tried again. "I thought I heard someone calling my name."

"It wasn't me. Maybe you were dreaming."

He couldn't stand it. With her hovering over him, there was no way his body would behave. He wanted to haul her into bed with him, cracked ribs and all. And he wanted to know why he was hearing things.

"Maybe I was. I guess it's the pills." Rance willed himself to close his eyes. He really was tired, and he hurt like hell, in spite of all his brave words and the doctor's painkillers. He hurt too much to be thinking about long, pleasure-filled nights. Even with the object of his thoughts so temptingly near.

Maggie woke up disoriented and confused. Her eyes were bleary, and she had a crick in her neck. She yawned and stretched and rubbed her eyes as she tried to remember what she was doing in a recliner in Rance's room.

Rance's room. Maggie glanced over to Rance's bed. If she hadn't been wide awake before, she was now.

The bed was empty.

Maggie tried to stay calm. After all, there could be a perfectly plausible reason for Rance to be out of bed.

Yeah, sure, Maggie told herself as she released the lever that lowered the recliner seat. The man was badly injured and filled with enough drugs to take him to La-La Land, and she thought there was a logical reason for him to be up? That would teach her to get too comfortable on the job.

Maggie's legs were decidedly rubbery when she hit the floor running. More than once she'd found one of her kids curled up under a bed after she made a frantic search of the house, certain they'd been kidnapped. She raised the bedspread to look, then shook her head. Rance wasn't five years old, and his bulky body would not fit under the bed, even with a shoehorn.

She did look on the other side, in case he'd fallen. He hadn't.

Think, Maggie. Think. Where would you go in the middle of the night?

The bathroom! Maybe he was as embarrassed as she, and had tried to go alone.

Maggie tore down the hall. She could see that the door was open in the dim light, but the small room was dark. She fumbled for the switch, steeling herself to find Rance's crumpled body in a heap on the floor.

He wasn't there.

Maggie sank down onto the toilet seat. Where could he have gone? And why hadn't she heard him?

If Rance hadn't moved Rusty and her pups back outside, maybe the dog would have alerted Maggie. But Rusty was outside, Rance was missing, and Maggie had to find him.

Her maternal ears weren't as finely tuned as they had been when the kids were babies. But how could she not have heard a one-hundred-and-ninety-pound injured man get out of bed?

Something made Maggie look down the hall, toward the back portion of the house. A dim light shone from a door she hadn't noticed before. The door was slightly open, allowing feeble rays of light to escape.

She felt an eerie chill as she pushed tentatively against the wooden door, fully expecting to hear it creak. This was the haunted Hightower house, after all. And it was the middle of the night. The musty smell of decay reached her nose, and Maggie prepared for the worst.

The door swung silently open at her touch, and Maggie discovered a flight of stairs that twisted downward. Without pausing to wonder what an injured man would be doing traipsing down a treacherous, rickety flight of stairs at midnight, Maggie followed them down, grateful for the dim bulb that illuminated the way. She was very relieved to reach the bottom without encountering anything sinister. Or Rance's bleeding body.

She supposed the dark basement had been a root cellar in the old days, before electricity, because the faint smell of long-forgotten fruit came to her as she began to survey the cavernous room. The weak light from the stairs didn't reach all the way into the interior, and her flesh crawled as sounds came from out of the darkness around her. Maggie chafed her bare arms to warm them, and tried to banish the thoughts about the origins of those sounds that ought to be—were—scaring her silly.

A movement to the far left caught Maggie's eye, and she turned toward it. A feeble ray of moonlight from the dirty window high on the wall above pointed to a standing figure.

Rance. As if frozen in time, he stood staring at a cinderblock wall.

Soft hands on his shoulder woke him. If he had actually been asleep. Rance reveled in the caressing touch, but then he realized the weirdness of the scene. He vaguely remembered getting to the basement, but not why he'd come. He looked at the blank wall, then at Maggie, blinking as he tried to clear the confusion from his muddled mind.

"What am I doing here?" he asked, wide awake now, in spite of the horse-size pain pills he'd taken. His side hurt less than before, but he shouldn't be awake. He shouldn't be here. Hell, he shouldn't be standing.

"I was hoping you'd tell me," Maggie whispered softly as she stood on tiptoe to feel Rance's head.

It was getting to be a habit with her, Rance realized. One that he liked. Damn if he didn't like having a red-haired angel hovering about him. It had been a long time since anybody had fussed over him in quite the same way. Not since his mother. Maybe getting run over by a tractor had its good points.

"You don't have any idea what you're doing down here?"

Rance looked at Maggie blankly.

"And do you have any idea how hard it's going to be to get you back upstairs?" Maggie looked at the stairs that seemed to stretch for miles above them.

Rance followed the path Maggie's eyes had taken and blanched. If the porch steps had seemed like Mount Everest, these looked like Mount Everest with Pikes Peak on top. He groaned. *How the hell did I get here?*

His eyes flickered back to the bare wall he'd been facing. Why had he been staring at a blank wall?

"Well?"

Rance turned quickly back to Maggie. He winced as his taped ribs reminded him why he'd been doped up in the first place.

Then something else made him turn back to the wall.

Rance, a voice called softly, clearly.

"Did you just say my name?" Rance knew Maggie hadn't.

"No. Maybe those painkillers are making your ears ring." Maggie's look of motherly concern drew Rance's eyes to her.

"I didn't hear ringing," Rance replied quickly. How could he explain what he'd heard, when he didn't understand it himself? "I don't suppose I'm dreaming and that I'm really upstairs tucked in my soft, warm bed."

"Nope. You got down here. I guess you'll just have to get back up the same way." Maggie's grip on his arm was firm as she gently led him toward the stairs. At the foot of the steps, Rance stopped and looked back toward the stark, bare wall. Gooseflesh covered him that couldn't be explained by the chilly cellar air.

Why had he ended up here?

Maggie appraised the situation carefully. Rance had gotten to the bottom of the stairs without mishap; surely he could make it back up. And this time, he would have help.

As far as she knew, Rance's legs were fine. More than fine, she thought distractedly as she eyed the corded muscles that displayed all their leashed power in spite of the bruised flesh. His powerful legs had carried him downstairs, Maggie reminded herself. They would take him back up. "Okay. Here's the plan," Maggie announced, hoping her brusque manner would mask the concern she felt.

Rance looked at Maggie absently, as if he hadn't realized she was there. "What?"

"You're going upstairs."

"Oh, yeah. But how did I get down here?" Rance looked blank, definitely showing the effects of his medication.

If it hadn't been so serious, Maggie would have laughed. Rance looked downright addled, but she knew an intelligent and very real man was in there, hiding behind the painkillers.

"You're going to have to walk up the stairs." Maggie waited for her statement to register. When it looked as if it had, she continued, "I'll be right behind you to catch you if you lose your balance."

That tactic always worked with toddlers, but Maggie was not at all certain she would be able to catch and hold Rance if he should fall. Her one hundred twenty-eight pounds were no match for his well-muscled bulk. She took a deep breath and prayed to whatever spirits were listening for help.

"Are you up to it?"

"I guess I have to be." Rance set his jaw and stared determinedly at the stairs. "Let's do it."

Maggie's eyes widened as Rance resolutely put his foot on the first step. That seemed easy enough. He pulled the other foot up. A spasm of pain marred his handsome face, but he lifted the other foot.

One step done and eleven more to go, Maggie thought as she watched Rance's determined progress. He advanced another step, and she couldn't help admiring the way his well-defined muscles worked together to propel him upward. His rate of ascent increased, and his determined efforts gained momentum. He actually charged up the stairs, making Maggie hurry behind him.

She reached the top and caught Rance, who was swaying dangerously. Whatever had given him the strength to negotiate the stairs had deserted him at the summit. Even in the dim light of the hallway, Maggie could see beads of perspiration on his forehead that hadn't been there before.

She offered her hand to steady him, and Rance took it, closing his long fingers over hers. His muscles trembled from the exertion, and Maggie wondered how much longer he could hold himself up. She willed herself to pass some of her strength on to his fatigued and trembling body, while she watched to see if he would fall.

"I think we made it," Rance muttered, his breath still coming hard.

"Don't talk, it'll just make it worse. Let's get you back to bed." Maggie wanted to put her arms around Rance to hold him up, but she didn't, partly because she was well aware of his taped ribs, and partly because of what she was feeling inside.

In spite of his pain, in spite of all the medication that kept him going, Rance Montoya was very much a man. And Maggie was just as much a woman. This enigmatic man, full of contradictions and masculine stubbornness, had touched her in a way no man had since Chet. She didn't even know who Rance really was, but she was physically attracted to him. And it scared her to death.

Her feet seemed to carry her to Rance's room without her consciously telling them to, but once there, her maternal instincts took over. She helped Rance lower himself to the bed until he was seated on the edge.

"Thanks, Maggie." Rance's strong, callused hands closed over hers.

"You're wel—" Maggie stopped, stunned, as Rance brought her hands to his mouth and kissed them. A faint tingle crept up her arm as she felt Rance's lips on her hand. If she had been the type of person to swoon, she would have. She looked into his dark eyes, darker now from the pain. His gaze locked with hers and seemed to pull her in as he let go of her hands and touched her face. He gently caressed her cheek, his thumb teasing her lower lip.

"I want so much to kiss you," Rance whispered, low and husky. "A real kiss," he amended. "But I won't. I don't think I'd want to stop with a kiss, and I doubt I could go further right now." With that, he released Maggie's trembling fingers and eased himself carefully into a sitting position on the bed.

"Hell," he muttered, and grasped Maggie at the curve of her neck, his clumsy fingers surprisingly gentle. "I won't be able to sleep until I know what I can dream about."

Rance pulled her to him with a strength she hadn't imagined he had. She knew better than to resist. Not because she feared him, but because a sudden movement might startle him and make him fall. She brushed a quick kiss across his lips and tried to ease away. He needed rest, she tried to convince herself, though the gentle ache deep inside her urged her to follow his lead. "That'll have to do for now," she told him lightly. "You need to sleep."

But Rance's will was stronger than hers, and he pulled her to him. "I won't. Not until I know how this feels..." His voice trailed off as he pulled her face toward his. Knowing it would be easier to give in than to resist, Maggie met him halfway. Not that it was a great sacrifice, for she needed the kiss as much as he wanted it.

His lips met hers, and Maggie closed her eyes, wondering how she could be drowning in waves of sensation, when he must be nearly dead with pain. But the way his lips moved over hers, taking and tasting, belied any discomfort he might have. And when his tongue sought invitation, Maggie parted her lips to let him explore. Then, all too quickly, it was over.

Rance sighed. Or groaned. He leaned back slowly, grimacing from the strain. "It was everything I'd expected and more," he whispered, his face beaded with sweat. "But I'm afraid I'm just not up to doing us justice right now."

She watched as Rance lowered himself gingerly to the mattress. That was better. All he'd needed was a goodnight kiss. Maggie reached over to adjust the covers, trying to ignore the hot breath that brushed her cheek as she leaned across him.

"I'd feel a lot better if you'd stay here beside me," he whispered. "What if I try to get up again?"

Maggie closed her eyes and breathed an aggravated sigh. Rance's argument was hard to ignore, and she reluctantly joined him on the bed. She lay on top of the light spread, as far away from him as she could be and still be touching him, her back modestly turned to him. He shifted slightly and draped his arm possessively across her. Maybe this wasn't such a good idea after all.

Or was it?

But it felt so good to be lying next to him in the quiet dark of night. Maggie convinced herself she would just stay with him until he fell asleep.

The hand caressing her hip so possessively stroked and teased and sent her nearly to the brink of madness. More than once she tried to get up, and more than once his languid ministrations kept her snug with him. Maggie closed her eyes, feeling the half-forgotten moves of love and wondering what it would be like to complete the act with this man who so intrigued her. And frightened her just as much.

Her breath grew ragged as his fingers wandered up her side to the curve of her breast. Her breath caught as he moved his hand closer to her heart, and her heart beat furiously when he stopped in response to her instinctive reaction. After an endless moment, he resumed his teasing exploration. His fingers probed and massaged until Maggie's traitorous nipples beaded into hard, throbbing nubs, and a once familiar aching trailed from his exploring fingers to the deepest part of her being. For one brief moment, she wished he was capable of making love to her.

Whatever Rance had taken to relieve the pain seemed to have relaxed his inhibitions. Almost as if he'd sensed her need for completion, his hand moved lower, stroking her hip, her thigh, until he reached the hem of her dress. Gently his fingers closed around the cotton fabric. Slowly, inexorably, the material inched upward in his grasping hand. Then he touched bare skin.

Maggie's breath stopped for an instant as she felt the warmth of his fingers on her skin. When she became accustomed to the heat there, she breathed again. But it was only a moment of ease, because his hand began to move again until he reached the brief scrap of cotton that covered her most private spot.

If he withdrew his hand now, Maggie would die of frustration, but she was certain that if it stayed she would never be able to look him in the eyes again. He paused. Had the sedating medication made him more sensitive to her needs than he would have been otherwise?

His searching fingers found the tender spot at the center of her being, and though a thin barrier of cotton separated his exploring hand from her, he began to caress and massage until Maggie found herself straining to increase the sensations of pleasure that were flooding through her. Her breath grew ragged and harsh, and she feared that the noise would stop him.

What was she afraid of? That he would stop? Or that he wouldn't.

Wave after wave of sensation flooded through her. Helpless to resist, Maggie felt herself drowning in a sea of dark and forbidden pleasure. She rode the waves, rising and falling, until she reached the climax, then the last giant wave lifted her higher and higher, leaving her breathless and gasping with shuddering release.

If only he could have joined her in the final moment of satisfaction.

He must have been feeling the same as she, for he groaned—it was a ragged, heart-wrenching sound of frustration—and withdrew his hand, leaving her cold and surprisingly bereft. He hugged her to him, and after what seemed like an eternity, his breathing slowed. Had he fallen asleep?

Maggie waited a few minutes longer to be certain he had sunk deep within the arms of sleep, then eased herself out of his possessive grasp, holding her breath for fear that her breathing might wake him. She rolled quietly off the mattress, wincing at the gentle creak, then stood for a moment and watched him. Certain that the gentle rise and fall of his chest meant he was safely asleep, she tiptoed back to her haven in the chair.

Rance looked across the room to where Maggie dozed. With the greatest difficulty, he had feigned sleep, allowing her to escape. Anything to keep her from tempting him further. As much as he wanted her, there was no way he could do anything about it in his present condition. And he wasn't fool enough to prolong the torture.

So he had let her creep quietly out of his bed and resume her position in the chair across the room. It was a sacrifice, but maybe the wait would be worth it, when he finally did make love to her. And he knew as surely as he knew the sun would rise in the morning that he would. And she would love him back.

He had accomplished something, though. Before now, he hadn't been sure how Maggie would feel about his attentions. Then he'd seen the light in her eyes as they gazed into his soul. She hadn't pulled away, and her response had told him more than volumes full of words could have.

Maggie wanted him as much as he wanted her. He hated that he would have to wait to make her his. He didn't just need time to heal; he needed to find out who he was. Everything would come together someday. Knowing that would have to hold him for now.

Rance closed his eyes and hoped to dream. Not the same dream that had haunted his sleep in recent days. He wanted to dream of Maggie.

Maggie woke with a start.

Feelings churned through her that she had once thought

she would never feel again. Her heart beat erratically in her breast, and she pressed her palm against it to still its frantic pounding. She feared that its insistent drumbeat would wake Rance and alert him to her distressed state. She willed herself to sit in the old recliner across from him and watch him sleep as she waited for her heart to return to normal speed.

That Rance wanted her was an exhilarating thought, but frightening at the same time. It had been so long since she gave herself to a man, and she didn't trust her roiling emotions.

For that matter, how did Rance really feel? He would probably remember nothing in the morning. He'd taken enough drugs to knock out an elephant. Elephants might never forget, but Maggie hoped Rance would. How could she have allowed him to caress such an intimate part of her? How could she have let him give her such pleasure when he was in so much pain?

Her face burned with embarrassment and shame at the knowledge that she had enjoyed the experience. What kind of wanton woman would allow a man she barely knew such access to her body and her secrets? And when the man was supposed to be in her care?

Please let him not remember, she prayed silently. Let him think this was all the effect of the painkilling drugs.

If Rance forgot what had happened between them, Maggie wouldn't have to deal with it, and perhaps that would be best. She wasn't certain she could handle those reawakened urges, after suppressing them for so long. And she wasn't sure she could face him.

Maggie glanced over at Rance. Her eyes caressed his brow and memorized the lines of his strong face, his jaw shadowed with night and a new growth of beard. She didn't know what to do about him when he woke up in the morning, much less at some unknown time in the future. The prospect was frightening. And wonderful.

Maybe if she'd taken one of those horse pills that Rance had, she would be able to sleep now. But she couldn't. She had a job to do. A responsibility. Maggie sat in her chair and stared across the room to where Rance slept. She knew she shouldn't envy his sleep; he needed it to heal his injured body. But she was tired, and she needed to sleep, too. She had a job to do, she reminded herself again, and she had to stay awake. She couldn't just assume that the next time Rance decided to walk in his sleep he would be able to negotiate the house safely.

Maggie sighed, picked up a newsmagazine, and tried to read it.

Help me. I'm here.

Maggie looked up, instantly alert. Had she heard something? Or just imagined it? She held her breath, hoping the sound would come again.

She hadn't imagined it. Maggie was positive that something had gotten her attention. And it wasn't Rance. The sound hadn't come from his direction. It hadn't come from any direction. Yet she was sure she had heard something. Or felt it. Maggie had the impression that somebody needed her. She cocked her head and listened again, straining to filter out the other night sounds.

Whatever it was, it was gone. Or at least now it was quiet. There was no sense sitting around scaring herself, like the last time she'd stayed in this house—in this very room, she remembered. But it was different this time.

The first time, when she was sixteen years old, something had frightened her. Frightened her so badly that she ran from the house, all the way back to her own home. What she heard this time wasn't really frightening. She turned back to her magazine.

I'm here.

There it was again! This time, Maggie didn't bother to look up. She had been listening for a sound, she realized, but she hadn't heard one. She'd felt it. It hadn't come from somewhere outside the room. It had come from within. Not from inside the room. *Inside her!*

Maggie shook her head, trying to expunge the notion she was formulating. She was a practical, educated woman, and paranormal experiences were things that she hadn't thought about since she was an impressionable kid. Yet since Rance Montoya had moved into this house, every bit of her grown-up sensibility had deserted her.

The longer she stayed here, the surer she became that someone was calling to her from the other side. Had called her years before, and was calling her now. She had sensed something. Call it ESP. Call it a hunch. Call it whatever you wanted.

Somebody was trying to get her attention.

And, more than that, whatever she'd heard beckoning her had a decidedly feminine aura.

Her scalp began to tingle, and Maggie reached up to smooth her hair down, although it wasn't really standing on end. She laughed nervously at the silliness of her impulsive action and quickly pulled her hand away.

"Get a grip, Maggie," she told herself. "There's no mysterious dead woman connected with this house." She started when the words hit the air. She hadn't realized she was voicing her thoughts aloud.

Rance stirred, and Maggie glanced over to him. The last thing she needed to do was wake him. He murmured something unintelligible, then settled again. Maggie breathed more easily. How could she have let her imagination run so rampant? Voices calling, indeed.

I need your help.

There it was again. The same thing she'd heard that night twenty years ago. A silent plea for help. Only then she hadn't understood.

Maggie scrambled to her feet, and was halfway down the dark hallway before she realized what she was doing. Yet the feminine entity compelled her to continue.

She crept down the unlit hallway, silently trying to talk herself out of this foolishness, but helpless to stop herself. She tugged open the cellar door and grimaced as the smell of decay and neglect assaulted her nose again. Maggie yanked on the light string as she hurried down the stairs. Almost as if she were being pulled, she found herself drawn to the same place where she'd found Rance earlier.

Had Rance heard the same entreaty? That must be it. He had obeyed the same unheard summons as she now did. More fascinated than frightened, she let her instinct draw her on.

Just like Rance before her, Maggie found herself facing the bare cinder-block wall in the cellar. She stopped and stared. She couldn't go any farther.

Remembering the slew of paperback ghost stories she'd read as a girl, Maggie first thought that there was a hidden door. She glanced around for any sort of protruding object that she could push or pull. But the wall was smooth. There wasn't a knob, there wasn't a knot, there wasn't so much as a mouse hole as far as she could see.

Maggie reached out and tentatively touched the wall.
Yes!
She glanced behind her, knowing that no one would be there. The internal voice had increased in intensity.

Gooseflesh formed, and Maggie shivered as she felt the dampness that had settled on the clammy blocks. No one was there. She shouldn't be here. She should be upstairs with Rance, where she belonged.

Knowing full well that her duty to Rance wasn't the real reason for her retreat, Maggie turned and hurried upstairs.

Chapter 8

Morning sounds filtered through the open window, along with the cool air. Birdsong replaced the sound of the rooster, waking Rance. He lay still, not daring to move his hurt and aching body. He listened in the half-light as the day began. A soft whimper from across the room drew his eyes to Maggie, curled up in the old chair.

Rance would not have believed it was possible for as much of him to ache as did at that moment. His ribs were still hot and sore, and most of his muscles cried in protest if he tried to move. So he didn't. He was content to lie as still as possible in his big, lonely bed and gaze across the short distance, which might as well have been a mile-wide chasm.

Vague recollections of his lips on Maggie's, of holding her soft white hand, played havoc with his conscious mind. Had he really told her that he wanted to make love with her? Had he dreamed of her writhing and arching in the throes of ecstasy? He focused on Maggie's sleeping face, beautiful in the soft light. If her passionate response hadn't been real, it was something to look forward to. If he hadn't told her of his desire for her, he should have. But for now he would be content with the memory—if it was a memory and not the fevered imaginings of delirium. If it *had* happened, he would only mention it when Maggie gave him some clue that it was all right.

The sun climbed above the trees and streamed in through the open window. It crept across the floor to the chair, caressing Maggie's delicate skin as intimately as Rance wanted to. He couldn't help envying the sunbeam as it had its way with her.

A mourning dove lit on a branch outside the window and crooned its sad lament. Had the morning symphony always been so loud? As much as Rance had enjoyed listening to those sounds each day in the past week, he didn't want them to wake Maggie now. After tending him all night, she deserved to sleep.

And if she woke, she might leave.

Had it been only one week since she stepped out onto her porch and stole his heart? Had it been just five days since she walked so lightly into his life, carrying a picnic basket? He chuckled as he remembered the way that Jennifer had let out the information that her mother was free. That day had been the beginning of the rest of his life.

He'd thought he would find all the answers to the questions that haunted him in back issues of the local newspaper, but he hadn't. If anything, the paper had just shown him how much he didn't know.

And the Chevrolet in the creek! Instinctively Rance knew that the car was a major piece in the puzzle that was his family's history. How could he prove it? With no identifying tags and with only a vague boyhood memory, there was no way to prove ownership. And years of being submerged had left its paint nothing but rust. Yet there had to be some way to identify the car.

Maggie stirred and murmured something in her sleep,

distracting Rance from his confused thoughts. The sun had touched its fingers to Maggie's tousled hair, setting it aflame. He focused on one tight ringlet that caressed her cheek and envied it the privilege.

She shifted, as if trying to avoid the sun's probing fingers. Reaching up as if to thrust the sun away from her porcelain cheek, Maggie dislodged the curl that had so entranced him as he watched her sleep. Slowly, Maggie's eyes opened. Her eyelashes fluttered and fell back against her creamy cheeks. She wasn't ready to greet the day, for she squeezed her lids tight. A morning bird called, insisting that she listen, and Maggie opened her eyes again, presenting their startling turquoise to the day.

"Good morning," Rance whispered, his voice husky from sleep and pent-up emotion.

Maggie's eyes opened wider, and color came into her cheeks as she looked across the room into Rance's watchful gaze. She blinked as her eyes adjusted to the bright morning light.

"Hi," she responded softly. "How are you feeling this morning?"

Rance shifted and grimaced as his muscles protested the slight movement. "Like a tractor rolled over on top of me." He grinned, his face being the only part of him that didn't feel the results of yesterday. "I ache, but I think I'll live."

Maggie crossed the room and stood over him. Was she going to feel his head again? He wanted to feel her cool hand against him, yet he wasn't sure he could control his body's reaction to her touch.

She didn't. "Do you want me to get you anything?"

You, he wanted to say. Not that he would be able to do anything with her if he had her. Last night had proved that. Discretion kept his mouth shut. A noise from the drive outside, and Rusty's bark of greeting, changed the subject altogether.

* * *

"What was that?" Rance's languid posture stiffened to coiled tension.

Maggie laughed. "I imagine it's the cavalry to the rescue."

"Cavalry?"

"Yup. You know, the day shift." Maggie stretched and yawned. "I *have* been here all night." She pointed. "In that chair. I'm long overdue a break."

Daisy Popwell's voice yoo-hooed from the front of the house.

"It's my mom." Maggie's stomach rumbled, reminding her how long it had been since she ate. "I hope she has breakfast."

"Breakfast. Oh, no, I was supposed to cook dinner for you last night."

"Don't worry, I haven't forgotten. I'm holding you to that invitation, but it won't hurt me to miss one meal." For the first time since the whole drama unfolded yesterday, Maggie remembered that she had skipped lunch the day before in anticipation of Rance's promised Tex-Mex dinner.

Maggie's mother appeared in the doorway, carrying a tray. The warm aroma of coffee came with her.

"Coffee," Maggie murmured appreciatively. "I could use some to jump-start my battery this morning." She reached for a cup.

Her mother jerked the tray away. "None for you," she told her daughter sternly. "You're going straight home and take a nap." Instead of coffee, she handed Maggie a tall glass of cold orange juice.

"Mom," Maggie protested. How could her mother still order her around as if she were six instead of thirty-six?

"Your mother's right, Maggie. You were up most of the night with me. You need more sleep than those few catnaps you got in the chair." Rance's eyes were direct and insistent.

Realizing that it was hopeless to argue with both of them, Maggie reluctantly gave in. "All right. You win, Mom. But can I have breakfast first?"

Chuckling, her mom nodded. She handed Rance the cup she'd kept from Maggie. "I'll go rustle up some eggs and grits." She turned to Rance. "How hungry are you?"

"I think I could do justice to whatever you fix, Mrs. Popwell."

"Call me Daisy." She grinned. "Mrs. Popwell makes me feel as old as I look." She handed Rance the other glass of juice and left.

"You will go home and get some rest, won't you, Maggie?"

Maggie yawned, finally realizing how tired she was. Belatedly she tried to cover her weariness. "I'll try. I've never been good at sleeping in the daytime."

"You'll sleep. You look tired enough."

Maggie didn't know whether to accept that remark at face value, but gave Rance the benefit of the doubt. He was in no shape to be gallant, and she *had* spent all night in the chair and the clothes she was still wearing. "What about you?"

"I'll survive. It'll take more than one tractor to keep Rance Montoya down." Rance turned his attention to his coffee.

Maggie looked at him and remembered what she'd discovered at the library the day before. It had only been yesterday, but it seemed as if forever had passed since then. She wondered if she should ask him about his connection to the Hightowers. Would he tell her the truth if she did?

She gnawed her lip as indecision changed to resolve. She would ask. If he said yes, then she would know. If he didn't...then what?

The coffee must have revived him, for his eyes seemed brighter. "Do you need another pain pill?" Why was she stalling? That wasn't the question she wanted to ask.

"I don't think so. I don't like what they did to me last night."

Last night! Did he remember what he'd said? What they'd done? Maggie felt a flush creep over her face. She turned away. As she reached the door, courage met resolve. "Rance?"

"Yes."

"Luther Hightower had a son named Rance who'd be about your age now."

The silence in the room was deafening.

"You're Rance Hightower, aren't you?"

The silence got louder as Maggie waited for Rance to reply, and she was sure she could hear her heart thumping against the walls of her chest. Maybe she was wrong about her assumption and she had shocked Rance with her question. Unable to face him, she stepped out of the room.

"Maggie."

She stopped.

"Come back. I need to see your face."

Maggie turned and walked slowly back into the room.

Though it must have been painful, Rance stretched his hand to her. "Come here."

She did, stopping beside the bed and taking Rance's hand. His warm fingers wrapped around hers and made it difficult for her to think clearly.

Rance didn't have to tell her the answer. His reaction already had.

"I *was* Rance Hightower, but that was a lifetime ago. I'm not hiding anything." He paused. "I took my grandfather's name when he became my guardian. It seemed right at the time."

The explanation seemed logical enough. An olive-skinned boy with an Anglo name would want to fit in with his grandfather's people. But why hide it now?

Rance brought her hand to his lips. "Just as I remembered," he murmured.

He hadn't forgotten last night! He kissed each finger and made Maggie's legs even weaker than they already were. *Oh, God, I don't think I can deal with this. If he admits he remembers everything that happened last night, I'll just die.*

"Wh-why didn't you tell anyone?" Maggie managed to stammer, before Rance's warm lips on her hand drove all rational thought away. *I can deal with this,* she reprimanded herself. *As long as he doesn't say anything.*

Rance took his lips away from Maggie's hand. He looked into her eyes with an expression that she couldn't read. "It's a long story."

Reluctantly removing her fingers from Rance's strong, warm hand, Maggie replied, "I have plenty of time."

"No, you don't, Margaret Rose." Daisy had returned to the room, unnoticed. "You're going to eat and then go home to bed."

Maggie sighed, defeated. "Yes, ma'am." She was too weary to argue, and she had the answer she needed. At least part of it. She could wait a little while for the rest of Rance's explanation.

"I promise, I'll finish this," Rance told her huskily.

Maggie was well aware that the promise bore a double meaning. She hoped her mother had missed it. Had she seen Rance kissing her? Somehow his lips on her hands had seemed ever more intimate than on her mouth.

"I'll hold you to that." Maggie adjusted Rance's pillow and helped her mother set up the breakfast tray. Then she followed Daisy out to the kitchen.

How long had Maggie suspected his true identity? Rance wondered as he watched Maggie and her mother disappear down the hall. It could have been as early as Tuesday, when they dug through stacks of newspapers at the library, he supposed, but he didn't think so. It seemed very unlikely that the open, friendly Maggie would have been able to sit on something like that for very long.

She had probably only figured it out yesterday. Yet she had kept her questions quiet all through his long ordeal and the even longer night. Why had she waited to ask him when she was ready to leave?

The smell of country ham and eggs reached Rance's nose and reminded him that he was hungry. With some food in his belly, he would be able to get on with his life. The sooner he got back on his feet, the quicker he would be able to move on. Or so he hoped.

Rance dug into a mound of fluffy scrambled eggs and scooped up a forkful of grits dripping with melted butter and chewed. He momentarily forgot his questions about Maggie as he savored Daisy's homemade buttermilk biscuits, slathered with creamy butter and peach preserves. Yes, he would have to get up to work off this meal. If he ate like this and didn't move, he would never be able to get out of bed again. But then, if Maggie was there with him, he wouldn't care.

In short order, he was finished, full and satisfied. He leaned back on his pillows and thought about what he was going to tell Maggie. There wasn't a hell of a lot to tell, he realized. He still didn't have all the answers. He still hadn't found Drake. He still didn't know why his mother had left him. Where she had gone. Or why she hadn't come back.

Rance shook away his questions, and his thoughts turned to Maggie's face. A smile crept over his face as he closed his eyes and remembered the feel of her lying beside him in the dark of night.

"That's what I like to see—a clean plate and a happy

man," Daisy Popwell announced as she bustled in to clear away the breakfast tray.

Opening his eyes with a guilty jerk, Rance realized Daisy was scrutinizing him with her clear, blue gaze. He felt like a teenager caught kissing on his first date. "I… You startled me."

"Sorry about that. I'm going to run back over to my place. Do you need anything else before I go?"

"I'm sorry, Mrs. Pop—I mean, Daisy. Thank you for breakfast. It was delicious."

"I can see that," Daisy replied, chuckling. "I may not have to wash the plate."

Rance grinned. "It was good, and I was hungry."

"Well, thanks. I guess I'll leave you alone."

"Daisy, is Buddy around?"

"No. Why?"

"I thought I'd like to…clean up. Soak in a hot bath to loosen up some of these stiff muscles." He shifted as she took the tray from his lap and grimaced with the movement. "I'm not sure how steady I'm going to be on my feet, so I might need some help." Why did Rance feel so awkward? He was sure Daisy had seen a naked man before. Still, the thought of Maggie's mother seeing certain parts of him didn't set well.

"Say no more. Joe said he and Buddy'd be over directly to set your tractor right-side-up. I'll tell 'em to stop in before they get started."

Maggie put the clock down and groaned. She had only intended to lie down for a minute or two to rest her eyes. Now it was nearly noon. Half her day was gone, and she was still wearing the same clothes she'd put on almost twenty-four hours before. They were a wrinkled, rumpled mess, and a quick survey found a torn hem and a large, dark grease stain. Maggie wrinkled her nose as she reached behind her to undo the buttons.

The house was strangely quiet, the only sound the insistent hum of the air conditioner. It drowned out the sounds of the birds and the day. Maggie stretched languorously and reflected on how much she missed by having a modern home that kept the heat and cold at bay and the sounds of nature outside. Modern life had a lot to offer, but Maggie realized now what she missed by closing her doors and windows and shutting out the world.

She decided to allow herself another moment of peace and solitude before she headed for a shower, but the jangle of the telephone shattered the quiet.

It was her mother inviting her to Sunday dinner at Rance Montoya's—make that Rance Hightower's—house. Daisy had certainly wasted no time in adopting Rance. "Yes, I slept. I'm just getting up now," Maggie assured her mother. "I have to shower and dress, then I'll be over."

Already Rance's old clapboard house seemed like home to her, certainly more than this plastic-and-aluminum convenience. Maggie liked the big, airy rooms at Rance's. The floor-to-ceiling windows let in air and light in the summer, and the fireplaces in every room would keep it warm in the winter.

She imagined how it would be to curl up in front of the big fireplace on a pallet of rugs and pillows. A feeling of warmth and urgency settled in the place between her thighs, and her face warmed as she envisioned herself and Rance making love by the crackling fire. She recognized feelings that she had long since thought dormant. Forgotten…never to be experienced again.

Even though she was alone, Maggie's face burned with embarrassment. She hardly knew Rance Montoya. How could she be fantasizing about a future with him?

After what had happened in the wee hours of the night in his bedroom, how could she not?

Rance gingerly flexed his tight muscles until they were working again. He wanted to go out into the yard to supervise the tractor-salvage operation, but Daisy had sternly forbidden him to go. So, fresh and dressed in a crisply ironed shirt, thanks to Daisy, he sat in the shade of the porch and swung in the old wooden glider.

Once the nighttime medication had worn off, he'd really begun to feel the results of his two hours trapped beneath the heavy farm machine. He'd be damned if he would take another one of those horse pills, but he had popped three aspirin tablets and washed them down with a tall, frosty glass of Daisy's lemonade.

Before he settled in the swing, Rance had made sure that he had a full box of matches in his pocket ready for him. He took one out and rolled it between his fingers as he watched Joe work on the tractor, tolerating Buddy's awkward attempts to help. Rusty strolled up onto the porch and permitted Rance to pet her, then ambled away to tend her litter. Everything seemed well with the world.

In spite of his sore and aching body, Rance felt truly contented. Daisy's humming as she worked in the kitchen and Jennifer's frequent trips outside to check on his progress seemed right. The Popwell family's presence made his big, brooding house seem like a real home.

It didn't take Joe and Buddy long to right the tractor. What Maggie hadn't done with post and fulcrum, they accomplished in short order with an electric winch and Joe's pickup truck. The tractor stood back on its wheels, looking none the worse for wear, from where Rance sat. He popped the match to his lips and chewed on it.

Buddy loped up and assured Rance that except for a few dents and scratches the body of the machine was fine. Joe had given it a quick once-over and declared it in remarkable condition. After some tinkering, he was going to try the engine.

As the tractor engine grumbled to life, Rance heard another sound. How he heard it, he didn't know. Maybe his ears were especially attuned, or it might be ESP. But before Maggie's gray minivan turned off the main road and into his lane, Rance knew she was coming. And the sight of Maggie's riot of flaming curls through the rolled-up window was more welcome than the sound of any machine could have been. He plucked the match from his mouth, broke it and tossed it away.

Maggie drew the van to a halt behind her father's pick-up. But instead of coming over to the porch, she walked around to the back hatch of the van, calling Buddy to her. He hefted out a large cylindrical container, and Maggie slammed the door shut and looked Rance's way. His heart soared as she raised her hand in a cheery wave.

How was it possible that he had become so dependent upon her to brighten his day? Maggie had become a definite ingredient in Rance's recipe for happiness. His heart beat faster as she hurried across the dusty yard.

She'd changed to a cool summer shift of lime green that skimmed her body and dipped at her hips to meet a slightly gathered skirt. It was shapeless and comfortable, but didn't hide the womanly swell of her breasts or her well-shaped arms. Rance would have liked to see her in something more revealing, but he understood the need for comfort in the Alabama heat. Besides, the skirt stopped just short of her well-turned ankles and sandaled feet.

"What's that?" Rance called when Maggie and her son were within hailing distance.

"My world-famous secret-recipe cherry-chocolate-chip ice cream. Or it will be when Buddy and Jen get finished cranking it." Maggie flashed a sunny smile and climbed the steps.

Rance held his breath as Maggie held the door open for Buddy. Would she follow her son in?

Maggie paused at the door. "I made a batch of it yesterday, but we never got to eat it."

"Yes, we did," Buddy called from behind her. "It was great!" He proceeded into the interior of the house.

"Well, Rance and I didn't get to have any. It was my contribution to dinner." Maggie let the door swing shut and turned to the glider. "Is there any room for me?"

If there hadn't been, Rance would gladly have made it. As it was, there was plenty. He slid carefully to the left and patted the bare wooden seat. "I've been saving you a spot."

Maggie dropped her purse by the door, then lowered herself to the swing. She leaned against the glider, one hand on her lap, the other palm down on the seat between them. Her fingers seemed to invite him, and Rance edged his own fingers closer to hers until they touched. She didn't draw away, and she smiled.

It was cooler than Maggie would have expected in the shade of the porch; those old-time home builders must have known what they were doing when they constructed these houses, with their wraparound porches and with glider swings. The gentle sway of the glider provided enough breeze to keep her comfortable, but the very close, all-male body of Rance Montoya was enough to heat her up again.

Since she had discovered Rance's birth name, Maggie wasn't certain what to call him. Hightower or Montoya. His dedication to the house and surrounding land declared him a Hightower, yet his exotic dark features said Montoya. But why had he hidden the truth?

Maggie retracted her fingers and placed her hand on her lap. She shifted slightly and turned to face Rance. "You promised me an explanation."

Chapter 9

Rance looked out over the brown lawn, over the trees, and toward the distant orchard. He was silent for a long moment. Then he turned back to Maggie and reclaimed her hand. "There's nothing sinister about my keeping quiet."

"Why, then?"

"I was seven when my father died. Later, when she realized we couldn't pay the huge debt, much less make ends meet, Mama and I moved to San Antonio. Too young to understand what had really happened. Maybe the emotional stress of Dad's death and the move caused me to forget things I knew." Rance dug into his pocket and pulled out a matchbox. He turned it over and over in his hand.

"I never really knew what led up to my father's suicide. My grandfather would mutter something about foolish scandal, and my mother would cry. Mama would just say that we were going to go home again some day. That it was my birthright. She worked long hours waitressing at my grandfather's restaurant, saving her tips to buy this place back.

"I held on to my mother's dream about regaining the place even after she was gone. And I finally bought the place back. To tell you the truth, once I had it back, I didn't know how the neighbors would react. I didn't know what I'd be walking into. For all I knew, that scandal Grandfather always spoke of could have been murder. Maybe I wouldn't be welcome."

"Why didn't you ask your mother?" Maggie asked simply.

"My mother disappeared when I was nine." Rance took a match from the box and rolled it between his thumb and forefinger.

No wonder he had wanted to dig through those dusty stacks of papers in the library storage room. "I'm sorry." Maggie squeezed Rance's hand. "Did you find out what you wanted?"

"Yes and no," Rance answered, after a moment of reflection. "I thought that the facts would ease my mind, help me to understand. But they just gave me more questions." He broke the match and tossed it over the rail into the stubbled brown yard. "I finally know why my father killed himself, but the information didn't put the past to rest. My mission is far from over."

Maggie sensed that intruding with words would hurt rather than help, so she squeezed Rance's hand and waited for him to continue.

"Dad lost it all on a failed business deal," Rance told her, confirming what she'd already discovered for herself. He laughed ruefully. "That's what happens when a farmer messes with something he doesn't understand.

"What I still don't know is who wrote the terms of the business loan. My father had put his land up as collateral, and apparently somebody—I think his name was

Drake—wanted it. I think he stacked the terms in his favor, and when Dad couldn't pay, he stepped in.''

''Is that legal?''

''Yeah, unfortunately. I expect he waited until the bank foreclosed, then he bought it cheap.''

''Well, it might have been legal, but it was hardly moral,'' Maggie stated indignantly.

''I agree. I think that's why my mother was so angry, and why she left me with my grandfather in San Antonio.''

''You don't know?'' Maggie angled her body around to look Rance squarely in the face. He clamped his mouth tightly closed, and a muscle in his lean jaw twitched. Maggie waited and watched as Rance's grim expression changed to that of pain.

Rance hadn't expected the question, and he was unprepared to answer it. It had taken him most of his life to deal with his mother's disappearance. He had managed to sublimate his feelings, but something still festered deep inside. He wasn't sure he wanted to bare those emotions to Maggie and risk opening up old wounds. He was in enough real pain without dredging up best-forgotten childhood anguish.

Maggie squeezed Rance's hand. She seemed to be offering gentle reassurance, yet demanding nothing. ''You don't have to go on,'' she whispered softly.

That clinched it. Maggie's sensitive understanding told Rance that she would accept what he needed to tell her with compassion and grace.

He drew a deep breath and looked out over the trees at the edge of the yard. Somehow it seemed easier if he didn't have to look at her. ''All I know,'' Rance mouthed slowly, ''is that my mother set off on the day before Mother's Day in 1968. She told me that she was going away, and when she got back, we'd be able to move back home.''

''But you didn't till now,'' Maggie murmured softly.

"She never came back for me," Rance finished, choking on the words.

"Did somebody look for her?" Maggie whispered.

Rance shook his head. "Of course. We reported her missing. There was an investigation, but in spite of my grandfather's insistence otherwise, they concluded that she disappeared because she wanted to go." He swallowed a lump of emotion. "I don't think anybody much cared about a missing Mexican woman."

Maggie opened her mouth to say something, but stopped herself. Rance knew what she was thinking. Or thought he did. Nobody wanted to doubt the intentions of those whose job it was to serve and protect.

After years of dealing with his mother's abandonment by himself, he'd thought he could talk about it. He'd even consulted a shrink about it when he was in the service. He'd thought he'd gotten past the hurt. But damn it, it did hurt. Then. Now. Still.

Rance looked over Maggie's head and blinked, struggling to force back the tears he had held at bay all those years. He gulped in great lungfuls of air until he could see clearly. Until he could speak.

"You know, I haven't heard a word from my mother in thirty years. I even manage not to think about her for weeks at a time." Rance sucked in a deep, shuddering breath. "Yet since I've been in this house, it's as if she's been with me. I can feel her. I don't know why, but I sense her presence."

Maggie looked surprised. "You know, it's odd, but I had the strangest feeling of a female presence here last night." Then she smiled and shook her head. "Silly, huh?"

"No, I don't think it's silly at all." He found himself tearing up, and he looked away until he could compose himself.

Maggie squeezed his hand, and Rance returned the comforting gesture. "Maybe it's because your family lived here. You probably have many happy memories about this place. It's natural that you'd think about her," she suggested quietly.

"Maybe." But how could Rance tell Maggie that it was more than that? He'd felt as if she were actually here. She'd spoken to him at night in his sleep; she'd welcomed him home. She had called to him last night. He didn't know how he knew it, but Rance was certain her spirit was here.

That the sun still shone and the sky was still blue seemed remarkable to Maggie, in the wake of what she'd just heard. Yet the birds still twittered in the trees, and life went on. She tried to imagine how lost the little boy Rance had been would have felt growing up alone. How could a child cope with two such devastating events as the death of his father and the disappearance of his mother—all in such a short span of time?

"I don't know what else to say," Maggie whispered shakily, unable to meet Rance's eyes. Not because she was repulsed by his revelation or because she was embarrassed, but because if she looked at him she would cry. And that was the last thing she suspected Rance needed right now.

"I know. What *can* you say?" Rance's reply was as soft as Maggie's had been. He angled his head, as if to look at the porch overhang, but Maggie knew he wasn't seeing anything. "I never wanted to believe she meant to leave me, but it's been so long with no word." He paused. His next words were soft, barely a whisper. "But now that I'm back here, I think there's a very real and terrible explanation why my mother didn't return."

Maggie looked at Rance, surprised. Rance's expression was calm. Serious. Resolute. "What do you mean?"

"I don't know yet. Call it a feeling, intuition, ESP. You know the car in the pool?"

"Yes," Maggie replied, puzzled about where Rance was taking her.

"I think it's part of the answer to this puzzle."

Cold chills traced icy fingers down Maggie's spine. "How?"

"The car is a Chevrolet, the same make as my mother's was." He shrugged, wincing as his injured muscles reminded him of their presence. "The final answer is here. In this house. I know it. I just have to find it."

The tone of the conversation had been getting too heavy. Rance wanted to steer it to another topic altogether. He would much rather enjoy his time alone on the porch swing with this pretty woman by his side. Yes, he wanted the answers to all his questions, too. But those were not to be found today.

Maggie was here beside him. Why not make the best of the situation? Rance maneuvered his arm around to the back of the porch swing.

The inviting aroma of fried chicken drifted to them, and Rance gratefully accepted the opportunity to think about food. Anything but Rose Montoya Hightower. Anything but the jumble of questions that were his past and present.

He blinked and shook his head and forced a smile. "I think your mother has dinner nearly done. It smells good," Rance announced heartily, in an effort to change the mood.

Maggie's pensive expression lightened. He hadn't intended to upset her with what he said. He hadn't expected to blurt out as much as he had, or he wouldn't have started at all. He was used to being strong and silent. He was used to keeping everything inside. For now, he was happy to see a shy smile brighten Maggie's clouded turquoise eyes.

"You don't know what you've been missing," Maggie said with an infectious grin. "My mom makes the best fried chicken east of the Mississippi and south of the Mason-Dixon line."

Rance returned Maggie's grin. "I hope she made lots. I'm starved."

"Lounging around on a porch swing can really work up an appetite," Maggie teased. "We're all in for a treat. Mom hardly fries anything anymore."

"I guess she heard about the evils of cholesterol, even way out here."

"Not to mention the dreaded fat and calories. Let's go inside." Maggie eased carefully out of the swing and held out her hand.

Rance took it, leaning on her more than his masculine pride would have preferred. He shoved himself out of the glider, sending it swinging wildly, and he bit back a grunt of pain as the seat walloped him in the behind. He'd forgotten his sore ribs for a while, but when he got up, they'd wasted no time in reminding him why he'd been lounging around on the porch all day.

Maggie would rather have returned to the swing after dinner, but Rance insisted on a walk. He had let Buddy and Joe help him down the steps, and was now pacing carefully around in the yard, working out the stiffness in his hurt muscles.

"I'm almost ready," Maggie called as she watched Rance move slowly around on the lawn below. She smeared on another glob of sunscreen and rubbed it in. How she hated to stop everything and slather sun-protection goo on her white skin every time she wanted to go outside in the daytime. But she liked it better than sunburn.

Screwing the cap back on the plastic bottle as she went, Maggie headed for the steps. She stopped at the top and tossed the bottle onto the swing seat and skipped down to join Rance.

He was looking pensively at the grounds. "You know,

I haven't really looked at the yard since I lopped off all the tall grass.''

"Well, let's do a short walkaround. You really have some nice shrubs here. They need some pruning and some T.L.C., but they should come back very nicely. Those old-timey plants have a lot more staying power than the hybrid nursery-grown stock we get today.'' She pointed to a straggly stand of orange blossoms. "There's a nice bed of day-lilies.'' Maggie changed directions and pointed to a clump of tree-size bushes that showed a riot of hot pink blossoms. "And look—those are crepe myrtles blooming over there.''

Maggie pointed to the west side of the house. "There are some azalea bushes,'' she exclaimed, and gestured toward a row of tall, leggy shrubs that grew up against the east wall.

"You can tell they're azaleas? How? There aren't any blooms,'' Rance exclaimed.

Maggie laughed as they ambled over to give the shrubs a closer look. "They are identifiable without blooms.''

"I'll take your word for it,'' Rance drawled as he carefully examined the row of bushes. They looked like a bunch of scraggly brush to him. He stepped back to take in the side view of the old house, a look of pride and contentment on his face.

The landscaping possibilities in Rance's yard were interesting, and Maggie strolled over to a dogwood tree nestled among the pines that stood on the periphery of what would be the lawn. She'd always loved the way the dogwoods spread their gnarled and twisted limbs beneath their tall, straight neighbors.

Rance ambled up behind her. Maggie smiled, oddly pleased that she could draw his attention away from the house. She spoke without turning to look at him, content to know he was there.

"You know, it's remarkable how much survived here,

in spite of the neglect.'' A warm tingle spread throughout her veins when Rance placed his hand lightly on her shoulder. She fought the urge to rub her cheek against the strong, tanned fingers.

''I hadn't given much thought to the grounds,'' Rance admitted. ''My first priority was to get a couple of fields ready for cultivation. I have my military retirement to live on, but it won't go far. I'd like to bring in a cash crop as soon as I can.'' Rance's hand fell from Maggie's shoulder.

Missing the warm caress, Maggie turned to see what had taken Rance's hand away. He had found another match, and was rolling it thoughtfully between his fingers. His eyes shifted from the grounds around the house to the dirt track that led to the dying peach orchard. ''You can still get the yard squared away and get the fields ready,'' Maggie suggested, feeling that she was intruding on his private thoughts.

Rance glanced absently at Maggie, as if he'd forgotten she was there. He smiled a gentle smile. ''But I don't know anything about flower beds or the difference between annuals and perennials. Sure, I'm self-taught about crop rotation and horticulture, but I don't have any practical experience.''

Maggie laughed. ''The basic principles are the same for both. You just can't eat the results.''

Rance laughed. ''I can't eat anything that grows around here now.''

''But you will. In the meantime, you can get your yard in shape, as well as prepare your fields.'' Maggie resumed her survey of the yard. ''Yup, you've got plenty of potential. In fact, it'll probably be easier to bring this back than the farm.''

Maggie steered Rance back toward the porch, where her parents and children had stationed themselves. Daisy had brought out a pitcher of lemonade, and she gestured for them to join the group. Joe was whistling and whittling, working hard at producing a pile of shavings at his feet.

"I guess I'll defer to your expert wisdom as far as the grounds are concerned. You obviously know more about lawn care than I do." Rance took Maggie's arm as she strolled toward the house.

Maggie stopped at the bottom of the porch steps. "It's a good thing you didn't say gardening is woman's work," she said teasingly, laughing at Rance's expression.

His face crinkled into a big grin, followed by a deep belly laugh. He cut the laughter short, and a grimace replaced his grin. "Don't make me do that."

Having the grace to feel sheepish, Maggie looked contrite. "I'm sorry. I forgot about your ribs. I guess it hurts, as they say, to laugh."

"They say? *I* say it hurts. Let's go sit down."

"I'm for it. Oh, by the way, you know who would be a big help with the yard?"

"I hope you'll tell me."

"Tess. She's very big in the Pittsville Garden Club. I know she looks like she never breaks a nail, but she's won awards."

"I'll defer to whatever you and your sister recommend," Rance said as he started up the steps. The top seemed a long way off, but he made it, though he clung to the stair railings for dear life. Gratefully he lowered himself into the swing, and Maggie settled next to him as naturally as if they'd been doing it all their lives.

Except for his ribs, Rance was feeling reasonably fit. His legs had been sore and stiff, but the walk had helped. If he didn't coddle himself too much, he would be almost up to speed in a few days. He leaned back, closed his eyes, and sighed contentedly.

Big mistake. Rance squeezed his eyes tighter as a spasm of pain shot through him. Deep-breathing exercises were definitely out for a while yet. He forced his breaths to come slow and shallow until the twinge had passed.

"Look, somebody's coming," Maggie announced. Rusty barked from under the porch, but was apparently too busy with her brood to investigate.

Rance opened his eyes and saw her pointing to a cloud of orange dust that accompanied a car as it bumped down the rutty dirt lane that meandered between the overhanging crepe myrtles.

"Who could that be? I don't know that many people yet, and most of 'em are already here."

"It looks like Bob Carterette's car to me," commented Daisy. "I'd best go get a couple more glasses." She scurried inside.

The name touched something in the back of Rance's mind, a long forgotten memory. "*Reverend* Carterette?"

"How'd you know that?" Joe drawled.

A Reverend Carterette had officiated at Luther Hightower's funeral. Could this be the same minister, coming to pay a call?

Maggie crossed the yard to greet the visitors. The man was in his early thirties, too young to have ministered to the elder Hightower, and Rance was vaguely disappointed. It had fleetingly occurred to him that Carterette might know something about his family. How strange it was to be so close to his answers, after so long a time.

Joe sat up a little straighter in his lawn chair. "Young Bob just took over Mattison Methodist. Old Bob's retired."

Maybe he would pay a visit to Old Bob and see what the retired minister knew. Rance figured if anyone would remember what went on back then, the preacher would.

Maggie ushered the clean-cut young minister and his pretty wife up the steps. Joe gestured toward the chair that Daisy had vacated, and the minister's wife took a seat.

Carterette leaned up against one of the roof supports as Maggie began the introductions.

"This is Bobby Carterette, and his wife, Lucy. Bobby just took over Mattison Methodist."

Rance started to rise.

Bobby waved him down. "No need to get up. I heard about your accident. Just thought I'd pay a call and see if we could help." He leaned forward and extended his hand.

"This is Rance Montoya," Maggie continued. "He's Luther Hightower's son."

Rance swung his eyes to Maggie, and he felt the color drain from his face. He hadn't told Maggie who he was so that she could announce it to the world. Hell, he still wasn't sure he wanted everybody to know. He shook the young minister's hand numbly as he resisted the urge to strangle Maggie.

Joe stopped what he was doing and laid down his pocketknife. Buddy gaped. Jennifer stared.

"Well." Bobby shook his head, as if to shake off his amazement. "That's one big surprise." He pumped Rance's hand vigorously. "Welcome home."

Maggie knew enough to tread lightly around Rance after she made the unauthorized announcement. Luckily, there were enough people around to diffuse the anger simmering just behind Rance's obsidian-colored eyes. By the time everyone had gone, Maggie sensed she would be safe alone in the same room with Rance.

The kids had gone with Maggie's parents, ostensibly to the pond to fish while the fishing was good. It was just a ploy on Maggie's parents' part to give her a chance to set things straight with Rance. She figured Rance knew it, too, but he wasn't making it easy for her.

Once everyone had gone, Rance made his way inside. He acted as though Maggie weren't there and switched on the television, positioning himself on the new sofa. Reception was never good this far out in the country, but Rance stared at the snowy double image on the screen as if his life depended on it.

Maggie hovered in the doorway, undecided. Should she hang it all up and go home, or should she force a confrontation? Always a coward, Maggie chose "None of the above." She gathered up the empty pitcher and lemonade glasses and carried them to the kitchen. He might not want to talk to her, but he wasn't going to run her off, either. No, sir, not Margaret Rose Popwell Callahan.

Maybe it was time to resume the kill-him-with-kindness campaign, Maggie thought as she washed the glasses and pitcher. She even dried them by hand, something she would never do at home. She knew it was a delaying tactic at best, but she needed time to come up with a plan.

The plan came to her as she finished straightening up the kitchen. She would simply act as if blurting out Rance's secret were no big deal and pick up with the southern hospitality where she'd left off.

She made a pitcher of iced tea, then looked inside the aged refrigerator. She found enough left from dinner to feed two, if they weren't gluttons, and prepared a tray with two plates of cold fried chicken, potato salad and coleslaw. Okay, so she was using somebody else's food to get through his stomach to his attention, she thought as she poured tea into glasses. It was the thought that counted.

Rance was still staring at the fuzzy television picture, trying to hear the nightly news, when Maggie came out with the supper tray. She placed it on the coffee table in front of him and took a plate and a glass of tea to a large high-backed chair that sat at an angle to the sofa. She was very careful not to block the television screen, not to talk, not to intrude. Acting as if nothing were wrong, she ate.

It pleased Maggie that Rance did not hesitate to avail himself of what she had set before him. He might be angry, but he had enough sense to know when he was hungry. Maybe on a full stomach, he would be reasonable.

Rance clicked off the set with the remote control and looked at Maggie with an unreadable expression. A dark lock of straight black hair fell across one coal black eye, and Maggie felt an unreasonable urge to cross the room and brush the hair away. She didn't. She just waited.

"I see it didn't make the local news" was all he said, as he picked up a chicken leg.

Success, Maggie thought. He was talking. How should she respond? She removed her dinner plate from her lap and set it on the tray again.

Brandishing her glass of tea, she confronted him. "Rance, the only reason people were surprised was because you'd hidden it from them in the first place."

It seemed that the chicken leg was more important than a response. Maggie shuddered at the feral way Rance chewed at the leg until it was nothing but a bare bone. He put it down and dragged a paper napkin across his mouth. He worked his mouth as if he were trying to form words, but nothing came out.

Maggie hadn't really hurt anything by blurting out an omitted fact, Rance realized. She hadn't meant to hurt him and, in fact, had probably helped. He also realized that he wasn't really angry about what she'd told everybody. He wasn't angry at them. He wasn't sure he was angry at all.

But he was damn sure confused.

He had made a life for himself as Rance Montoya. He knew all about Rance Montoya, retired air force major and all-around good guy. He didn't know who this Rance Hightower was, or who he was supposed to be.

Rance looked across the room to Maggie. Maggie, who had stepped into his life just one week ago, who had kept him off balance all week, had just upset another apple cart, with him in it. He knew he had frightened her with his moody silence, and he had to make it right.

But doing that meant he would have to bare himself to her again. How could she respect a man who always seemed to be advertising his insecurities? How could anyone love him? He stopped short with his introspection and reached for a match. Did he really mean *love?*

He realized that he was falling in love with her, had already fallen, but he didn't feel worthy. How could he give himself to a woman when he wasn't sure who he was anymore? When his own mother hadn't bothered to hang around to see him through life? Rance put the match down on his plate and struggled to his feet.

"Maggie, come here." He held his hand out toward her.

She came and stood in front of him, her blue-green eyes wide and questioning. She offered him her hand.

Rance folded her small, white, sun-dappled fingers in his. He looked deep into her eyes and felt he would drown in them before he could finish what he had to say. To save himself, he looked away.

"I'm not angry at you. I'm not angry because you told them my name. I was at first, but I'm over it." Rance squeezed his fingers tighter around hers.

Maggie started to speak, but Rance stopped her, placing two fingers gently against her peach-colored lips.

"Let me finish," he continued huskily. "I'm not sure who I am. Yesterday I was Rance Montoya. I knew where I'd been, and I thought I knew where I was going. Today I'm Rance Hightower, and I don't know who he is at all." He sighed long and deep.

"I'll help you find him," Maggie whispered softly.

Rance worked his fingers loose from Maggie's and cupped her face in his hands. He looked into her eyes as he caressed her lower lip with his thumb. His first urge was to kiss her, but he pulled away.

He brought his fingers down to his side, clenching them, then opening them again. Away from distraction, temptation. Her. "Why do you care?" he asked hoarsely.

Chapter 10

Maggie backed up and tilted her head so that she could look into his dark eyes. She breathed deep, then spoke, hoping her words would be the right ones. "I see a strong man who has worked hard and long to be where he is. I see a man who is gentle and kind and sometimes tries to hide it. I see a good man who can take whatever life has to throw at him, deal with it, and come out stronger. Why wouldn't anybody care about that kind of man?"

Rance looked hungrily into Maggie's eyes, his deep, dark eyes delving into her soul. She resisted the urge to look away, and met his gaze head-on. She had to show him she wasn't afraid.

She found the courage to step forward, and reached up to touch his lean jaw. She felt the raspy contrast between his coarse cheek and her own hand. Senses that had long been sleeping had been wakened by his touch, and now she couldn't bear not to touch him.

How could she not react to him after what happened last night? Then again, how *could* she? Had his actions last night been intended, or were they merely those of a man too heavily medicated to know what he was doing? Until she was sure, she would just pretend nothing had happened.

If she could.

The man gazing so needily down at her reminded her of how it was to be with a man. She remembered how it felt to see a man, to touch him, to hear him, to feel him. She drank in his male scent, mixed with soap and aftershave and a touch of fried chicken.

Then she released herself from her own tangled web of emotions and backed away. Whatever was to be between them could wait for another day. A day when he was stronger.

When she was stronger.

It was too much for Rance to take in at one time. The smell of her musky perfume, her delicate white skin dusted with freckles and that riot of red hair formed a trap into which he would willingly fall. But he didn't have the strength. He wasn't ready.

He knew that Maggie had expected him to kiss her, but his body wasn't able to do what he wanted, willing as his spirit might be. He'd found that out last night. He was so grateful that she had taken that step backward, so that he wouldn't have to push her away. He didn't know whether he would have been able to do it.

His heart wasn't yet strong enough for him to give it away. That was the main problem. He still had too much healing to do. In spite of what Maggie had told him, Rance felt unworthy. There were too many unanswered questions about his past. Until he resolved them, he could not move on.

He groaned from somewhere deep within his soul. It was best not to start anything he couldn't finish.

Rance stepped back to put more distance between them,

then stepped back again. It was just too easy to reach out and touch her. He kept backing away until the high-backed chair stopped his cowardly retreat. He could still see Maggie's beautiful, caring face, hear her, and smell her. Maybe it would be enough.

"I'm sorry," Rance finally rasped. He wasn't sure whether he was apologizing for starting this emotional confrontation in the first place. Or for stopping it. Let her read into it what she needed.

Maggie looked at him expectantly, waiting. For him to kiss her? Or for an explanation?

Rance raked a hand through his hair, confused. He didn't know what to say. He certainly couldn't tell her that if she didn't go soon, he would beg her to stay. Would it be that much easier on him to dream of her while they both lay alone and separated by half a mile and a narrow strip of macadam? Or to lie with her and be able to do nothing, as he had last night?

"I think I'd better go home," Maggie finally said, relieving Rance of the responsibility of sending her away.

"Please thank your family for everything they've done for me in the last few days," he rasped. Rance hated the stiff and formal way they were speaking. He wanted to call her back. "Thank you, Maggie," he whispered.

Maggie turned and smiled. A wan smile, but a smile nonetheless. Then she slipped outside.

"What do you mean, you haven't seen him in a week?" Tess stopped grabbing the gardening supplies from the back of Tom's El Camino.

"I think he's avoiding me," Maggie answered quietly as she began unloading where Tess had left off. How had she let that little fact slip? Now Tess wouldn't leave her alone until she'd ferreted out the whole story. And, if truth be known, after what they'd done that night alone in his bedroom, she'd been avoiding him.

"After what you've done for him? What a jerk!" Tess put her hands on her hips. "Why am I fixin' to be his yardman?"

Maggie started to respond to Tess's outburst, then stopped. She felt someone watching her. She looked up and noticed that Rance had appeared. He was chewing on the ever-present match, and his dark eyes bored into hers so hard that she had to look away. When she looked up again, he was coming toward her.

His gait was still deliberate, but he looked much better than he had the week before. He had one arm hitched against his side as if it still hurt, but apart from that, he looked pretty fit. Maggie's heart made a tiny leap of joy. *Did* he remember, or did he think it had only been his imagination that night? Or had he decided in the clear light of day that he didn't want her?

"Shh. He'll hear you," Maggie said in a stage whisper.

Tess glanced up, then turned back to her work. "Okay," she whispered. "Tell me what's wrong before he gets here."

Maggie forced herself to the task at hand. "It's nothing, really, Tess." She tried to gauge how much of it she could safely confess. Her sister had been the biggest blabbermouth at Mattison Consolidated High School, and Maggie wasn't sure Tess had improved with age.

"Well?"

Sighing resignedly, Maggie told Tess, with as little embellishment as possible. "We just started something last week that we couldn't finish."

Tess's eyes grew wide, and her mouth formed a silent "Oh." She turned her gaze toward Rance, and her mouth widened into a grin. "Really?"

"He was injured, Tess! I knew I shouldn't have said anything." Maggie hoisted the last bag of fertilizer out of the truck and onto the ground.

"Well, fill me in on the details before he gets here."

Tess smiled brightly and waved in Rance's direction. He returned her wave and tossed the match away. Tess turned back to Maggie.

Maggie hesitated, watching Rance from the corner of her eye. "He said he wanted to make love to me. But he was too injured to do anything about it." For all practical purposes, he had made love to her, but she wouldn't tell Tess that. "He probably doesn't remember it, because he was heavily medicated, but he did kiss me."

"Oh. That's all?" Tess sounded as disappointed as Maggie had been at the time. Then her face brightened. "But that's not so bad. It shows he's interested," she finished hopefully.

"He was probably delirious. He'd just had a tractor pulled off him."

Tess made a face. Then, wiping her hands on her denim-clad thighs, she turned to greet Rance. "Hi, handsome. I thought I'd work on that row of azaleas around the side of the house this afternoon." She waved her hand in the direction of the overgrown shrubs.

Rance glanced toward the spot and frowned.

"Would you rather we work someplace else?" Maggie hoped the expression wasn't for her. Rance had asked Tess over to help; he hadn't actually included Maggie.

"That's fine. I was just thinking." Rance's frown deepened as he scanned the row of bushes.

Maggie gathered up the equipment they'd unloaded.

Rance rubbed his chin as he studied the row of shrubs. Then he looked up, eyeing the bags of fertilizer. "I can't help you with the heavy stuff." He shrugged apologetically. "Still not cleared for heavy lifting."

"Don't give it no nevah mind, sugah," Tess announced in a syrupy-sweet phony drawl. "We didn't bring nothin' we couldn't carry our little ol' selves."

Maggie grimaced and shook her head slowly. She trudged up the slight embankment and across the yard to

the azaleas, grateful to be as far away from Tess's dra-
matics as possible. Rance picked up a rake and hoe and
followed. Tess brought up the rear with a box of hand
tools.

"Rance, honey, can you run us a hose over here?" Tess
asked as she deposited the box at the middle of the row
of azaleas.

Maggie was close enough to notice that Rance's bruises
had faded to the point of being barely visible. She probably
wouldn't have seen them at all if she didn't know they
were there. And she was too close to keep her heart from
beating wildly.

Rance nodded and looked thoughtfully toward the back
of the house. "I guess I can connect some hoses to the
old water line."

"Would you mind?" Tess fluttered her eyelashes.

Maggie thought she would toss her cookies, and told
Tess so as soon as Rance was out of earshot. "What are
you doing simpering like Blanche Du Bois?" she hissed.
"And why did you send Rance off? We won't need water
for hours."

"Tell me about what happened the other night," Tess
demanded as she glanced toward Rance's retreating figure.
"He'll only be out of earshot a few minutes."

"He'll be sick if you spill any more of that saccharine
southern-belle talk on him." Maggie tugged on her gardening gloves. "Let's get started."

"We will. What about it?"

"It's simple. Rance and I both got carried away." Maggie yanked at an enormous dandelion. "It isn't a big deal."

"Details, sister. Details."

Maggie sighed and gave the G-rated version of the story,
including the two trips downstairs. The love scene she
omitted.

It occurred to Rance about the time he reached the pump
house that Tess and Maggie were probably in no hurry to

use any water. He wondered if Maggie was trying to tell him that his attentions weren't welcome. Considering what had happened the week before, he really wouldn't blame her.

But then, Maggie hadn't sent him on the wild-goose chase; Tess had. Maybe Maggie wasn't angry.

He tinkered with the pump as long as he could, then made a final check of the water pipe. It was rusted, but it would work for now. He looped a coil of hose, hung it over his shoulder and stepped outside.

The two women had made a surprising amount of progress, he noticed as he came out of the dark pump house and into the bright afternoon. He stood for a moment, allowing his eyes to adjust to the light. He hadn't noticed before that Tess was wearing dark sunglasses to protect her eyes from the bright sun. The look was just right for Maggie's sophisticated older sister. But what interested him more was the Huckleberry Finn straw hat that Maggie wore. No sunglasses for her; she looked perfect in her country hat and yellow work gloves.

Rance made plenty of noise as he came up the hill, just to make sure he didn't catch them talking about him. He was pretty sure that Tess would send him off, because she wanted to talk with Maggie, so he gave her a chance to finish.

They'd already used the weed trimmer to hack down the tallest weeds around the shrubs. Now both Maggie and Tess sat cross-legged on the ground, attacking the soil with trowels and cultivating tools.

Rance shrugged the coil of hose off his shoulder and let it fall to the ground beside them, then showed them the pressure nozzle. "Just turn it on when you're ready," he said, and prepared to leave.

Tess nudged her sister, and Maggie shot her a dirty look. "Ask him," she urged in a stage whisper.

Maggie flashed her anger. "You want to see it so bad, ask."

"Ask me what?"

Both women turned guiltily to face him. Tess had the grace to look embarrassed, and Maggie colored from the roots of her hair to the vee of her buttercup gold work shirt. She looked at Rance apologetically, wiping a strand of damp, red hair away from her cheek and leaving a smudge of dirt behind.

"My darling sister wants to get a look at your cellar. She doesn't understand why we both went exploring the other night."

"Hell, neither do I." Rance laughed. "There's nothing down there except dust and spiders."

"I can withstand a few bugs," Tess said, gracefully pushing herself to her feet. She peeled off her gloves, then looked down at her muddy jeans. "I don't think a little more dirt will make much difference. Let's go."

"Has she always been such a steamroller?" Rance asked, watching Maggie scramble to her feet and peel out of her own set of bright yellow gloves.

"From the day I was born," Maggie answered dryly.

"Not from birth?"

"She's three years older than I. For the first three years, she didn't have anybody to push around."

"Don't rub it in about my advanced age, little sister." Tess put her hands on her hips. "Well?"

There was nothing else to do but humor her.

A sense of foreboding assailed Maggie as soon as she stepped off the bottom step and onto the cold cellar floor. The musty, decayed smell was as strong as ever, and she noticed cobwebs hanging thickly everywhere. How had she missed them before? She shivered in the unnatural chill as she dodged a particularly thick bunch of cobwebs.

Maggie shuddered. "Ugh! Just like a horror movie."

Something skittered across the floor and into a dark corner, doing nothing to calm her already nervous state. It was probably a field mouse, Maggie tried to convince herself. Or a rat. *Or the ghost of the long dead.*

It was cool downstairs, but not cool enough to account for the dense layer of gooseflesh that had formed on Maggie's bare arms. Enough goose bumps for two large geese, not to mention one medium-size woman. She rubbed her hands against her arms to warm them.

Rance was the last one down, and he pulled on the light as he passed the cord. Why hadn't she thought of that? The bare forty-watt bulb did little to illuminate the cavelike room, but it was better than nothing.

Maggie took a moment to orient herself, then pointed toward the east side of the house. Dirty windows, high on the walls, blocked more light than they let in.

Another unidentified animal scuttled through the shadows. "Is it just me, or does this place give anybody else the creeps?" Tess asked, her voice more timid than Maggie remembered ever hearing it. Tess looked warily around.

Maggie started to agree with Tess's pronouncement, but her sister interrupted her. "Okay, end of subject. I didn't think it was going to look like a mausoleum." She shuddered. "I'm going upstairs where it's warm." She turned and clattered loudly up the stairs.

But it wasn't the end of the subject. It would have been if Maggie hadn't heard the voice, she realized as Tess fled. And Tess's comment about the mausoleum didn't help. Tombs? Corpses? Disembodied voices? Maggie shuddered and looked at Rance. Even in the dim light, she could see that his handsome face was marred by a frown.

Maggie shivered. "Do you feel a draft? It shouldn't be this cold in July. Even down here." She tried to convince herself that Rance's proximity had made her tingle, and she resisted the urge to follow Tess.

A shadow crossed over one of the windows. Then the other grew dark, returning the space to near sepulchral gloom. A sharp rapping sound startled Maggie, and she jumped.

Rance chuckled as Rusty barked a greeting, and Maggie sighed with relief. It had only been Tess's and Rusty's shadows blocking off the light. Maggie smiled sheepishly and waved.

"Rance, I'm going back upstairs." Cowardly it might be, but Maggie couldn't think of one good reason to stay in that dark, creepy cellar for another minute.

No!

There it was again. The voice. Maggie backed toward the stairs. Even in the daytime, the place was spooky.

"Rance?"

The cinder block was cold and gritty to the touch, Rance realized as he ran his hand lightly along the wall. *Damn it,* he thought. "That wall shouldn't be there," he murmured.

"Rance!" Maggie's tone sounded urgent.

He swung around to look at her. Maggie's fair complexion seemed even paler than usual, and she chafed her arms.

"I'm going upstairs," she told him, not trying to hide her panicky look. Her turquoise eyes were shadowed and gray now. "Come on. That wall's been there forever. It isn't going anywhere."

"Okay. I'll be right up." Rance turned back to the wall. That was just it. That wall *hadn't* always been there. There was something wrong down here, and he knew it. He had played down here in this cellar on many a rainy day as a child, and he remembered it well. He was certain the place had been bigger. But then, he was a grown man now, a large man. Maybe the room just looked smaller to his adult eyes. He looked around again. No. It had changed.

Rance took one more long look around before he left, and shook his head. "I guess we can go up," he muttered.

Please!

"Maggie?" A chill, like the touch of cold, clammy fingers, crawled down Rance's spine, and he shivered.

He was alone in the cellar. As he hurried up the stairs, he could have sworn he heard a disappointed sigh.

Maggie collected the straw hat from where she'd left it on the swing. Even on the well-shaded porch, it was far warmer than the tomblike cellar. She stood in the shade for a moment longer, collecting herself, then hurried down the front steps, jamming the hat on her head as she went.

Rusty greeted her at the bottom of the porch with a wag of her tail and a joyful bark. Maggie stopped to fondle the dog's head and laughed as Rusty jumped up and bestowed on her a wet doggy kiss. It was just what she needed to rid herself of the creepy feeling the dank cellar had imprinted on her mind. "How are you, Rusty girl? And how are your babies?" The pups would be about two weeks old now, soon big enough to come out to play.

Rusty answered with a short bark and raced away toward her burrow under the front porch.

The fleeting respite from the creepy feeling ended when a hand clamped down on her shoulder. The shivery feeling returned with a vengeance.

"I guess we'd better see what Tess is up to." Rance's rich baritone voice filled Maggie's ear. His breath warmed her and sent cold shivers through her at the same time. She would have pneumonia by the end of the day, if she couldn't stop her blood from running hot and cold.

"You...you..." Maggie's tongue tripped over her surprised response.

"Startled you?"

There he went again, finishing her sentences, not that Maggie minded. It was pleasant having another person know what she was thinking. Especially since that person was Rance.

"I didn't mean to." Rance's strong hand on Maggie's shoulder urged her to move forward.

Enjoying the tingling sensation she always got when Rance touched her, Maggie followed him to look for Tess.

They found Tess on her hands and knees, wiping at the dirty glass of one of the basement windows. She shielded her eyes with one hand as she peered inside.

"What do you see?" Maggie asked as she and Rance came up behind her.

Tess gasped and scooted away from the window. She sat up on her haunches and clutched at her chest. "God, you scared the life out of me! Don't sneak up on a person like that!"

Maggie chuckled. It served Tess right for starting the whole thing in the first place. If she hadn't insisted on going down to look at the cellar, they wouldn't both be spooked now. "Fine. Next time I'll call ahead."

"Go ahead and laugh," Tess muttered. "You've probably scared me out of ten years of life."

"Gosh, I'm getting younger than you by the minute," Maggie said teasingly.

Tess made a very unbecoming face and turned toward Rance. "Maybe if you cleaned those windows, it wouldn't be so creepy down there."

"A couple of hundred-watt light bulbs wouldn't hurt, either," Maggie commented, knowing almost before she finished that it wasn't likely that more light would silence the voice.

The sound of a vehicle coming up the dirt drive distracted Rance, and he went to investigate.

Joe's old pickup, the one he used for dirty work and fishing, drew to a halt, and Buddy leaped from the passenger side. "Look what I found in the woods down by that pool," he shouted, displaying a lumpy brown object.

"That's nice," Rance said without really looking. He turned to Joe. "How were they biting?"

"Damn good." Joe reached into the bed of the truck and opened an old foam cooler and pulled out a good-size string of fish. "I reckon there's some good come out of that old logjam. I found me a new fishin' hole."

Buddy hefted his discovery in his hand, and something about the motion triggered a memory from a dark corner of Rance's mind. A memory that had taken shape the day they located the car. A vague memory that was becoming more vivid by the moment.

Maggie and Tess appeared from around the corner. "I thought I heard you, Buddy. How many did you catch?" Maggie circled her arm around Buddy's waist and squeezed.

Rance envied Buddy the hug as he answered, "I got five."

Tess eyed the string of fish her father was still displaying. "Not bad, Bud."

Buddy's face fell. "Grampa got six, though." Then he brightened again. "But look what I found." He again held up the object he'd displayed earlier.

It seemed smaller somehow, to Rance's adult eyes.

"It looks like a rock or something, but Grampa says it's made of fired clay." Buddy's eager eyes looked up into his mother's. "Do you think it's an ancient Indian bowl or something?"

Maggie shrugged. "I don't know, son. Let me see." She took the encrusted object from Buddy and turned it over in her hands.

"I don't think it's Indian pottery, Bud," Maggie finally said, after looking at it carefully. "At least not like anything I've ever seen."

"Maybe I've discovered a new kind," the boy suggested hopefully.

"I don't think so, Buddy," Tess told him gently. "But it's real neat, anyway. Maybe you can clean it up and use it for a paperweight."

"Maybe," Buddy echoed dejectedly.

Rance knew he should say something, but what? It wasn't as if he were sure. And if he was, it would change everything.

Drawing a deep breath, Rance waved to Joe as he drove away, then turned his attention to Buddy's find. Though he tried to be nonchalant, his heart pounded. "Can I see that?"

"Sure." Maggie tossed it over.

Rance's heart lurched as it came flying toward him. He caught it. It felt familiar, as he'd known it would, and he didn't have to look to know what it was. He knew every inch of it by heart. Chilly fingers played against his spine again as he remembered.

"Wait!"

She stopped.

Rance spun around and ran back toward the house. He stopped in the doorway and turned back. "Don't go yet. I have something for you."

He hurried inside to his bedroom, skidding on the throw rug on the slippery tile floor. Rance righted himself and charged on. He threw open the lid of his toy box and dug out a small wrapped package. He lifted it carefully and smoothed the bright Sunday-comics wrapping and then raced back to his waiting mother.

"Don't you remember what tomorrow is?" Rance shouted as he raced out to the car.

Mama sat in the driver's seat, the door still open. She looked puzzled. "No. What's special about tomorrow?"

"It's Mother's Day!" Rance yelled gleefully as he skidded to a halt in front of the open car door.

He held the package out to his mother and explained shyly, "I made this for you in school. It's for Mother's Day."

"Oh. Rancito, I had forgotten." She wiped a tear from her cheek. "And you made this for me?"

Mama undid the colorful newspaper wrapping and looked at the lumpy clay object.

"Do you like it, Mama? It's an ashtray." Rance admired his handiwork proudly.

"Oh, yes. It's the most beautiful ashtray I've ever seen. Thank you, son. Thank you." Mama leaned out of the car and enfolded him in a long embrace.

"If you like it so much, Mama, then why are you crying?"

"I'm crying because I like it. And I love you." She ruffled Rance's hair and kissed him on the forehead.

Rance wriggled out of his mother's grasp and stepped back. At the advanced age of nine, he was too old for all this mushy stuff. "You're welcome," he said gruffly for lack of anything else.

"Oh, you're getting so big," Mama said, her voice wobbly. "You be a good little man for your grandfather."

"I will." Rance stepped back so that his mother could close the door.

"I love my ashtray," she called over the sound of the starting engine. Rance watched her place his gift beside her on the seat. Then she eased the car toward the road.

"Bye, Mama. See you in a week," Rance called as the car pulled away. He watched as the car reached the main road and sped off. He had never noticed before, he realized as the car disappeared from sight, that his mama's license plate spelled ROSIE H.

"I know what this is," Rance said quietly.

Chapter 11

"How do you know what it is?" Maggie asked, grabbing back the thing she'd just relinquished.

"I made it when I was nine years old," Rance replied quietly, his voice more subdued than Maggie had ever heard it.

Three pairs of eyes stared. Three mouths gaped. Three people didn't say a word.

"If you'll turn it over, you'll see some letters scratched on the underside. *RMH*," he told them.

Rance's suggestion nudged Maggie out of her shocked state and into action. She turned the object flat side up and looked at it carefully. Barely visible beneath a crusty layer of mud and dried algae were the letters. Maggie drew in a sharp breath. "I see them."

Tess and Buddy crowded around her, jostling Maggie's arm in their efforts to see.

"What is it?" Buddy finally asked.

"It's an ashtray. I made it in school when I was in the third grade. I put my initials on it. *RMH* stands for Rance

Montoya Hightower.'' Rance took the ashtray from Maggie and looked at it again.

"I gave it to my mother for Mother's Day. She took it with her when she left," he added softly. Rance handed the ashtray back to Buddy. "Here, take it."

Buddy shoved the crude ashtray back at its maker. "Gee, Mr. Montoya. I can't take it. It looks too important to you," he said, with more perception than normally belonged to a thirteen-year-old. Maggie's heart swelled with pride at her son's gesture.

Rance closed his big hand over the ashtray and clutched it to his chest.

"But how did it get here? You were in Texas when you were nine, weren't you?" Leave it to Tess to ask the right question at the wrong time.

Rance's handsome face grew almost as pale as it had that day when Maggie rushed him to the hospital. Wrinkles furrowed his brow, and a frown stretched his full lips into a flat, straight line.

"You don't have to talk about it if you don't want to," Maggie told him, sensing that the subject was more painful than Rance might be ready to admit. She touched his arm in a gesture of support. Or comfort.

He was silent for a long, slow minute. "I don't honestly know how it got here," he answered, his voice husky with pain and emotion. "The last time I saw it was the day I gave it to Mama. Thirty-some years ago. The last time I ever saw her."

Rance turned away. For a moment, his shoulders shook, but then they stilled. He straightened, pulled his shoulders back, and turned around again. "I think we'd better call it a day," he told everyone quietly.

"Okay." Maggie swatted Buddy on the rear. "Go pick up the tools we left around by the house. We'll come back another time and finish up."

Tess started to say something, but Maggie shot her a

warning look and jerked her head toward the side of the house. Tess and Maggie followed Buddy, subdued after what they'd heard. They gathered up the abandoned equipment, and when they came back around to the front of the house, Rance had gone inside.

It would have been easy to convince himself that the car in the creek was a coincidence. There were hundreds of cars of that make and model, made that same year. But Rance couldn't shrug off the ashtray as happenstance. He looked down at the misshapen lump of clay and smiled sadly. It was one of a kind.

This was no coincidence. He had to admit it. He sat in the dim living room and turned the piece over and over in his hands. He pressed it against his ear, as if it might be able to give him an answer to any of his many questions. There was only one explanation for that unique piece of handmade pottery having fallen from that particular car.

It had to mean that Rose Montoya Hightower had been here some time after she left San Antonio. And considering the sudden appearance of flowers on Luther Hightower's grave about that same time, there was no other conclusion he could make.

This must have been where she was headed that day so long ago. But what had happened to her? Where was she now? Rose Hightower had been no stranger in Mattison, Alabama. She'd lived there for years, given birth to her son and buried her husband. How could her presence have gone unnoticed?

Maybe nobody had known she was here. Rance tried to convince himself. But how could she possibly have bought flowers, probably in Pittsville, gone to the cemetery and then come here, and have not one solitary person see her?

But somebody had to have known. At least one person did. The person who had driven the car through the woods and hidden it in the creek. The person who'd had the presence of mind to remove the identifying personalized car tag. It was no accident that the car had ended up in that pool in the stream, hidden away from the light of day for three long decades. That one person had to have known. And every time he thought about it, his conclusions always came down to Drake.

Rance wasn't certain what good it would do now that so much time had passed, but he had to report his suspicions. At least, with the ashtray as evidence, he had some corroboration of his theory, for what it was.

Rance reached for his newly installed phone. Without hesitating, he dialed the sheriff.

A week passed before Maggie and Tess were able to finish the job they'd started at Hightower's Haven. They'd stayed away to give Rance time to deal with the startling find. He hadn't said anything about the ashtray when they arrived, and neither Maggie nor Tess had pressed.

Several times during the past week, Maggie had wanted to call Rance to ask him how he was. But every time she picked up the receiver, she'd put it hastily down. It wasn't something to discuss over the phone. And she hadn't been sure he was ready for her to intrude. When he called on Friday to see whether she and Tess still wanted to work on the shrubs, she'd said yes, but chickened out when it came to asking about his feelings. Was she ever going to get over the streak of cowardice?

Now the three of them stood, tired and dusty, in front of the pruned and weeded row of azalea bushes. They had done all that they could for now, and Maggie was well satisfied with her day's work.

"Well, boss man, what do you think?" Tess gathered up her long blond hair, twisted it up and held it away from her neck as Rance looked over her handiwork.

A slight feeling of irritation wound its way through Maggie as she watched Tess's provocative pose. Tess was a happily married woman. Why was she flirting with Maggie's man?

Maggie flushed as she realized what she had just admitted to herself. *Her* man? Was Maggie staking her own claim to Rance? The thought was ridiculous. She'd avoided him like the plague for the past two weeks. And he'd barely spoken to her today. Was it because he was embarrassed about what had happened that night in his bedroom? Or was he still bothered that she'd told everyone who he really was? Her man, indeed!

Maggie and Tess had weeded, cultivated and pruned the leggy, overgrown azalea bushes into submission. At the moment, the shrubs looked like nothing more than scrawny sticks. But Maggie and Tess had fertilized and watered them well. When they were done, they had blanketed the ground around the base of each plant with a layer of pine straw, to protect the roots from the heat of the sun and to hold the water in. The shrubs didn't look like much now, but they would be something next year.

Rance shrugged. "I guess they look fine."

Maggie took one look at Rance's disappointed face and had to laugh. What had he expected, miracles? "You don't have to be so diplomatic. They do look pretty bedraggled right now. Come next spring, these sorry specimens will surprise you. We may have sacrificed some of the blooms by cutting them back so severely at this time of year, but it was best in the long run."

Rance's relief was obvious. "Okay, I defer to your superior judgment on this. Now what about the lawn?"

"It already looks better since you've been watering it, but we're not done yet," Tess informed Rance. "I'm leaving you some weed-control fertilizer to use, but my part of the job is pretty much done till fall. Maggie will show you how to spread it, then you'll just have to keep it watered."

Tess pushed her sunglasses to the top of her head and

let her hair fall to her shoulders. She rubbed her eyes. "I've got to get home, Rance. You and Maggie can handle the fertilizer detail by yourselves."

"Thanks for leaving us the best job, sis." Maggie grinned and saluted. Tess returned the salute with a wave of her hand and headed toward her car, dusting off her jeans as she went.

Maggie glanced at Rance. He seemed to be scrutinizing the shrubs, but Maggie knew better. She would have bet money he was still hung up about the cellar wall, and why they had been drawn to it.

"There's probably a very logical reason for one of the previous owners to have walled up the cellar," Maggie told him. "Maybe they were going to make a rec room and wanted it to be a specific size. They didn't need the rest of the room, so they walled it off."

Rance narrowed his eyes, squinting as if he were trying to see through the wall into the space behind. He rubbed his lean jaw absently. "Yeah. Could be," he said slowly.

"I don't think there's anything sinister about it. It's just puzzling." Even as she said it, Maggie remembered the eerie feeling she had gotten when she was down in the cellar. The place certainly did not feel benign. A shiver cooled her hot, sticky skin as she remembered.

"You know, I called Sheriff Potts about finding that ashtray."

Another stronger tingle replaced the one that had just faded away. "Oh?" Maggie said carefully. "What did he say?"

"What *could* he say? He might be able to use the information indirectly as justification to check on the ownership of the car. It gave them a direction to look, but it's damn little to go on. Even if they did believe my theory that the car had belonged to my mother, could they prove it after such a long time? How long do they maintain records on old cars?"

Maggie wished she knew, and she wished Rance would drop the subject. She hadn't made the connection that the car might have been Rose Montoya's. Now the creepy, cold feeling wouldn't go away.

It was ridiculous to feel this cold the last week of July. Maggie crossed her arms and hugged herself to try to ward off the chill. "I have no idea. You'll have to ask Sheriff Potts."

Rance tossed his head as if to shake the questions from his mind and turned away from the side of the house, the row of shrubs and the window. "Let's go tackle the lawn."

"Let's." Maggie hurried away, hoping to distract herself from the unsettling thoughts as fast as she could.

The yard didn't look much different now from the way it had before, Rance thought as he crossed to Maggie's van to help reload the supplies they hadn't used that day. Maggie had assured Rance that he would see results soon. Already he realized Tess had been right when she told him about watering the weedy lawn. He was sure she was right about the weed-control fertilizer, too. It just seemed pretty silly to him to throw good fertilizer on a bunch of weedy junk grass that he was going to plow under in a few months.

It was true that the yard resembled a real lawn now, instead of the brushy field of knee-high weeds he'd mowed down weeks before. And the water and fertilizer would take it from brown to green.

"Do I sense some doubt in you?" Maggie asked, coming up behind him.

Rance turned and tried to formulate a response. It wasn't easy to do, with those lovely, luminous eyes staring up at him. He tried to focus on the mop of curly red hair showing beneath the straw hat instead. A tinkling chuckle interrupted his thought processes.

"I felt the same way a year ago when Tess and I were trying to whip that old cornfield into shape. Two years ago that lawn my mobile home sits on used to be full of corn. Look how nice it looks now."

It was hard to believe that Maggie's well-tended yard had been a field only a year before, but then, it had been under some form of cultivation before it became a lawn. His yard had been neglected for decades. Rance started to voice his doubts, but changed his mind.

And he changed the subject. "Remember that Tex-Mex meal I promised you a few weeks ago?" Rance asked suddenly.

"Sure. I salivated all that day, just thinking about it. My stomach still hasn't recovered from the disappointment." Maggie patted her belly and grinned.

"Well, tell it to hold on. What say I do up a real Texas-style barbecue and invite everybody who's been so helpful to me?" Already the idea sounded good to him. He figured he owed at least half the population of Mattison. His ribs were feeling pretty good now, and cooking would hardly be a strain on him. Yes, sir, the idea sounded pretty damn good.

"What, no Mexican food? I had my heart set on it." There was no mistaking the disappointed expression on Maggie's face.

"There's more to Mexican cuisine than tacos and refried beans. I promise, you won't be disappointed."

"You're on. When?"

"How about next Saturday? That'll give me the better part of a week to invite people and get ready," Rance said, making a mental list of what he needed and whom he owed.

"So long?" Maggie looked crestfallen, but then she brightened. "That'll give me time to diet ahead of time. That way I can afford the extra calories." Maggie waved and headed toward her minivan.

Rance watched her go, noting her well-rounded bottom

as she climbed into the vehicle. Why did she want to look like that walking-stick sister of hers? She was perfect just the way she was.

But he didn't dwell on her cute derriere for long. He was still stuck on the hidden car, the voice and the hand-made ashtray. He rubbed his chin as Maggie drove away. When would it all come together?

It seemed to Maggie that she had just experienced a week that could be a candidate for *The Guinness Book of World Records*. She felt as though she'd never endured a longer seven days. Even during the dark days after Chet died, time had not passed so slowly. But then there had been plenty of necessary things to do. This week, all she'd done was wait. Today at the library had been no exception.

Maggie eyed the milky white sky with apprehension as she hustled her kids into the minivan. The day had dawned hot and clear, but as it progressed, the heat had built and the blue sky had quickly been clouded with heat haze. By the time Maggie was ready to go to Rance's party, the sky had filled with the murky white clouds that often presaged a storm. Thunder grumbled ominously in the distance.

An irrational thought struck her. "This is not exactly the best time to be visiting a haunted house," she muttered. "With a storm brewing and all." A cold chill cooled her hot and clammy flesh. She squelched the thought with a nervous giggle and tugged the van door open.

The temperature had soared to around a hundred, and the humidity pressed against her like an unwelcome blanket. It had been weeks since it last rained, and they could use it. But did it have to happen now? The last thing they needed was to be stuck over at Hightower's Haven during a power failure.

The desultory westerly breeze distracted her from fretting as it brought the spicy aroma of herbs, garlic and mesquite.

"Umm. Do you smell that? Rance must already be cooking. Let's hurry, before it's all gone," Maggie told the kids as she climbed into the van.

"What if I don't like it?" Jennifer asked, a worried frown creasing her elfin face. "You said he wasn't making tacos."

"You'll like it, Jenny." Maggie reached into the back seat and patted her daughter on the knee. "I'm sure Rance will have plenty of stuff that you'll like."

"Yeah, and if he doesn't, you can always run home and fix a peanut butter and jelly sandwich later," Buddy said.

Maggie wasn't sure whether Buddy was trying to be reassuring or mean with his remark, so she let it ride. Her son had been making an effort to get along with his younger sister lately, and she was grateful. Maggie buckled her seat belt, switched on the ignition and backed into the lane.

Her parents' Sunday-best pickup truck pulled up behind her and tooted a greeting as Maggie steered the minivan onto the paved road. If it wasn't so hot, they could have walked the half mile to Rance's. They could walk off the meal later, but the thickening clouds that threatened rain urged her onto the side of caution now.

It took just a short minute to drive down the macadam and turn into the shady lane lined with fading crepe myrtles. Bobby Carterette and his family were already there when Maggie drove up to Rance's big old house. Bobby and Old Bob were supervising Rance as he worked over a smoking barbecue grill that had been stationed under one of the stately pecan trees. Rusty lay quietly by the porch steps, proudly watching her pups frolic. Lucy had taken a position on the long veranda that shaded the west side of the house. She guarded three tables laden with heaped and covered platters of food.

Maggie chuckled as she pulled in behind the Carterette

family car. "Look there, Jen. I think you'll be able to find something to eat in all that."

The kids dashed off, joining Rusty and her brood of puppies tumbling about on the lawn. Maggie closed up the car and waited for her dad to park the truck and her parents to join her. The three of them strolled slowly up, trying unsuccessfully to stay cool and dry in the oppressive afternoon heat.

"*¡Buenos días, señoras y señor!*" Rance called from his position at the grill. He poked at a couple pieces of chicken and lowered the lid.

Maggie studied Rance appreciatively. He was dressed more like a cowboy than anything, but his garb fit the occasion. He wore an off-white western shirt trimmed with turquoise piping. A string tie fastened with an intricately designed silver-and-turquoise slide matched an equally ornate silver belt buckle. Tight, faded jeans hugged his muscular thighs and skimmed all the way down to the tops of his cowboy boots. A tightly woven western-style straw hat with a turquoise band topped the outfit. His only concession to the heat was that he'd rolled up his shirtsleeves to expose his tanned forearms.

Rance was one hell of a man, and he made something deep inside Maggie stir. Her heart fluttered, and she smiled brightly as Rance tipped his hat and came toward her.

Actually, he was aiming for the three of them, Maggie reminded herself as she watched Rance's approach. She had to keep reminding herself that her parents stood on either side of her.

Rance showed no effects from the accident he'd had just three weeks before. His bruises were gone, and his arms swung freely. He rolled down his sleeves and buttoned his cuffs as he came.

A tingle of excitement surprised Maggie as Rance tipped his hat to Daisy, shook Joe's hand, then directed his dark, smoldering eyes to her. Rance took her hand lightly into his and spoke. He must have said something, but Maggie didn't register the words. She was too entranced with the music of his rich baritone voice to hear anything else.

Suddenly it occurred to Maggie that the music had stopped. Rance looked at her, amusement in his dark eyes. Had he asked her a question? Heat colored her cheeks crimson.

A rich, deep chuckle tickled Maggie's ear as the color faded from her face. She looked up at Rance, panicky and embarrassed. Finally, she stammered, "I'm sorry...."

"We're almost ready," Rance repeated.

Rance had already said that once, Maggie realized, blushing again.

"Tess called to say they were running late and to start without them," Rance continued. He crooked his arm. "Shall we?"

"Thank you," Maggie said with relief. Relief that lasted only a few fleeting seconds. She had been able to escape Rance's hypnotic eyes and melodious voice, only to fall under the spell of the heat radiating from his strong arm into her hand.

He relinquished his hold on her moments later, when he showed Maggie to the shaded porch. Her eyes feasted on the colorful bounty in front of her. "It looks like I'll have to diet all next week, too," she commented shakily as Rance steered her to the side steps.

"I have to put the chicken and peppers on plates, then we can eat." Rance strode off to the grill.

Lucy Carterette grinned as Maggie climbed the steps. "Whoever snags that man is going to be one very lucky lady."

Maggie laughed. Anything to cover her embarrassment. She'd been thinking the same thing...with one difference. The whoever who snagged him was going to be her.

The tantalizing display of food astounded her in its variety. There were tacos and all the fixings for Jen. But there

were spicy seasoned green beans, roasted corn, bowls of
sauces ranging in colors from red to green, and a steaming
pot of chili, as well. For dessert there were churros, a fried
pastry, and several varieties of sliced, chilled melons. Maggie sighed as she tried not to think of her waistline.

The heavy clatter of masculine feet on the steps heralded
the approach of the menfolk. Rance carried a huge platter
heaped high with steaming grilled chicken. He was followed by Bobby Carterette, who was carrying a tray of
roasted green peppers. Old Bob and Joe brought up the
rear.

Rance set the brimming platter on the table and made
room for Bobby's. Then he turned to the assembled group
and spread his arms expansively. "*Mi casa es su casa. Mi
comida es su comida.* Eat!"

Maggie's children wasted no time in responding to
Rance's invitation, and scurried to the food-laden porch,
she noted with an apologetic smile. Both kids showed no
embarrassment when they began piling food onto paper
plates. And Jen had worried that she wouldn't like anything!

Maggie held back until most of the others had loaded
their plates and found places to sit on the porch. Then she
let Rance guide her through a tour of the dishes he'd prepared.

The breeze had changed, Maggie noticed later as she
settled on a lawn chair. It wasn't lazy now, and it brought
with it the smell of rain.

A sound from the drive called Maggie's attention from
the wind and her plate. She looked up to see Tess's family
Oldsmobile pull in behind her van. Tess's crew hurried
across the lawn and up to the porch as the first big drops
of rain sprinkled the grass. Raindrops sizzled as they found
the heated metal top of the grill.

Happy that everyone had made it before the rain, Maggie glanced at Rance and grinned. He returned the smile

with a thumbs-up, and motioned for her to eat, but Maggie could see the same smoldering hunger in his eyes that she felt. And it had nothing to do with the food.

She bit into a succulent, tender chicken breast and chewed, trying to distract herself from increasingly erotic thoughts. From the shelter of the porch, comfortable and dry, with plenty of good food within arm's reach, all seemed well. Thunder rumbled, seeming closer than before, and Maggie glanced apprehensively at the falling rain. Then a burst of laughter from a clutch of the gathered guests eased her mind.

Maybe it would be all right. With all the people who were gathered here, maybe the ghost of Luther Hightower would stay put.

And, at least, the lights hadn't gone out.

Chapter 12

This storm wasn't as bad as the one that had jammed the creek and flooded the bridge, Rance thought. But it had been enough to send everyone running inside in a flurry of activity, grabbing bowls and platters as the wind whipped the driving rain under the shelter of the porch roof.

Just when they thought the worst of the storm was over and that they had gotten away without losing the lights, the electrical power had gone to parts unknown. The thunder and lightning had moved on by that time, but the rain still fell steadily. Rance had rummaged around until he found candles and used some of his ever-present matches to light them.

When the meal was over and everyone sat, full and satisfied, he'd gone upstairs for his guitar. It hadn't taken much to sweet-talk the reluctant group into joining him in song. One song had led to another, and soon they had sung every song Rance knew and some he didn't. He had even tried to teach them several songs in Spanish.

Flexing his cramping fingers, Rance decided that there had been enough singing. He hadn't played in ages, and the hard calluses that had once protected the tips of his fingers were all but gone. His fingertips only tingled now, but they had screamed in pain as they pressed down on the metal strings during the last couple of songs. He lifted the guitar strap over his head and ducked under it, then placed the instrument carefully in its case.

"Don't stop now," Jennifer begged with a dreamy voice.

"Yeah. Play something by Sheryl Crow," chimed in Little Tom.

Tess made a face and shook her head slowly at her older son. "I don't think she's in Rance's repertoire, son. Besides, he's been playing for quite a while now, and he's probably worn out."

"Rance, you are a man of many surprises. First a gourmet meal, then entertainment. It's too bad I didn't see you first," Lucy said, nudging her dozing husband.

Bobby Carterette woke with a start to the sound of laughter, having missed the joke that had been at his expense. "What's so funny?" He stifled a yawn.

His question only provoked another round of chuckles. Lucy patted her husband on the knee and told him she would explain later.

"Mighty fine meal, son," Joe Popwell told Rance as he hoisted himself out of the rocker he'd wedged himself into. "We enjoyed it, but I reckon me and Daisy'll head on home now. It looks like the rain's about quit."

Maggie's and Tess's children had formed a huddle and were whispering softly among themselves. Teeny, Tess's twelve-year-old daughter, emerged from the knot of kids and acted as spokesperson for the group.

"Can Buddy and Jen sleep over at our house tonight? They haven't seen the latest Batman movie yet, and Tommy rented the video this morning." Several eager faces looked expectantly at their parents. "And you don't know when the electricity will come back on way out here in the country." Teeny's added logic clinched it.

"I'm for it," Maggie replied readily. "What about you, sis? You're the one who'll get all the noise and appetites."

Tess chuckled and looked at her husband. "I guess we can stand it just once. Besides, Rance stuffed 'em pretty full. Maybe they'll go right to bed after the movie."

Little Tom and Buddy snorted.

"Is that okay with you, old man?" She patted her husband affectionately on the knee.

"I think we'll survive," Tom drawled, feigning a frown. "The rec room is on the other end of the house, and I have earplugs somewhere."

"It's settled, then. Buddy, you and Jen can stop by your place on the way out for a change of clothes and toothbrushes." Tess clapped her hands together in a businesslike manner and hustled the kids out the door.

Lucy nudged her sleepy husband and father-in-law toward the door, too. *The evening is definitely looking better,* Rance thought. In a couple of minutes, his guests would be gone, and he would have Maggie all to himself.

Maggie looked even prettier than usual tonight. Rance hadn't thought it possible for her to be even more beautiful than she already was, but the backless yellow sundress she wore brought out the best in her. It hugged her curvy body just the way he hoped he would tonight, and her curly red hair tumbled around her creamy white shoulders in wild abandon, begging him to play in their tangled strands.

Rance felt certain that tonight he would finally learn the real secret of Maggie's lips. The one other kiss so long ago hardly counted. And he still wasn't certain he hadn't dreamed it. No, those feelings had been too real, too heartfelt.

A sudden thought stuck him and sent him reeling. *What if she wanted to go home, too?*

"I guess I'm drafted to help with kitchen duty," Maggie murmured as she watched the Carterettes back out and head down the drive. "I've never done dishes by candlelight."

Doing the dishes was the last thing Rance had on his mind, but they had to be done, and they had given Maggie a reason to stay.

"We may just have to scrape and stack them for now. The new water heater goes out with the lights, so we won't have hot water." He laughed as he assessed the heap of dirty serving dishes. It would have been worse if they hadn't used paper plates. "This may be the only time I'll regret spending the money on the electric water heater."

He let out a deep breath and looked at the dishes again. "I think they'll hold till morning." But he didn't know if he would. He listened to the awkward silence in the room.

"Or the lights come back on, whichever comes first," Maggie quipped, filling in the echoing quiet. She stooped to pick up a dirty paper plate from the floor, where one of the kids must have left it.

The soft light from the candles gave Maggie's complexion a golden glow the sun could never begin to compete with. Her coppery hair glistened in the warm candlelight. Rance paused, drinking in her beauty.

"Candlelight becomes you," he finally whispered, huskily.

Maggie looked up, a question in her eyes. A pleased smile formed on her peach-colored lips. "Thank you," she murmured softly. She turned quickly back to the table and the dirty dishes.

"That can wait," Rance whispered. He took the plate she'd been scraping and captured her delicate white hands in his and raised them to his lips. He heard Maggie's sharp intake of breath and registered the surprise in her eyes. He almost stopped what he was doing, but then Maggie smiled.

Her shy smile issued an invitation that Rance gladly accepted. He kissed her soft hand, then cupped her chin in his palm. How delicate and pale Maggie's skin appeared in contrast to his own dark hand. Rance struggled to keep his emotions in check and his touch light against her porcelain skin. He fought to keep his caresses tender, lest he hurt her. Or frighten her away.

Maggie's lips parted slightly, and Rance caressed the full lower lip with his thumb. Her tongue flicked out to wet her mouth, sending tremors of excitement coursing through him.

Rance tilted Maggie's captured chin up toward him, and he leaned forward and touched her lips with his own hungry mouth. He felt her tremble, but she didn't pull away.

Her lips, soft and yielding, tasted slightly sweet, like the melon she'd eaten earlier. Rance thought he would be content with just one kiss, but that one taste only whetted his appetite for more. His ardor built and his hunger increased. He had to explore the depths of her passion and share his own.

Maggie's lips parted, inviting him in, and he plundered the mysterious depths. A groan escaped from deep within him, or had Maggie moaned? How had he survived so long without her sweet lips?

His hand left Maggie's soft face and tunneled through her mass of flaming hair. His fingers plowed through curling waves and didn't resist as tendrils of silken fire wound themselves around his seeking fingers. Maggie's hands found the buttons of his shirt, released some, and explored his fevered chest with cool, sure fingers.

How long could this go on before he went totally insane? How long could it go on before he would have to have her?

She undid the rest of his buttons and pushed the shirt roughly, urgently, off his shoulders. He released his hold on her only long enough to shrug off the distracting garment, then gathered her back into his arms.

Her hands tangled through the hair on his chest, teased at his nipples until they knotted and tingled with desire. Then she took one beaded nub into her mouth and laved it with her tongue.

Rance moaned with pleasure as she repeated the process with the other one, and then her hands moved on, leaving his skin flaming and sensitive wherever her cool fingers touched. He felt her hands on his back, tracing the muscles, sending shivers down his spine with each new touch.

He reached for the clasp at the back of her neck that held the yellow dress closed. He had to explore her the way she had him. He paused, hoping that she wouldn't push him away.

Maggie stiffened suddenly in his arms. "What is it? Why did you stop?" she murmured, her warm breath heating his fevered flesh yet more.

Relief flooded through him. "I thought..." He shook his head and looked down into her questioning green eyes. "I don't know what I thought. I want you to be sure..." He left the thought unfinished. This time, it had to be her idea, if they were going to complete what they'd already begun.

"I'm sure, Rance," she whispered, her voice breathy and shallow with need. "Make love to me, Rance. Love me now."

Ignoring the twinge of pain from his healing ribs, Rance swept her into his arms. Pausing only to fling open the heavy wooden door, he carried her into the bedroom. He laid her gently on the queen-size bed they'd shared once before and lowered himself to the mattress beside her.

The room was dark. No softening candlelight here. Only the occasional flicker of lightning from the dying storm. Maggie breathed a silent prayer for that. She'd never before entered a man's bedroom with this purpose in mind. Not a man she wasn't married to. Perhaps it was better that she not be able to see. Only to feel.

She heard the rustle of the bed linens as Rance turned down the spread. Then he cradled her in his arms and moved her to rest on the crisp, cool sheets. Maggie lay there, wondering what to do, until the pop of his jeans' snap startled her, and she drew in a quick, shallow breath. Gentle fingers touched her lips.

"It's okay," he whispered, his warm breath fanning the fires of desire that burned deep inside her.

She heard the rasp of his zipper as it went down, then the soft slithering of his jeans as they slid down his long, muscled legs. She reached to touch him as he kicked out of his shoes and made quick work of removing the rest of his clothing. Maggie had never realized how arousing it was to lie in the dark and listen to the sound of a man removing his clothes. Warmth spread through her, leaving her aching and moist and ready.

Maggie held her breath as Rance turned to her and released the catch at the back of her dress. The fabric fell free, leaving her breasts exposed to the warm night air. She shivered, not from cold, but from excitement, and she heard him gasp. Or had he grimaced with pain? She had to help him; it hadn't been that long since he was injured, so she quickly undid the closure at the waist of her dress and pulled the concealing fabric down and off her legs.

She felt more than saw Rance's heated gaze as he took in her naked body, exposed briefly in the strobing lightning flash. She forced herself to lie still as his trembling hand gently traced a path down her waiting body from her flushed cheek to the spot at the juncture of her thighs. She waited as he studied her, wanting to turn away from his gaze, but not wanting to miss a moment of it.

Then he reached for her face, sending the scent of his spicy aftershave wafting toward her. His lips found hers while his hands caressed her, bringing her aching body yet more alive than it already was. "I thought this would never happen," he murmured, more a moan than words.

"I've waited for this, too," Maggie whispered back, her voice thready and weak under his skillful ministrations.

"I don't think I can hold back much longer," he muttered. His urgent throbbing against her thigh underscored his need.

"Then don't."

Rance crushed her into his arms, and Maggie felt herself rise above everything that made her life seem real.

Bare flesh against flesh. Skin to skin. How long had it been? Maggie closed her eyes as Rance lowered his lips to her neck, then moved lower. He traced gentle circles around each breast with his tongue, teasing each hardened nipple with his teeth. He suckled until he had his fill, then returned his attention to her mouth.

Rance's kisses tasted sweet and hot. Partly from the seasoned food he'd had earlier, partly from him. Maggie savored the spicy flavor, running her tongue lightly over his lips. Rance moaned and pulled her tighter to him, crushing her with his body.

She was so aware of his hardness throbbing against her arching body, and she responded with a sweet aching within her very core. Rance's exploring fingers found the spot and sent her writhing with pleasure. Maggie pushed him away. She wouldn't settle for anything less than his complete possession this time.

"I want to feel you deep inside me," Maggie barely managed to gasp. Her heart pounded, matching the rhythm of Rance's, so close to hers.

He rolled to cover her, nudging her legs apart with his knee. Maggie felt the hot pressure of his shaft at the opening to her inner self. He pushed, and she let him in.

Tremors of pure sensation washed through her as he filled her, pushing, demanding, sending her rocking and arching against him. She clutched at his back, drawing him closer, urging him deeper, until they'd climbed to the heights of passion. Then, with a shuddering moan, she felt his release, and they tumbled over the edge.

Rance lay still, weak and sated, his limbs heavy and languid from his exertions. How right it felt to hold this woman in his arms after making love.

Maggie lay snuggled against his chest, her head nestled against his shoulder. He gently massaged the yielding flesh of her hip pressed to his and listened to her soft, rhythmic breathing. Was she asleep, or simply sated, as he was? Her warm breath caressed him, sending comforting and cooling chills through him, threatening to reignite fires not yet extinguished, only banked and waiting for more fuel.

He squeezed her to him, sighing with satisfaction at the gentle murmur of pleasure that came in response. He would happily lie this way forever.

Then it was gone.

The lights came on suddenly and filled the night with the stark light of day. The silence that had been broken only by the sounds of lovemaking was now filled with raucous canned music from the radio in the other room.

Maggie's eyes flew open, and she pushed him away and pulled out of his arms. She turned quickly.

Damn! Any other time, Rance would have welcomed the restoration of the light and sounds that made modern life easier. But tonight he cursed it. He muttered another oath and reached to pull her back to him, but she wriggled away.

"I have to go home," Maggie whispered, her voice wobbly, her tone desperate. She smoothed her tousled hair with trembling fingers and avoided his eyes. Then she gathered up her scattered clothing and, with her back to him, dressed. Fully clothed, she rose, aimed one panicked, pleading look at him, and scurried away.

The moment shattered by the rude intrusion of the modern world, Rance could do nothing but follow Maggie's example. He dressed.

And then he watched her leave.

The clock made the only sound in Maggie's little bedroom, and it ticked in the quiet like a time bomb. She covered her ears, but she could still hear it. It had seemed like a good idea to wind the old clock, just in case the electricity went again. But why? Tomorrow was Sunday; she would surely wake up long before it was time to go to church.

She stuck the clock in the drawer of the nightstand, but it seemed to echo in the enclosed wooden box. Finally, she stuffed it into the other pillow and shoved it to the floor.

Then there was blessed silence.

Though it was late and she'd had a hectic day at work, Maggie couldn't sleep. She wasn't used to being alone at night. She was accustomed enough to sleeping alone. Even when Chet was alive, he'd had to go away for weeks and months at a time as part of his military duties. But she'd always had the children. Just being able to sense their presence had been comforting, in its own way.

She'd never been the panicky type, and she wasn't afraid. But she could count the times she'd been alone at night on one hand. It was different. And strange. And she didn't think she would ever get used to it.

The night and the house were quiet. Too quiet. The storm had cooled the hot summer air so that not even the droning hum of the air conditioner interrupted the silence. The only sound Maggie heard was the erratic beating of her heart.

Why did Rance Montoya affect her so? She was a grown woman. She'd been married, borne children, and buried a husband. Why had she been so drawn to him that she all

but threw herself into his bed? She should have been im-
mune to those adolescent feelings that made her heart
pound and kept her from sleep. She'd had her turn at life
and love. Why couldn't she accept her widowhood and
grow old gracefully?

Because she wasn't old! She was thirty-six, still young.
She didn't relish the thought of spending the rest of her
life alone in a little house, with the children gone, and no
man to share it with. Whom was she fooling? Even after
two years, the lonely nights still got to her.

And having Rance stir up all those feelings and desires
that were better forgotten had only made it worse.

Maggie tossed and turned and tangled in the bedcovers.
The rustling of the sheets provided welcome relief from
the quiet, but when she lay still, the silence returned. Then
the only sound she could hear was the beating of her heart.

Why was she kidding herself? She wasn't lying awake
because the house was too quiet or the kids weren't there.
It was Rance and the memory of making love with him
that caused her heart to pound and her mind to work fe-
verishly. *Why hadn't the lights come on sooner?*

Maggie rolled over and pulled her pillow over her head.
All she accomplished was to make the quiet of the night
even quieter and the arguments inside her brain even
louder.

Suddenly Maggie had an irrational urge to hear crickets
and birds and the rustle of the breeze through the old mimosa tree that shaded the mobile home. The last time she
listened to night sounds, she had been lying half-asleep
beside Rance in his bedroom after he was injured. On his
bed, she realized distractedly. That wasn't exactly the type
of thought she was trying to encourage. And no matter
what she did to the contrary, she couldn't keep her mind
from straying in his direction.

He had been injured and in pain then, but it had been
the first time he kissed her. He'd been drunk with pain-

killers, but he'd promised to make her his someday. She'd thought it was only fevered ramblings then, but tonight he had acted on that promise.

But she had stopped him. Prevented him from holding her all through the night. Denied him, when her body was aching to join again with his. *If only the lights had stayed off.*

She suddenly realized that she was up and out of bed. Maggie reached for her light cotton wrapper and put it on, groping with her feet for her slippers as she tugged the sleeves over her arms. She slid into the slippers and crept down the hall, careful not to wake…whom? She reminded herself that she was completely alone.

The night air was cool, and a gentle breeze blew in from the west. The sky was still overcast, and heat lightning flashed in the distance, coloring the bottoms of the thick clouds with a fluorescent glow. The storm, if it was a storm, was too far off for the sound of thunder to send its voice her way.

Maggie brushed the moisture off the glider swing in the yard and sank onto the damp seat, grateful for the welcoming squeak it gave her. She settled back and swung gently, listening to the symphony of night sounds.

Abruptly, the evening chorus stopped, and it was eerily quiet. Something had made the night creatures stop and listen. Maggie stopped, too, cocking her head to hear.

There it was. A muffled, distant, pounding beat, drifting in on the lazy breeze. It was as steady and insistent as her heartbeat, and Maggie's heart sped up as she realized where the sound was coming from.

It came from Hightower's Haven!

She tried to ignore the persistent drumbeat. The night creatures had already deemed it harmless and resumed their chorus, but she couldn't ignore the sound. Now that she had noticed it, it seemed relentless in its rhythm. It wasn't a natural sound she was hearing, and Maggie could think of no logical explanation.

I'm here.
The voice was stronger than he'd ever heard it. Calling to him. Begging him to come.

Rance stood in front of the bare cinder-block wall, heedless of the damp chill in the musty basement. In spite of the pervasive cold, his body dripped with sweat, and he breathed heavily as he rested his arms by leaning against the cool wall.

I'm here.
It called again. Rance didn't know how he heard it, or even if he heard it. Of one thing he was certain. Whoever—whatever—was calling was behind that wall. He reached for the heavy maul that he used for splitting wood. He'd leaned it against his leg while he rested. Now he winced as his not-quite-healed ribs protested the motion of picking it up again.

He clenched his teeth and bit against the pain as he wrenched the heavy maul up from the floor. He swung, grimacing as the maul found its mark with a dull thud that reverberated through him. The pain didn't matter. Nothing mattered except this wall and what it hid.

He swung again, automatically, as if driven by remote control. Chunks of cement flew free, striking him. In his fervor, he ceased to feel the pain. He was powerless to stop long enough to examine what he'd done; he just swung. Again. And again. Matching the rhythm of his pounding heart.

With Rance's next swing, the heavy hammer exposed a small hole. He'd finally broken through. He paused, gasping for breath.

Yes. Here!
Panting, Rance wrenched the mallet free and swung again. A shower of broken cement and cinder blocks

rained down on him as a crude mouth opened in the wall. It was only a tiny opening. Too small to enter. Too small to see.

Yes!

Rance drew back and swung again. Now the mouth yawned and gaped wider. He swung again and again.

A clattering noise behind him broke Rance's concentration, and the maul missed its mark. The mallet swung wide and thudded dully against the wall.

"Rance!"

He tried to swing again, but the unexpected voice had upset his rhythm, and thrown him off balance. He staggered as the weight of the maul pulled him around.

Maggie stood halfway down the stairs, fear and concern etched on her pale face. Her eyes were wide. He vaguely noticed that she was dressed for bed.

"What are you doing?" Maggie stepped warily down the remaining steps and picked her way through a field of cement chips and rubble. She stopped just short of where Rance stood.

Don't stop now.

"The wall. She's calling me. Don't you hear it?" Rance gasped brokenly as he swung blindly around to face the now broken expanse of wall.

"Hear what? I don't hear anything. What do you hear?" Maggie touched Rance's arm lightly, calming him.

He turned slowly around to face Maggie's frightened, questioning eyes. God! Was he going crazy? What was he doing down here in the middle of the night, pounding on a wall like a fool?

I'm here. Don't forget me.

If she hadn't had any doubts about what she was doing running over here in the middle of the night, Maggie sure had them now. What was she thinking, coming to a haunted house at midnight with lightning flashing in the distance? In a B movie that would be funny—exciting, even. But this wasn't a movie; this was very real.

Rance looked like a madman, an untamed gleam in his dark eyes, gasping in front of the crumbling, mysterious wall. Had Rance Montoya gone completely off the deep end? He wore only his jeans, his feet were bare, and his magnificent body was drenched with sweat. Trickles of crimson traced patterns down his chest. He'd been nicked by the flying chips, and his blood, mixed with sweat, made him look fierce and wild.

Rance cocked his head, his eyes moving in the direction of the hole. "Don't you hear it? She's calling me." He turned to swing again.

"Who's calling you, Rance? Who? I don't hear anything." Then she realized what he had just said. He had said *she*. He'd heard a feminine voice calling, too!

"I don't know. At least, I don't think I know. I just have to get through this wall. Now." He spun around and wrenched the heavy wood maul up and off the floor.

Maggie stepped back out of the way. She should have been alarmed. She should have turned and run. But she stood rooted to the spot. She didn't know why, but she knew she had to stay. To help. Though at that moment she felt helpless.

What could she do? Nothing. Nothing but be there for Rance.

She realized as she watched Rance beat against the crumbling wall that the eerie feeling she'd had when she was down here the two times before was missing. Gone. Yet she sensed something. Not the terrifying desperation she'd felt before. It was almost...relief.

Rance pulled back and made yet another assault against the wall. Maggie could tell that this blow was different. The hammer had found its mark, sure and true.

With that blow, the wall came tumbling down.

*   *   *

Sobbing for breath, Rance sank to his knees amid the
rubble. Dust flew everywhere, clouding the room with
smoky particles. Rance waved his arms to clear the dusty
air away from him. He coughed as too much filthy air
found its way to his lungs. There was nothing else he could
do until it settled.

I'm here.

The voice was different now. If it was a voice. Triumphant? Relieved? As if a long wait were over.

"I've found her," Rance whispered as Maggie's cool
hand settled on his shoulders. He looked up into her luminous turquoise eyes.

"Who have you found?" Maggie knelt beside him and
circled him with her arms.

Rance turned into her embrace and buried his face in
her soft shoulder. He realized with detached interest as he
nuzzled into the bend of her neck that Maggie wore only
a nightgown and a thin robe.

"What are you doing here?" he whispered into the soft,
coppery curls. "Why did you come?"

"I couldn't sleep," Maggie answered huskily. "And it
was too quiet in the house. I went outside and...I heard
something...you." Maggie's cool fingers caressed the
back of his neck and played with his hair, sending cooling
shivers down his spine. "Next thing I knew," she murmured, "I was here."

Rance pulled away. "I couldn't sleep, either," he said,
his voice rough and ragged from his exertions. How could
he tell her he'd responded to a voice calling him
from...where? "Something made me come down here and
tear down the wall. It was almost as if I were being manipulated."

Rance struggled to his feet and worked his way through
the dusty rubble to the gaping hole. He stared long and
hard into the cavelike opening. He had no idea what he
was looking for, what he expected to see, yet he did. And

as much as he could under the circumstances, he hoped he was wrong.

He waited for the dust to settle so that he could see. But he didn't need sight to know what was hidden there. His heart beat faster as he realized with sudden certainty who he would find.

Chapter 13

"I know she's in there," he said huskily as he stared into the opening.

Maggie stepped up behind him. "Who?" she repeated.

"My mother."

She should have been more surprised, Maggie realized as what Rance had told her sank in. But she wasn't.

It all made sense now. Finally, the clues were falling together. From the female "ghost" that haunted Hightower's Haven, to the car in the pool, to the ashtray that Rance had given his mother the day she disappeared from his life forever. Even the mysterious wall in the cellar made sense now. The secret lay almost exactly beneath Rance's bed, hidden in the house for all that time.

Though it had been natural for people to make the assumption, it wasn't Luther's ghost that people had been sensing in this house for the past thirty years, but Rose's. Luther had always been safely tucked away in the family plot in Mattison, but nobody knew where Rose was. Nobody knew she was dead. At least not for sure!

Well, somebody did. The person who had put her here and left her waiting to be discovered all this time.

As the dust settled, Rance continued staring into the hole in the wall. After several long moments, he grabbed a flashlight, ducked his head and stepped inside.

Maybe if she was thinking clearly after a good night's sleep, she wouldn't have followed Rance as he stepped, flashlight in hand, through the opening in the wall. But she did, as if it were the most natural thing in the world.

Rance didn't stop to get his bearings. He seemed to know exactly where he was going. Was he following the same unheard voice that Maggie had recognized in the still of the night? He aimed his flashlight to the left, as if he knew exactly where he would find what he was looking for.

The flashlight beam skimmed over a mound in the dusty earthen floor behind the wall. Rance swung the flashlight back and fixed the beam on the mound. A shiver of excitement that had nothing to do with fear heightened Maggie's senses.

There it was. The grave that neither of them was really surprised to find.

It looked like a fresh grave on Boot Hill, as depicted in any old western movie. Dry red dirt was piled high to accommodate the added bulk of whatever lay below. The only things missing were the empty boots and crossed sticks forming a crude marker.

"Hold this," Rance said tersely as he handed her the flashlight.

She did. It didn't even occur to Maggie to protest being left holding a flashlight in a dark basement that contained a grave. Rance stepped out of the cavernous room through the hole in the wall and back into the artificial light of the cellar, leaving Maggie alone in a dark tomb filled with creepy crawlers and at least one grave. And the only defense she had was a flashlight!

In spite of all that, curiosity got the better of her. As her eyes adjusted to the dim light, she began to play the weak beam around the shadowy cellar. The floor was hard-packed dirt, dry, and smooth except for the mound. The exterior walls were earth up to the level of the ground. Rough beams rose from the floor to support the ceiling and part of the cinder-block wall.

No wonder Rance had had so much trouble tearing it down, Maggie realized. The first place he chose to break through had been strengthened by a wooden support beam. When Maggie distracted him, he'd missed his aim and struck a much weaker spot. The wall had fallen within minutes.

Rance returned with a portable kerosene lantern and a shovel. He handed the shovel to Maggie and silently lit the lantern with a match from his pocket. He adjusted the wick, and this room that hadn't seen the light of day in thirty years filled with light. Maggie blinked in the sudden brightness and watched as Rance set the lamp beside the mound. Why did she feel so calm? Maggie handed the shovel to Rance, and he started to clear the heaped dirt away.

Rance worked easily with the loose dirt. It had not been touched in years. Without rain and sun and the tramping feet of man to tamp it down, it was probably as loose as the day it had been mounded. Perhaps looser, for the soil was bone-dry, and barely resisted as the shovel dug into it.

Rance dug deeper into the mound, making a new pile beside the old one. Maggie was so mesmerized by Rance's rhythmic movement and the rippling play of the muscles in his back that the sharp scrape of the metal shovel blade against something hard snapped her to attention as if a hypnotist had snapped his fingers. A shiver painted her arms with gooseflesh.

Rance dropped the shovel, hunkered down and began to

scrape at the dirt in the hole with his bare hands. In spite of her curiosity, Maggie held back, afraid to find out what was beneath the surface. Rance seemed to dig forever.

Finally, he stopped his fevered scrabbling in the dirt and tugged at something. Something flat that didn't give as Rance pulled. He yanked again. The object came free.

Rance scrambled to his feet, holding the flat object in his hand. Wearing triumph on his face, he spent no time celebrating his victory, but sank back on his haunches and brushed at the dirt-encrusted relic.

"What is it?" Maggie made herself ask. Visions of coffin lids and treasure chests had flown out of her mind. What Rance held was too small to be either of those things.

Rance shoved himself to his feet again. "Come on." He crossed the dirt floor and went back through the hole in the wall.

Maggie followed, sensing that it wasn't the time to ask questions. And Rance wouldn't take the time to answer them. He strode up the cellar stairs two at a time and across the hall to the kitchen. He was already running water in the sink by the time she caught up with him.

"I knew it!" Rance swished the object under the water and rubbed it with his hand. He rinsed it again. "I knew she didn't mean to leave me." He held up the rectangular scrap. "See?"

It was a license plate, Maggie realized as a chill traveled down the short length of her spine. Considering that the date was thirty years old, it was in remarkably good condition and easy to read. The personalized car tag announced its owner's name: ROSIE H.

"I knew she always meant to come back for me," Rance murmured, his voice cracking. He hugged the muddy plate to his chest.

"Rance?"

Rance looked up at Maggie. He had forgotten that she

was there. "This is the license plate that was on my
mother's car the day she left me. I knew she never meant
to stay away."

Maggie's face was too pale, Rance realized. Had he
frightened her? He had been gathering bits and pieces of
this mystery for weeks, and had almost been prepared for
what he'd just found, but this must have come as quite a
shock to Maggie.

He finally had incontrovertible proof that Rose Montoya
Hightower had been to Hightower's Haven after she left
him in San Antonio. He finally had some concrete evidence to give to Sheriff Potts. Though Maggie needed him
at this moment, the contents of the earthen grave demanded his attention first.

"I've got to go down and finish digging." Rance laid
the license tag on the table and wiped his muddy hands
on his jeans. He turned toward the door and made it halfway down the hall.

"I think you'd better leave the rest of this to Sheriff
Potts," Maggie told him, softly and calmly, as she followed him into the hall and placed a hand on his arm.
"There's probably proper police protocol that has to be
followed in this type of case."

Rance tried to shake free and reached for the door to
the cellar stairs. He knew Maggie was probably right about
procedure, but right now he wasn't sure he cared about
regulations. "I have to find her. Don't you see? She's been
waiting all this time...."

Maggie's hand was surprisingly strong on his arm.
"You have found her. You've done your part. Let Sheriff
Potts do his job now." She grabbed him again and pulled
him back from the stairs, wrapping him in her arms. Maggie's arms felt so right around him, even as she restrained
him from what he wanted to do. She held him securely in
her arms, murmuring soft nothings to him, as if he were a
child. The crooning sounds calmed him.

"Come on. Sit down." Maggie led him by the arm to a kitchen chair and pushed him gently into the seat. Rance was too drained to resist; he sat and waited while Maggie rummaged through cabinets and found the bottle of bourbon he kept. She poured three fingers of the amber-colored liquid into a water glass and handed it to him.

"Drink this. It'll calm you down. I'm going to call the sheriff."

The bourbon burned his tongue and warmed his blood as it went down. Rance needed the fiery, sweet liquid now as much as he had needed his mother thirty years ago. He drained the glass and set it down.

Then he went to find Maggie. He needed her, too.

Rance paced and prowled around the parlor like a caged animal. He stalked to the top of the cellar stairs and stared down into the darkness below. It had taken Maggie several long minutes to convince him that the situation would best be served if he let the authorities finish the job the right way. It hadn't been easy, and only Maggie's presence was keeping Rance upstairs.

Rance had seemed to accept her logic and submitted docilely as she set him down and doctored his wounds and insisted that he dress. That done, he had sprung to his feet and begun to pace again.

"You know, it's probably going to be a while before anybody gets here. Lyle Potts'll probably have to roust half the department from their beds," Maggie said, feeling she needed to explain to Rance why the wheels of justice moved so slowly in the middle of the night in Alabama.

He stopped pacing, turned and stared. But he said nothing.

"It's a long way out here from Pittsville. You might as well sit down before you're a nervous wreck," she continued, trying to ease the high tension in the room. *Before I am,* she should have said. Rance already was.

It was much too late to calm him down, Maggie realized. Maybe thirty years too late. Rance had been heading for this moment for decades. He was already a wreck, and nothing she could say would change it now.

If only this had happened earlier. In the daytime.

Rance continued pacing, and Maggie helplessly watched him. The clock ticked, and Rance paced. The clock ticked, and Maggie watched.

A shrill summons interrupted the tense monotony. When the phone rang, everything stopped. Rance stopped pacing. Maggie stopped breathing. Even the clock seemed to skip a beat as time stood still. The phone rang again, its voice shrill and insistent.

Maggie reached it first and grabbed it off the cradle. Sheriff Potts's voice boomed out of the receiver before Maggie had a chance to pronounce a greeting. "Any of my boys make it there yet?"

"No sir. We're still waiting," Maggie told him.

She held the receiver away from her ear as the sheriff uttered a curse. Then he instructed Maggie to tell whoever arrived before he did not to touch anything.

"I'll tell 'em," Maggie said, not at all sure she would be able to get the deputy on duty to do her bidding. She listened as Sheriff Potts finished his instructions. Then she hung up.

"The sheriff's on his way. The deputy on patrol has already been dispatched and should be here pretty soon." *I hope,* Maggie didn't add.

"Good," Rance muttered, and resumed pacing, obviously at the end of his tether.

A light blinked outside the window. Maggie hurried over to the screen door and looked out. More lights winked through the trees as a patrol car pulled up to the house.

Maggie stepped out onto the porch to greet the deputy, only to remember that she was standing there in her nightgown and robe. She pulled the lapels closer together and tightened the sash around her middle. It was too late to change now. Let him think what he wanted.

Truman Higgins climbed out of the car. He would have been easier to face if he wasn't someone Maggie had known forever.

He waved a greeting and climbed up the steps. "You still trying to collect on that bet we made twenty years ago?"

Maggie looked at him blankly. Of course. Truman Higgins and his then girlfriend, Nancy Nelson, had been in cahoots with Tess and Tom all those years ago. Maggie blushed and smiled sheepishly. "It's not what you think, Truman."

"Hell, Margaret Rose, it ought to be. You been alone more'n two years now. I wouldn't begrudge you, even if you did pick him over me." Truman jerked his head in Rance's direction.

Blushing furiously, Maggie countered, "I'm sure Emmalyn would object to that. Didn't I hear there was a fourth little Higgins on the way?"

Truman chuckled. "Yes, ma'am. We aim to get us a girl this time and then quit."

"Well, good luck." Maggie glanced at Rance, grateful that he'd taken the time to put on a T-shirt, and reminded herself why Truman had been summoned. It wasn't to hash over old times with her. With an apologetic smile pasted on her face, she turned to Rance.

Maggie introduced the good ol' boy in the gray uniform. Did the woman know everybody in Pitt County, or just the men? Rance wondered irrationally.

This was not the time to be jealous. There was a concealed grave in his cellar. A grave that held answers to questions that had plagued him for thirty years.

"What say we go take a look at this here grave you

think you found?'' Higgins said after the introductions were done.

Well, that was more like business, Rance thought, clenching his teeth. He wasn't sure he liked this yokel, or the way he'd leered at Maggie. But he was here to do a job, and Rance guessed he'd better help him. He turned to lead the way.

"Wait," Maggie called after them. "I forgot to tell Truman. Sheriff Potts said not to touch anything. He was going to call in investigators from Montgomery."

"I reckon I know that, Margaret Rose. I just want to take a look," Higgins drawled.

Rance led the way, vaguely irritated at the way Higgins seemed to be taking it all so lightly. Hell, he was more than just irritated; he was damned mad. He yanked on the light string at the top of the stairs with an angry swipe.

Higgins let out a long, low whistle as he followed Rance down the stairs. "How'd this happen? Looks like you had an earthquake!"

Maggie touched Higgins's arm. "It's a long story, Truman."

"Okay. I reckon it'll wait." Higgins ducked through the hole.

The lantern still flickered inside—Rance had forgotten to retrieve it and turn it off—and the mound of dirt and the fresh hole were plain to see.

Truman stood, looking over the area, and scratched his head. "Well, you sure found something, all right." He walked over to the lip of the hole. "What made you go looking down here?"

Maggie touched him again. "You wouldn't believe it if I told you."

Higgins turned away from his inspection of the grave. "Old Luther's ghost tell you to look here?"

"Something like that," Maggie responded dryly.

If Maggie hadn't stepped between them, Rance would

have wiped the smirk off Deputy Higgins's face. Higgins had leered at Maggie one time too many. And that remark about Luther was the last straw.

"Truman," Maggie said softly. "Have some respect." A short burst from a siren outside kept her from continuing.

Higgins looked contrite. "Sorry, man. I forgot he was your father."

Rance uttered a curse. Damn! Had his life story been told in every living room in Pitt County?

Higgins stepped out through the hole in the wall. "I reckon the sheriff's here."

By the time Maggie, Rance and Truman made it back up the stairs, Lyle Potts was hoisting himself out from behind the wheel of his car.

He mounted the porch steps, then looked at Truman. "Tell me what you got."

Truman turned all efficiency and business. "Well, sir, we have what looks to be an old grave in a concealed room in the cellar of this house."

"You find a body?"

"No. Not yet," Truman admitted.

"I'd bet my life she's there, though," Rance said as he held the screen door open for everyone to file in.

"You mean you got us all up at zero-dark-thirty a.m., and you don't have a body? What the hell makes you think there is one?"

Maggie held her breath as she watched Rance struggle to control his emotions. How long would he be able to keep them in check? She placed her hand gently on his arm. It seemed to calm him, at least for the time being. "Go get it," she urged.

While Rance was out of the room, Maggie tried to explain how she and Rance had been drawn to the cellar. "I know you probably don't have any more faith in psychic phenomena than I did before tonight, but I truly believe that whoever is buried down there has been calling for help. I sensed it twenty years ago, when I took a dare to spend the night here. All the previous owners of this house must have felt it, too, and run scared. Rance was the only one who understood what the message was.

"It wasn't Luther Hightower trying to scare people off," she continued, "but someone else, calling for help. Rance thinks it's his mother, who's been missing for all of those thirty years." Maggie stopped her explanation as Rance returned.

"I never personally took advice from psychics, but I'm not gonna rule 'em out right yet. A police force can use all the help it can get." Potts turned to look at Rance. "What you got to show me?"

Rance handed the license plate to the sheriff. "That's the personalized tag that was on my mother's car when she left San Antonio. I don't know for sure, but I have reason to think she was headed here. That license plate was buried in that hole, and I believe it came off the car that we found in the pool."

Sheriff Potts looked thoughtful. He slapped the metal tag against his hand. "You got you a bunch of evidence that sure places Miz Hightower, or at least the car, here. But we ain't got no body. Hell, she mighta run off and done hid this stuff here to cover her getaway."

Maggie shook her head and sighed as she watched the impact of Potts's statement hit its target. Rance sagged as if he had been punched. It was probably the worst thing that anybody could have told him in his present state. Maggie held her breath as she waited for Rance's response.

He drew a deep, shuddering breath before he answered. "I can't believe that, Potts," he said with measured tones. "I don't know how I know, I just do. Mrs. Larson said somebody came to town and put flowers on my father's grave after we left. I think that person was my mother."

He closed his eyes and drew in a deep, calming breath. "My mother is in that hole in the basement, and she's been waiting for thirty years for someone to set her free. And if you won't do it, I will." Rance spun around and headed for the hallway and the cellar door.

"Now hold on. I didn't say I don't believe you. I was just presenting another possibility. I didn't mean any disrespect. I got forensics experts coming in from Montgomery. Let's let them do the looking. They know how to do this a whole bunch better than my little country police department."

Rance stopped at the end of the hallway. He hesitated, then put his hand on the knob of the cellar door.

Maggie hurried after him. She reached him as he turned the knob. "You don't want to do this yourself, Rance," she told him softly, trying to soothe him. "Let them do it, so you can remember her as she was."

Rance looked at Maggie uncertainly. He looked at the cellar door, then back again. "I don't know what to do," he said weakly.

"Come with me." Maggie held out her hand, hoping he would take it; he didn't. "Come to my house and wait. You don't have to be here. You've done your part. You found her grave. Let the experts do their job. Sheriff Potts can call my house when they've found her. Or anything that might tell us where she is."

Maggie turned to the sheriff. "Is that all right? Can he go to my place?"

"Sure, Margaret Rose. It'd prob'ly be the best thing he could do right now."

Maggie recited her number for the sheriff, then took a deep, calming breath. She closed her eyes and took a moment to collect her thoughts. What did one do in a situation like this? She could hardly browbeat the man into coming with her, but neither could she leave him here when he needed her. When he needed to be out of the investigators' way.

She looked to Rance and held out her hand to him once more. "You can't do anything to help right now. You're exhausted. Let Sheriff Potts and Truman do their work. We'll only be in their way."

Rance looked puzzled. His dark eyes clouded, and a confused frown marred his handsome face. For a moment, it looked as if he would dig in his heels and insist on seeing the excavation through. But then the uncertain look eased, and the stubborn lines on his face smoothed. He looked at Maggie as if he were waiting for her to tell him what to do.

But she knew she couldn't tell him. Maggie sighed and opened her hand. Rance had to make that final decision himself. "Those cuts on your chest need more attention. They're still bleeding. I have everything we'll need at my place. Will you come with me?"

Maggie held her breath.

Chapter 14

He had never felt so tired and helpless in his entire life, and he hurt all over. Not just his body, but his mind. Rance sucked in a lungful of air and winced as his chest muscles and ribs reminded him of the abuse he'd given them. It had only been a few weeks since he was hurt, and though he had recently felt sound, he must not have healed completely. He closed his eyes and tried to think.

Going with Maggie was a tempting thought. But didn't he owe it to Mama to stay here? *Somebody tell me what to do.*

"You can't do anything here that the rest of us can't. Go with Margaret Rose. If we do find your mother, believe me, you'll be the first to know. Go on. You don't need to be here," Sheriff Potts urged. "You told us where to look. You did your part."

Rance forced his eyes open. He looked at Maggie's outstretched hand. Then he looked at Potts and Higgins. The oafish grin was gone from Higgins's face, replaced with concern. He looked at Maggie again.

"Okay," he said slowly. "I'll go to Maggie's." Rance reached for her hand, and she squeezed her fingers around his. He closed his eyes and breathed a long, broken breath. Then he dropped Maggie's hand.

"I need to get something," he said, and headed for the kitchen. Rance located the bottle that Maggie had left on the table and unscrewed it with shaking fingers. He poured a good two inches into the glass and tossed it back. He hadn't been much of a drinking man, but he needed the stuff now. His body felt chilled to the bone, and he would do anything just to ward off the cold.

"You can bring it with you if you want." Maggie had come up behind him, and Rance spun around guiltily. "It's okay," she said reassuringly. She took the bottle and tightened the cap. "We'll take it with us."

Mutely Rance followed her to the door. Potts and his deputy had seated themselves in the living room and were discussing something in low tones. Rance didn't want to think about them or what they were thinking. He didn't want to think at all.

Maggie waited at the door, and Rance followed slowly, grateful to be spared any more discussions. When he reached her, she pushed the door open and stepped outside. Rance started to follow, but stopped and looked back.

Potts glanced up. "It's all right, son. We'll call you as soon as we find something."

Rance nodded and followed Maggie outside to her minivan. He watched as she took the driver's seat, and then he tugged open the passenger door and settled in beside her.

The little trailer house looked warm and welcoming in the late-night darkness as Maggie pulled the van into the lane and drew to a stop in front. She'd left the lights on in her earlier haste, and now the cheery glow invited them in. Such a contrast to the eerie Hightower place.

"I know it won't be easy for you, but I think you should

try to get some sleep,'' Maggie told Rance as they walked up to the door.

Rance didn't respond, but Maggie hadn't expected him to. She wondered if he was in shock, and she wouldn't have been surprised if he was.

"You can sleep in my bed," Maggie told Rance as she opened the door. "I'll be just down the hall in Jennifer's room, if you need anything."

He nodded slowly as Maggie showed the way.

The bed was still rumpled, the covers tossed and tangled from her sleepless thrashing earlier. Though it would be perfectly normal to find a bed rumpled at this time of night, Maggie fought the urge to blush. The only man she'd ever had in her bedroom before was her wedded husband.

She glanced at the clock, half hidden on the floor. It was 2:00 a.m. Had it only been two hours since she heard the sounds that sent her running to Rance's house?

Maggie set the bourbon on the nightstand and smoothed the bedclothes. She turned down one side. When she bent to retrieve the pillow she'd tossed to the floor, the clock thumped to the carpet. "I'll just take this and put it in the kitchen," she murmured, displaying the clock. "It makes an awful racket when you're trying to sleep."

"Fine." Rance sank heavily onto the bed, hugging his arm to his ribs. He reached for the bottle and grimaced. It was plain as day that he'd reinjured himself. He unscrewed the lid.

"I'll bring you a glass."

"Okay."

"And some liniment, if you need it," Maggie added as she saw his jaw clench and his face harden as he raised the bottle to his lips. "I'll be right back."

The liniment was not where she thought it was, and it took several minutes for Maggie to locate it finally on top of the refrigerator. Carrying it and the glass, she hurried back to the bedroom.

Rance had gotten undressed and into the bed. His clothes lay folded neatly at his feet, and his shoes were lined up carefully along the side. He had propped up the pillows behind him and lay on his back, with the sheet pulled up over his hips and arranged carefully at his waist. His eyes were closed, but Maggie knew he wasn't sleeping.

Her breath left her at the sight. As needy as Rance might be this night, he was still a magnificent man. And it had been a long time since there was a man in her bed—even if she wouldn't be there with him. She would have had to be dead not to appreciate the sight of him, and Maggie was definitely not dead.

She paused at the door, taking a moment to control her speeding heart. She tried to banish the erotic thoughts that had suddenly come charging to mind. *Yes, Maggie,* she told herself. *He needs you tonight, but not for that.*

"Do you want me to pour you another drink?" she asked breezily as she tried to pretend that she was not looking at a nearly naked man in her bed.

Rance opened his eyes and lethargically waved her away. "I don't need any more," he said languidly. "Just give me the liniment."

Maggie handed him the bottle and watched as he tried to unscrew the top. The bottle was old, and the cap stuck. Rance's face paled as he tried to wrench the top free.

"Let me run some hot water on it. That should loosen the lid," she told him. He handed the bottle back to her, and Maggie hurried out.

It took a moment for the water in the bathroom to run hot, so Maggie took a quick inventory of herself in the mirror. She wished she hadn't. Her hair was disheveled, and she wore no trace of makeup to darken her pale lashes or to cover her freckles. She resisted the urge to powder her nose, reminding herself that she was there in the capacity of nurse, not...lover?

Tossing her head in an attempt to banish the errant thought, she found it hard to ignore since she and Rance had already become lovers. Maggie tested the water. It was hot enough. She let the scalding water run over the sticky lid, and after a moment it was loose enough to open. Unscrewing the top, she padded back to the bedroom.

"Got it open," she announced as she entered.

"Thanks." Rance reached for the bottle.

"Well, I'll go now." Maggie started to leave, but a muffled groan of pain called her back. "Are you all right?"

"Yeah," he said through clenched teeth. "I just got some of that stuff into one of the cuts." He sucked in another sharp breath.

"Maybe I can do it. I can maneuver around the raw spots better than you can," Maggie volunteered.

Rance hissed again. Had he found another cut with the stinging medicine? Maggie didn't think that was the only reason he had made that sound, but it was too late to back out now. Was he reacting to the medicine? Or to her?

"Thank you," he said huskily.

Rance placed the bottle of liniment in Maggie's outstretched hand, careful not to touch her porcelain skin. He was conscious of the rising color in her face; she had the kind of complexion that made it hard for her to hide anything, and he knew she was remembering what had happened earlier. Had that just been a few hours ago?

It seemed as if a lifetime had passed. And now everything had changed. He knew she was as uncomfortable as he was about the situation, but there was nothing he could do now. They'd started on this path; they would have to finish the walk to see where it went.

Maggie's eyes widened as his fingers briefly touched hers, but she lowered her eyes quickly as even more color flooded her face. Was she sorry she'd made love with him?

Why was it that every time he was alone in a bedroom with Maggie, she was nurse and he was her patient? Well, almost every time. He was in the right place but the wrong situation again. Rance felt a tightening in his groin as he watched Maggie pour some of the liniment into her cupped hand. He willed his body not to react as she rubbed the pungent liquid into her hands to warm it. He wasn't successful.

"Tell me where to put it," Maggie said, her voice breathy and soft.

Pointing with his hand, Rance indicated the lower right side of his chest, just below the nipple. He had situated himself on the left side of the bed and Maggie had to climb across the sheets to reach him. That was a mistake, but it was too late to change it now. He watched as she inched across the mattress toward him.

Rance sucked in a lungful of air as Maggie's fingers, slick with the warming balm, touched his chilled flesh.

"Did I hurt you?" she asked, alarm on her face.

"No," he answered huskily. *You definitely put me in pain, but not the kind you meant,* he didn't say. He closed his eyes and tried to think of anything unpleasant enough to keep his body from reacting to her gentle touch.

Maggie's fingers caressed him lightly, massaging the healing liquid into his sore muscles. Her touch was light, but still he flinched as the liniment occasionally found the raw spots left by the flying chips of concrete and cement.

Her anointing fingers forced the soreness out of his muscles as she caressed and massaged. The liniment worked quickly, and Rance should have told Maggie to stop, but her soft fingers on his bare skin felt too good to refuse. He reveled in the sensation as her fingers tenderly worked heat into his muscles and into his soul, and he could not prevent a low moan from escaping his tortured lips.

Maggie stopped abruptly. "Did I hurt you?" she asked, alarmed.

Rance drew in a deep, shuddering breath. "No. It feels too good." He pulled the sheet up to disguise his all-too-evident desire for her. "I think that did it," he whispered huskily. "Thank you."

The door closed behind her. The gentle click of the mechanism belied the finality of the simple action. Maggie had seen Rance pull the covers up to conceal his body's response to her. She sighed. Was it regret or relief? It was all too apparent that Rance did not want to stay, in spite of his body's reaction.

If he had only asked, she would have stayed. But he had all but sent her away.

Maggie paused in the hallway, undecided. Should she go back to Rance and try to change his mind? Or should she just shrug it off and go to bed—alone?

She did neither. Instead, she went back into the bathroom and gazed at her reflection in the mirror. Had seeing the "real her" doused the flame that had burned so bright earlier in the evening?

Her light robe was streaked with dirt and traces of Rance's blood. Maggie grimaced and resisted the urge to peel it off. She might need to check on him again, and she wanted to be appropriately covered. Even if he had already seen everything the garment concealed. She washed the pungent-smelling ointment off her hands, soaping and rinsing twice. Then she splashed water on her face, repeating the same ritual she had performed hours before.

She always washed her face, brushed her teeth and combed the tangles out of her hair before she went to bed. She might have done it already tonight, but she was starting over, trying to sleep again. She knew there was no chance of success if she didn't perform her regular night-time routine, no matter how late it was. She looked into the mirror again.

She tugged the comb through her unruly curls with more

force than usual, catching it on every tangle and snarl. Tears sprang to her eyes as the comb snagged on yet another knot. Finally it ran through without encountering obstacles. Maggie put the comb down.

Only then did she realize that tears were streaming from her eyes. She wiped at them with the back of her hand and blotted her face with a towel, trying to convince herself that the pain from the tangles had made her cry. Or maybe she'd gotten some liniment in her eyes. But she knew that neither excuse was the real reason. Maggie had experienced her first rejection since those awkward days as a teenager. Funny, it seemed to hurt even worse now.

She looked again into the mirror and forced herself to smile. Not that it would help much. Now she not only had invisible eyelashes and visible freckles, but puffy, red eyes, as well. She snorted in disgust.

There was no way she would sleep at all.

Get a grip, Callahan, she told herself. *Stop acting like a lovesick teenager.* She drew in a deep breath that turned into a sigh and stepped into the hall.

The hallway was dark except for a thin sliver of light leaking from under her bedroom door. Could he not sleep, either? Maggie started toward Jennifer's room, then stopped. She turned, mentally debating the pros and cons of going to Rance.

Her common sense won the argument. She turned back toward Jennifer's room.

"Maggie?" Rance's voice came soft and muffled through the closed door. He sounded as tenuous and uncertain as she felt. Or did the distance and Maggie's imagination give her hope?

"Yes?"

There was a long silence. Too long. Maybe Rance had only called her name to identify the sound he'd heard in the hall. Curiosity satisfied, he had no other reason to talk.

Maggie started back toward the other room, and the empty bed meant for one.

"Please don't go."

Maggie stopped. Did he want her? Or did he need something? Like aspirin, or a drink of water?

She responded slowly, not certain what Rance wanted of her. She turned the knob and slowly pushed the door open.

Rance's handsome face was drawn and pinched, but he smiled as she stepped into the room. Maggie's heart leaped as she positioned herself at the foot of the bed, waiting. "What do you need?"

"I need you," Rance said softly, barely loud enough to hear. Had she only imagined what she wanted him to say to her? "I don't want to be alone. Not tonight. Stay with me, Margaret Rose." He offered his hand to her.

Her full name sounded like a caress on Rance's lips, sensuous and soft. He pronounced it lovingly, smoothing out the syllables and giving it a life of its own. How could she refuse him?

Maggie harbored no illusions that Rance needed more than a warm body to help him through the night, but for now it was enough. There had been no talk of love, no whispered promises. Earlier, they had just been two people alone in a romantic situation. Now he needed nothing more than comfort. But she needed it, too. She stepped forward and accepted Rance's outstretched hand.

Rance's breath caught in his throat as Maggie's soft fingers touched his. How easily a man could get used to this—and he was a man weary of being alone.

Maggie's trembling fingers were cool on his heated flesh. Or was it he who was shaking? Maggie slid onto the edge of the bed and waited, primly, almost virginal in her demure white nightdress. She had an ethereal, Victorian look about her, with her simple gown and her softly flowing mantle of carrot curls, but he remembered the passion she'd displayed in his bed. Had it only been a few hours since she was there? So much had happened in such a short time.

She must have sensed his thoughts. Self-consciously Maggie reached up and smoothed her hair, as if to douse the flames.

"Turn out the light," Rance whispered huskily.

She did.

"I'm a little new at this," Maggie murmured softly. "In spite of what happened earlier."

Good. She had brought it up. Rance held his breath and took a long moment to ponder his next move. "It's all right," he told her carefully. "I'm a little shaky, too."

The curtains were open, and moonlight bathed her in enough light for him to see her smile. He reached out and gently touched her velvety-soft face. He traced the outline of her lips with uncertain fingers. "Lie beside me, Margaret Rose. I need to hold you."

"I like the way you say that," Maggie whispered breathlessly. She turned away and fumbled with the sash of her robe.

"You like what?"

"The way you say Margaret Rose," she explained as she loosened the tie. "I always hated it when I was growing up, but you make it sound different. Intimate." Her voice was soft and breathy.

The fabric covering her nightgown slid away from Maggie's shoulders and pooled around her feet. She turned shyly back to Rance, drew a shaky breath, and lifted the sheet, sliding under it in one graceful motion.

It took all the self-control he had to keep from grabbing Maggie and clutching her to his pounding chest, but he forced himself to wait until she had settled beside him. She rolled to her side and faced him, pillowing her head with one bent arm. With the other, Maggie found Rance and touched his hand.

"Hold me, Margaret Rose. I need you." Rance hardly recognized his own raspy, emotion-filled voice.

Maggie pulled him to her and enfolded him in her arms as she would have a child, but he felt like anything but that. He breathed in her soft, womanly scent and nuzzled into the bend of her neck, burying his face deep in her luxuriant hair.

The tightening returned to his groin, and Rance groaned. Maggie shifted in his arms and angled herself until they were face-to-face. She worked her hand up his back and to his neck. Her fingers were gentle but strong as they urged him toward her slightly parted lips.

Rance wasn't sure who kissed whom, but then, did it really matter? Maggie's lips were soft, yielding, yet returning his passion with more of her own. His hand found the curve of her neck and traveled lower. He cupped her full breasts in his hand, feeling the nipples beneath the thin layer of cotton harden in response to his exploring fingers.

"Margaret Rose," he breathed between kisses. "I want you."

"I know" was all she said. Maggie snuggled deeper into his arms and gave herself to him. "I want you, too."

And with infinite care not to worsen his injuries, she showed him just how much.

Later, when his breathing slowed and she thought Rance must be asleep, Maggie rolled onto her side and with her head pillowed on her bent arm, she stared out the window. The clouds had long since evaporated, leaving the moon and the stars shining bright in the dark summer sky.

Maggie sighed. This would have been wonderful if there had been any sort of declaration or promise. But there had been nothing. The first time had been pure, unbridled desire. The second time had been...what? Need? Comfort?

How could such a beautiful, giving experience leave a woman feeling so satisfied yet so confused at the same time?

She wished she could wake Rance and ask him all the questions for which she had no answers, but she knew that after what he'd found in his cellar—or thought he had—he needed to rest. Tomorrow would be soon enough for answers.

She lay for a long, long time, watching him sleep. Wondering how it must have been for a small boy to believe for so long that his mother had abandoned him. No wonder he had grown to be such a guarded person. He'd given his unconditional love to two people in his young life, and they'd both left him. Both by death—one by his own hand, but his mother…?

Maggie shuddered at the thought of Rose Montoya Hightower being buried for so long in the grave in the concealed portion of the basement. For so long, she had called and called for someone to help her. And finally Rance had heard.

Why was it that so many people had heard her, but only one had known what to do? Was it the power of a mother's love, reaching out beyond the grave? Had her power been only strong enough to reach her son?

But no, Maggie had heard that voice, too. First as a teenager, when she been dared to spend the night in the abandoned home. Then again, the night she had kept vigil over Rance's injured body. She had heard, but she hadn't understood. Though she wished she had, she couldn't fault herself for not understanding.

She hadn't been the only one to hear her all those years ago. A succession of people had lived in the house, heard Rose calling, and fled. If only one of them had understood and found her….

But then, if Rose's body had been found years ago, would Rance Montoya be here today? Would he have grown into the man who had to come back to his roots, looking for his past? Probably not. Maggie consoled herself with the notion that the delay in discovery had been meant to be.

Rance would not be lying beside her. Would never have made love to her. And she would never have met him and fallen in love. Maggie rolled to her back and sighed. She had to admit it—she had fallen in love with the man.

And she had no idea whether what he felt for her was anything more than friendship or gratitude. Or basic need.

With that disquieting notion nagging at her brain, she finally settled into shallow, restless sleep.

Rance rolled over and settled on his back, spent and happy. He propped his arm beneath his head and stared up at the ceiling. He had given Maggie all the love and passion he had to give, and she had given him the same in return. If only for this one night. Did he dare think there would be others? That yesterday and tonight could lead to a tomorrow?

He lay in the warm darkness, listening to the gentle rhythm of her breathing. Maggie snuggled closer and found a spot in his arms. With her nestled in the crook of his elbow, it was possible to believe that she'd been there forever. That she belonged to him. Was meant for him.

Maggie's eyes were closed in sleep, and she couldn't know how that shaft of moonlight found her face and lit on it, giving it an unworldly beauty only the night could. Rance brushed a tendril of tangled hair from her forehead and leaned over to kiss the silky-smooth skin of her brow. She murmured in her sleep, and Rance's heart swelled at the trusting sound.

"I love you, Margaret Rose," he whispered more to the night than to her.

"Hmm?" Maggie's sleepy voice responded, sounding warmly contented from within her restless slumber. She nuzzled his chest, and her fingers found his chin and then explored his lips.

Rance kissed her clumsy fingers and lowered his head to find her mouth. He covered her lips with his.

Maggie made a mewling sound way back in her throat, kittenish and soft. Then she returned the kiss, all the while still wrapped in sleep, snug in Rance's arms.

How easy it would have been to stay that way forever. Rance hugged Maggie to him, careful not to wake her. As he pressed her to his heart, his loins tightened, and he felt a resurgence of his need for her.

He resisted the urge to wake her. Maggie looked so unguarded and trusting lying there asleep, it would be a crime to disturb her. She'd had as long a day as he; at least one of them should sleep.

The phone rang, and Rance was instantly alert. It could only mean one thing at that time of the morning. Rance reached across Maggie's sleeping form and silenced the phone before it could ring again and wake her. But he'd forgotten that her kids were away from home; her maternal ears would be as attuned to the phone as his. She was awake as he.

"Yes," he said softly into the mouthpiece. Then he listened. "I'll be right there."

He placed the receiver carefully back on the cradle and eased himself out of Maggie's tender grasp. "It was for me. You go back to sleep."

She murmured a protest, but Rance placated her with a gentle kiss.

"I'll come back in the morning and tell you what Sheriff Potts found," he whispered, brushing a soft strand of hair away from her ear.

"I'll be waiting," Maggie murmured. Then she sighed, settled, and curled into a childlike ball.

Rance found his jeans and slid them on as quietly as he could. He groped for his shoes and socks, retrieved his shirt and then rose. He stood for a long moment, clothing clutched haphazardly in his arms, gazing down at Maggie. She was beautiful, even half asleep.

Deep inside him, Rance felt the urge to kiss her awake and make love again. Anything to postpone what he knew he was about to learn. What he already knew. But he resisted. He knew that if he touched her again, he would never be able to go. She would understand why he had to leave. And as much as he wanted to stay, Potts's summons drew him even more strongly.

Chapter 15

"Goodbye, my Margaret Rose," he whispered. "I have to go, but I'll be back soon." He turned to leave.

Maggie murmured something, and he turned back to her. She didn't repeat it, and he had to go. "I love you, Maggie," Rance told her, one more time. Then he slipped quietly out of the room, closed the door and crept down the hall, as silently as the fog drifting in on the night air. He stopped in the living room long enough to finish dressing, then let himself out the door.

After all that had happened the night before at his house and here at Maggie's, it seemed remarkable that the earth still turned and night still became day. Darkness was just beginning to give way, and the sky was no longer black, but a misty gray that outlined the ghostly silhouettes of the trees.

Rance took a deep breath of the fresh morning air and looked around. When he failed to find his truck, he remembered that he had come in Maggie's minivan. He shrugged. It was only a half mile; the walk would do him good.

He took one last look at the window behind which Maggie lay sleeping. How could one night have made so much difference in his life? He'd found his mother and the love he'd lost. And he'd found new love in the form of Margaret Rose. Or so he hoped.

Odd. Even her name held part of the past he'd known so little about. Margaret *Rose.*

After so many years of not knowing, the tangled threads of his life were finally coming undone. Potts still hadn't confirmed it, but Rance had no doubt that the grave in his cellar contained Rose Montoya Hightower's body.

The walk to his house was short, due more to Rance's rapidly working mind than to the length of his strides. As he mulled over the implications of Potts's summons, the distance between Maggie's home and his house disappeared. Before he had a chance to work it all out, he turned into the lane.

Rusty greeted him at the mailbox with an excited bark. He had forgotten about the dog in all the excitement of the night's developments. Rance paused to scratch her head. "I don't have time for you now, girl," he said as he drew his hand away from her coppery, silken fur and hurried toward the house.

Potts hadn't said anything about finding a body, but he had told Rance about finding some effects. Effects that he wanted Rance to identify. That was the only other reason that could have dragged Rance away from Maggie so soon. And if Potts had found effects, he would find Rose, too. Rance just knew it.

Several more vehicles had arrived. There were two un-familiar civilian cars, and another that bore the markings of the Alabama Special Investigations Branch. As he threaded his way through the jam of cars, another vehicle pulled in, a hearse bearing the legend of the Pitt County coroner.

The hearse confirmed his certainty and his worst fear. They had found her.

"Potts! Higgins!" he shouted as he jogged the rest of the way to the house. No one answered, and he made it up to the porch in two long steps.

The front room was empty, and Rance hurried beyond to the kitchen. Higgins and two men Rance had never seen before were sitting at the table. Spread out in front of them on a sheet of plastic were a woman's purse and its contents. One of the strangers was sorting through the items and describing each, while the other compiled a list. Truman Higgins was overseeing the process.

Rance was torn. Should he stay to find out what Higgins had? Or should he seek out Sheriff Potts? Higgins solved the dilemma for him.

"You ever seen this before, Montoya?" Higgins indicated the purse.

It looked familiar. But it had been thirty years, and he hadn't spent much time scrutinizing ladies' handbags at age nine. Rance couldn't be sure. "I don't know. Maybe. What about identification?"

Deputy Higgins indicated a woman's wallet encased in plastic beside his elbow. "I got a billfold. I'm waiting for Sheriff Potts to come back up before I go into it. And he ain't coming up until the coroner gets here."

"I saw the hearse outside. The coroner isn't here?"

"No. Jimmy Shelton drove it over. We're waiting for Ollie Patterson to make it back in town from a fishing trip down to Cahaba."

Rance was damn sure tired of hearing people toss around names and excuses he didn't have time for.

"I don't give a damn about procedure," Rance muttered, and grabbed for the wallet. "I want to look."

Then he spotted it.

A pearl-handled revolver. Small, compact. A woman's gun. Rance had definitely seen it before. Had held it. And it was definitely something that would stick in a small boy's mind. He had found the pistol in his mother's room the day she disappeared. He'd thought it was a toy. A present for him, for his birthday the next week. But it hadn't been a toy; it had been very real.

He picked up the small, white-handled revolver and held it carefully in his hands. What was Mama doing with a gun? he wondered as he examined it, his childish curiosity piqued. His birthday was coming soon. Could it be for...?

"Rance Hightower! Put that down right now!"

He dropped the gun back to his mama's bed and whirled around guiltily to see his mama swoop down upon him and snatch him into her arms.

"I'm sorry, Mama. I didn't go into your purse," Rance said from his position tight in his mother's arms. "It was on your bed. I was just looking."

Rose Montoya Hightower released her tight grip and held her son at arm's length. "It's all right, hijo. *I shouldn't have left it there for you to see."*

"But what is it for? Is it for my birthday next week?" Rance squirmed under his mother's grave scrutiny.

"No," she replied sharply. "You forget that you ever saw it," she continued as she swept the gun into her opened purse and closed it tightly.

He hung his head in shame. "I'm sorry, Mama."

Rose ruffled her son's hair and sighed. "I didn't mean to upset you." She drew a deep breath. "Come, help me take this bag to the car."

Rance sucked in a deep breath. "I've seen that gun before. My mother had it."

"You sure?"

"Positive as I can be after thirty years."

Somebody banged on the front door, probably the coroner, and Higgins went to answer it. The sound of feet on the stairs and in the hall ended Rance's wait for the sheriff and the discussion about the gun.

"You know, Margaret Rose always claimed that she'd heard a ghost in this house," Truman Higgins said as the coroner's men made their way past with the gurney that carried his mother, zipped into a black, plastic body bag.

Rance didn't know what he expected to feel after finally finding out what had happened to his mother. What was he supposed to feel?

Grief? No. Through the years his grief had long been spent. There was sadness, but not the debilitating anguish he had felt as a child when the emotion was still strange and new. Rather, sad because in spite of it all he'd held out a tiny hope that he would find her some day.

Anger? Oh, yes. There was anger. Anger that Drake— whoever he was—had taken everything from him that had made his young life happy and safe. And he would bet that Drake was out there somewhere. Fat, happy. Living, while everyone Rance cared about was dead and gone.

Maybe not everyone. Rance remembered the warm, vibrant woman who had comforted him last night. He drew in a breath of relief that he still had someone.

Regret? How could he mourn for something he'd never really had? He hadn't had a mother for thirty years. He had learned to live without one.

Relief? Why wasn't he relieved? It was finally over, wasn't it?

Rance swallowed and focused on Higgins. "Did you say something?"

The deputy shook his head. "It wasn't important."

What was important, Rance realized, was that he still didn't have all the answers.

He forced himself to watch the gurney being wheeled out.

He still had questions. And as sure as he was standing here, he knew one man had the answers.

Drake.

Sun streaming through the opened curtains poked at Maggie late in the morning. She tried to brush the warm, teasing sunbeam away, but it persisted, kissing her cheek as if it were a new lover.

Maggie woke slowly, stretching languidly, mildly surprised to discover that she was naked beneath the sheets. Then she smiled, remembering the feel of Rance's strong hands on her trembling body and what had happened the night before. Sighing contentedly, she stretched and yawned.

How nice to wake with Rance lying beside her.

She lay there in the moment between sleep and waking, with her eyes closed against the bright light of day, and remembered each kiss, and the feel of his skin against hers. She could still feel the way his hands had caressed her, making her skin tingle and her pulse throb.

Maggie nuzzled her pillow and recognized a vague hint of wintergreen that clung to the smooth cotton fabric. The liniment. Would he need more this morning? She smiled. More liniment, or more of what had come after?

She finally opened her eyes and reached for Rance. But her fingers encountered the empty pillow. She moved them lower, to the rumpled sheets, but they were cool and bare.

Rance sat alone in the kitchen, a half-empty cup of black coffee in front of him. For the first time since he'd been back at Hightower's Haven, he felt truly alone. Not just because the horde of investigators was finally gone, but because Rose Montoya was no longer here. The presence he'd felt since the first day of July was gone. He listened for the voice that had called to him, but there was only silence.

There had been a body in the grave in the cellar. Or what was left of one. *Skeletal remains,* the coroner had called them. They had yet to be officially identified, but Rance knew who the small female skeleton belonged to. The wallet had contained Rose Montoya's driver's license; the comparison of the local dental records still on file would only make it official.

His mission should be over, but Rance felt no sense of closure. Every time he thought he'd solved the puzzle, he would find another piece missing. He'd thought he would be able to end his search for roots and home when he reclaimed Hightower's Haven. He'd thought when he discovered why his father had taken his life it would be over. He'd thought that finally finding what had happened to his mother all those years ago would put an end to his uncertainty. It hadn't.

He still didn't have all the answers. He had finally found his mother, true, but Rance knew beyond a shadow of a doubt that it had been murder, and he was pretty sure he knew who had done it.

The mysterious Drake.

He just didn't know why. It had to have something to do with the way Drake had gotten his hands on Hightower property. And Rance would have bet anything that Drake was the one who was living at Hightower's Haven when his mother had returned.

People had only begun to talk about the house being haunted after the first owner left. Rance had gotten that much out of the few people who'd told him about the place. He was more certain than ever that Drake was that first owner, and the final part of the puzzle.

Rance wondered if the man was still alive, and something deep inside him assured him that he was. Now all he had to do was find him.

He rubbed his eyes and realized that he hadn't slept. It was midday, and he was tired, hungry and heartsick. He could eat and he could sleep, but his heart would not mend until he knew the whole truth. He reached for the coffee cup.

The coffee was cold and bitter, but Rance drank it anyway. The noxious taste made him grimace, but the caffeine would give him enough energy to do what he needed to do. He downed the rest of the horrible black stuff.

There had to be someone who knew how to find this Drake, but in Rance's fatigued condition, he was too muddled to dredge up a name. He dumped out the contents of the coffeemaker and started a fresh pot. He needed lots of coffee, black and strong, to clear his head and help him make it through the day. It didn't matter that it was already ninety degrees in the room and would probably get hotter. He needed the coffee.

And he needed a shower.

Rance forced himself from the kitchen, rummaged in his room for fresh clothes and hurried down the hall. Only then did he notice the bright yellow police tape that had been stretched across the cellar door. Why were there so many reminders? When would he be able to put it all to rest? When would his life go back to normal?

His life had never been normal, he realized painfully. Would it ever be that way? he wondered, trying to ignore the yellow tape as he passed it on the way to the bathroom.

The stinging spray did much to clear his head, but the hot water hit the welts on his chest and reminded him of what else had happened the night before. After he found the grave and before the sheriff's crew uncovered the body, there had been Maggie. The hot water irritated the wounds and reminded Rance of the way Maggie's gentle hands had stroked and caressed his aching flesh and tried to ease his pain.

How much he had needed her last night. Maggie had made the long night bearable. She had eased his suffering, body and soul. He owed her more than he could ever express. Maybe he owed her his life. And he wanted to share that life with her forever.

He still couldn't make plans for his tomorrows until he'd dealt with his yesterdays. Rance turned off the water and reached for a towel. Somebody had to know where to locate the man called Drake.

It came to him as he toweled himself dry. Old Reverend Carterette. Rance wrapped the towel securely around his middle. Without bothering to take the time to dress, he hurried to the phone.

One minute Maggie was as high as the birds in the sky from relishing what had happened with Rance the night before. The next she was lower than a flat-footed snake, remembering that he was gone. She knew that what was unfolding at Hightower's Haven was more pressing than she, but, selfishly, she would have preferred to be the center of Rance's thoughts right now.

She wanted to be able to sing and shout to the clouds that she loved Rance, but she couldn't. She had no doubt that he loved her in return, for she had a vague impression of him saying the words in the dark of morning. But right now, clearing up his past came first on his list of priorities. She did understand, she told herself. She really did.

As the mature woman that she was, Maggie understood. But as a reawakened woman, she craved more. She poured herself another cup of coffee and laced it generously with milk.

Maggie had slept well and late, and wasn't tired at all. Still, she remained in a languid mood. She'd showered and dressed and read the Sunday paper at her leisure, but it hadn't been enough. She had a secret to tell, and no one to share it with.

A horn sounded from outside.

Funny, she had been so wrapped up in her thoughts that she hadn't heard a car approach. She looked out the window to find that Tess had returned from town with the kids, and they were all piling out of her car. Maggie took a long swig of her coffee and went to the door.

A gaggle of kids—some Tess's children, some hers— waved and trooped past the house and down the dirt lane toward the Popwell place as Tess hurried in with an armful of clothes and the kids' toothbrushes.

"Not even a 'Hi, Mom, we missed you'?" Maggie murmured as Tess brushed past her and dumped the load on the floor.

"I sent them all down to the folks. We're having dinner with them this afternoon. You're invited, too," Tess explained as she handed Maggie the toothbrushes.

"Without Tom?"

"He'll be here later. Prudy Meeks's basset hound is having puppies, and he has to hold her hand. Not the dog's, but Prudy's. You'd think Pru'd never seen a dog drop puppies before." Tess poured a cup of coffee.

"If you'd paid as much for that dog as Prudy did, you'd be in a snit, too. Besides, you've been married to a vet forever. You should be used to it."

"Pooh. Pru is just looking for attention since her divorce. Does she seriously think he'd look her way?" Tess put the coffee down. "Forget that, Prudy really is worried about her investment. Tell me about last night."

Maggie looked at her sister, then quickly looked away, but not quickly enough to hide the blush that had come unbidden.

Tess noticed. "That good? You don't think I let the kids spend the night just because of the video, did you? I want details."

Blushing even more, Maggie tried to explain. "More happened than just a kiss."

Tess raised an eyebrow and cocked her head. "Better and better."

"Take your mind out of the gutter. This is serious."

"Between you and Rance? That's terrific. Give me all the details."

"Tess! Listen to me. Something major happened last night. I'm surprised that you haven't heard it on the news."

"I'm sure it was a red-letter day—night—sis. But the news? Really."

It was like trying to stop a speeding train with a trip wire. Maggie wasn't sure she could make Tess stop without being blunt. "Tess, Rance and I found a grave in his cellar."

That stopped Tess's charge. She slowed down immediately and listened while Maggie told her about the events of the night before.

Reverend Carterette had known right where to find Drake Headly. Rance's childhood mind had remembered a name, but he'd believed it was a surname all along. Even if he had gotten the name right, everything still would have played out the same way.

The Wee-Care Rest Home bore a superficial resemblance to Hightower's Haven, Rance noticed idly as he pulled the truck into the visitors' parking lot in front of the shady porch. The irony of Headly's choice of residences was not lost on Rance as he walked toward the house.

The long wraparound porch was populated by a group of elderly people busily rocking, whittling, or otherwise biding their time. As Rance mounted the steps, a dozen interested eyes followed his progress, and half as many curious mouths murmured speculatively. Rance straightened and pushed open the door.

There was a desk just inside, the occupant talking so animatedly into the phone that she didn't bother to look up. She hardly looked old enough to be out of orthodontia or acne medication, but she was apparently in charge. Rance waited for her to terminate her conversation.

She kept talking to someone named Randy, and it was obviously not a rest-home-related call. Rance cleared his throat, but Randy continued to get an earful.

Patience had never been one of Rance's strong points. He cleared his throat again, louder this time, and waited for the woman to take a breath. When she finally stopped for air, Rance cut in. "Excuse me," he said, barely attempting to disguise his sarcasm. "I'm looking for Mr. Headly."

"Hold on. Can't you see I'm on the phone?" the woman replied icily, without looking up.

"Yes, I can see that," Rance replied smoothly, enunciating each word carefully as he reached across the desk and pressed the disconnect button on the phone.

"Hey!" she yelled angrily. Then she looked up at Rance. Instantly her expression changed to sweetness and light. "How may I help you, sir?" She smiled seraphically.

"You can tell me where Mr. Headly is." Rance reached into his pocket and found a match.

"Do you know what room he's in?"

Rance snapped the wooden matchstick in two before it ever made it to his lips. "If I knew that, I wouldn't be wasting my time here, talking with you," he replied, as levelly as he could.

The woman shrugged and had the grace to look apologetic. "I'm sorry. I'm new here. What is Mr. Headly's first name?" She turned to flip through a card file.

"Drake. Drake Headly."

"Oh, yes, he's assigned to room 4-C. But he's probably not in there at this time of day." She consulted the card again. "It says here he likes to sit in the solarium." She shut the file box and scooted out of the chair. "Follow me. We'll check in there before we look in his room."

She led Rance through a dim corridor to the back of the house and into a glassed-in chamber on the south side of the building. The room was filled with blooming plants and vines and was as hot and humid as a tropical rain forest. Yet the lone occupant was huddled in a chair and wrapped in a blanket.

The woman's tone was patronizing as she addressed the old man. "Mr. Headly?"

He looked up, as if surprised to hear his name. He blinked and stared at Rance blankly, his eyes dull and his movements listless.

"You have a visitor, Mr. Headly." The woman backed away. "I'll just leave you two to talk."

Rance appraised Headly as Headly did the same to him. Rance hadn't expected to find such a frail old man. He should have been about the same age as the hearty, robust Joe Popwell. But this wizened old man seemed aged beyond his years. He looked like a man whose soul had died already, but whose body hadn't yet caught on. Just the opposite of Rose Hightower.

"You aren't Bob Carterette," he said, his voice thready and weak. "Who are you? Nobody ever comes to see me but Bob." The old man started to cough and wheeze, but motioned Rance away when he moved to help.

"I'm all right," he finally managed. "Who are you?" Headly peered up into Rance's face, as if trying to read a name somewhere between his ears. "You look familiar. Do I know you?"

The brittleness in Rance's heart softened. "No," he replied quietly. "But I think you might have known my mother."

A flicker of something crossed Headly's face. "Who was your mother, son?" The old man's voice strengthened, and he sat up straighter.

"My name is—was—Rance Hightower. It's Montoya now. My mother was Rose Hightower."

Headly sucked in a quick breath of air, then looked down. He shook his head slowly. When he looked at Rance again, he waved a clawlike hand toward a chair. "You know, don't you?" he said simply. It wasn't a question, but a statement of fact.

Rance pulled up a chair and settled into it, using the time and the activity to compose himself. He finally had his answer. His heartbeat slowed to a crawl, and a chill settled over him in spite of the greenhouse effect in the solarium. "We found her early this morning," he finally said.

"You favor her, you know," the old man said irrelevantly. "I thought I knew you when you came in. You got his size, but you favor her more than you do your daddy."

Rance had no idea what to say. He didn't have to say anything. The old man continued.

"She was a pretty little thing." Headly's voice was a rasp. He chuckled, and the laugh turned into another rasping cough. "She was wild as a cat on an anthill that day." Headly looked across the room to nowhere in particular, as if he were trying to see into the past and make his recollection clearer.

"I spent the last thirty years trying to forget what happened. Now I suppose you want to know it all."

Rance nodded.

"Hell, I've been holding it in so long, maybe getting it off my chest will do me good." Headly sighed long and deep.

"I didn't mean to do it. It was an accident." The old man shut his eyes tight, intense concentration on his face. He shook his head. Finally, he opened his eyes and looked at Rance, as if he had forgotten he was there.

"She had scraped together enough money to make a respectable down payment on the place. She came flying down the lane in that old Chevy of hers, radio blaring, all excited and happy. Said she'd pay me off the rest bit by bit.'' Headly shook his head sadly. ''I don't know what got into me, but I had it in my head that I had to be some big landowner. I told her I knew she didn't stand a chance in hell of paying me back, and I turned her down.''

Rance swallowed and tried to analyze what Headly had just told him. It sounded as if his mother's accusations had been true. He drew a deep breath. ''You mean you really did dupe my father out of the place?''

Headly shook his head regretfully and sighed. ''I didn't set out to. At least, at first. But when that note came due, I could've—hell, should've—worked something out with your daddy. But by that time, I wanted that land so bad I could taste it.

''We were nothing but poor white trash when I was growing up. World War II and the GI Bill were my way out. I worked hard to get where I was at the bank, but I still didn't think I had the respect I deserved. Figured owning all that land would give it to me.'' He shook his head again.

''Rosie didn't take my turning her down too well. She chewed me out about Luther's death, then she pulled that gun out of her pocketbook and started waving it like she was going to shoot. She did get off one shot.''

Rance had been desperate to find out what happened way back then, but now he wasn't so sure he wanted to.

''She didn't hit me, but the bullet stuck in the windowsill in the living room. I covered up the hole, but the bullet might still be there.''

Headly stopped and sneezed. ''Damn pollen in here. The only room in the place where I can almost get warm enough, and they fill it with weeds,'' he muttered.

He continued. ''I just tried to get the gun away, but she fought harder'n a banty rooster. I finally managed to snatch the gun from her, but she lost her balance. She stumbled backward and caught her heel on the hearthstones. She fell up against the fireplace and hit her head on that big rock that sticks out on the left side." The old man shook his head regretfully. "One minute she was yellin' her head off, the next thing she was dead."

Rance had to remember to breathe; somewhere during Headly's narration, he had stopped. Now he pulled in a big gulp of air.

"But why didn't you get help? She shot at you. It would have been ruled self-defense." Rance stopped abruptly. It seemed disloyal, somehow, to put it in those terms.

"I guess neither one of us was in our right mind that day. By the time I came to my senses, it was too late. I'd already hid the evidence. Nobody would've believed me. Ever'body believed I had cheated your daddy out of that property. Just what your mama thought. I wasn't exactly very popular around Mattison after I bought that house of hers."

Headly snorted ruefully. "Instead of the respect I wanted, I got nothing. If anything, it was worse. Hell, I wish I'd never heard of Luther Hightower and any of his kin."

Now that he had the answers, Rance didn't know what to do. He sagged in the chair and buried his face in his hands.

"You gonna tell 'em?"

"I don't know," Rance said slowly. He struggled to his feet. "I just don't know."

Rance turned to leave; he was accomplishing nothing here. He had to think. "Thank you for telling me," Rance muttered as he stumbled out. His path was blocked by someone else at the door. Sheriff Potts, he noticed, but he didn't stop. He supposed that Potts had reached the same conclusions he had.

The way the newscaster presented the story had made it sound as lurid as a tabloid headline. She could just see it displayed on the rack beside the checkout counter in the grocery store. Son Finds Corpse Of Long-Lost Mom In Cellar Grave! the headline would read. Maggie shook her head sadly and switched off the television set.

She hadn't heard from Rance all day. Or anyone who would know the real truth about the find in the cellar. It wasn't so much that Maggie needed more details; she'd already figured out most of it before it was confirmed on the ten-o'clock news. She was worried about Rance.

Rance's condition the night before had been tenuous at best. No balanced man would have gotten up in the middle of the night and bashed down a wall in the cellar on a whim. Voices or no voices.

Maggie had been able to calm him, to make him forget for a little while. But that had been hours ago. A lifetime. Before his worst fears were confirmed.

She reached for the phone and dialed the number she had committed to memory after her repeated attempts to reach him. Rance wasn't home. Or he wasn't answering the phone. It rang and rang.

Maggie replaced the receiver on the cradle and peered anxiously out into the dark void. There were no lights from the direction of Hightower's Haven, so she guessed he was gone. There was nothing to do, so she closed up the house for the night and pointed her feet toward her bed. Just before she sank into the cool cotton sheets, Maggie looked outside one more time. There was nothing to see. No lights, nothing. Not a clue to tell her if Rance was all right.

She turned out the lights and tried to make herself comfortable enough to sleep. After a battle with the sheets, tossing and turning, she realized it was futile. Flopping over on her back, Maggie stared up at the patterns that the moonlight was painting on the ceiling and sighed.

She had told herself that the few moments they'd shared in this very bed were only temporary. At the time, she thought she'd convinced herself. But the way Rance whispered that he loved her had suggested that he wanted more than just a moment's peace. Had she been so wrong to believe him. Or had she only dreamed she'd heard what she wanted to hear?

She rolled over and punched the pillow. There was something else she hadn't taken the time to think about in her haste. They had taken no precautions. After so many years of married love, she'd stopped worrying about such things. Was she a candidate for pregnancy? Why had she been so impulsive?

She vowed to leave dating to the young. She was too old for this, and too many of the rules had changed.

There was no chance she was going to sleep tonight. Not without a stiff drink. And she wasn't about to resort to that.

"Where are you, Rance?" she whispered into the night. "Why haven't you come home...or come to me?"

Chapter 16

The thick evening air weighed down on him like a soft, warm blanket. Rance sat alone, his back propped against one of the few surviving peach trees in the old orchard as he stared up into the star-spangled night. Come Christmas, he would put in new trees, the promise of new life. But now there was nothing here except the derelict remains of a time long gone.

He'd intended to go home. To sleep. To catch up on the hours he'd missed the night before. But when he entered the house, the quiet had been so pervasive that he couldn't stay. He had gotten used to the voice and the feeling that he wasn't alone. Now he was.

The silence in the house had echoed loudly in his mind and reminded him of everything that he had lost. His father, his mother. Would he ever be able to fill the void?

And the yellow police tape burned in his memory like so much salt in an already festering wound. When would his life become normal? Ordinary. Sane.

Rusty nuzzled his neck and whimpered, kissing him with her cool, damp nose. Rance scratched the animal behind her ears and hugged her tightly to him. The dog squirmed and broke out of his grasp. She stood just out of reach and barked once, then stared at him gravely.

Rance chewed on a match until the stick splintered in his mouth. He plucked it from his lips and threw it away. Rusty darted after it, but lost it in the dark. "Go on home, Rusty," Rance murmured as he watched her. "Go to your babies. They need you more than I do."

The dog looked at him as if she understood and ambled away. She turned once and seemed to ask, "Are you sure?" Then she dashed off.

As Rance watched Rusty go, he hugged his knees to his chest and sighed. The tree trunk behind his back wasn't comfortable, but it was something familiar and old. Old, but not replete with the haunting memories the house contained. He'd played in this orchard as a child, swiped green peaches to lob at squirrels, savored the succulent flesh of the sweet, ripe fruit, so juicy that rivers of nectar ran down his chin. Now, even that was gone.

He felt completely alone, lonelier than he'd ever been before. He couldn't help wondering whether it would have been better never to have come back here and never to have known what really happened. Already he knew the answer to that. If he hadn't come here to look into his yesterdays, he would never have met Maggie.

He remembered back to that hectic first day he'd met her. The day he'd threatened that gaggle of kids over some stupid firecrackers. Now that he looked back on it, Tess had introduced herself and told him Maggie was her sister; she hadn't even mentioned Maggie's first name. He learned that from Mrs. Larson at the library.

They were some pair.

But one thing Rance Hightower Montoya was certain

of: Margaret Rose Popwell Callahan was the key to his tomorrows. If only he could be sure that she felt the same way.

Black was not her best color. Maggie stared at her reflection in the mirror and frowned, creating lines in her pale complexion, which was already dulled by the somber color she wore. She looked like the living dead.

She had never known Rose Hightower and she barely knew her son. Well, maybe in the biblical sense, Maggie reminded herself irritably. So why was she worrying so much about appearances? She brushed a piece of lint off the front of the simple black dress and shrugged.

It was a funeral, after all. Not a date. And considering that she hadn't seen or heard from Rance in the three days since they found Rose's grave, Maggie probably wasn't obligated to attend the funeral at all. But she would go. For Rance, she told herself. *No,* she finally had to admit, *I'm going for me.*

Maggie brushed another layer of blusher onto her pale cheeks and saw little improvement. She shook her head slowly and smiled weakly. "Let's face it, Callahan. People are going to mistake you for the dearly departed."

"Did you say something, Mom?" Buddy poked his head into the room. He looked stiff and uncomfortable in his starched white shirt and black tie. And so grown-up.

"No, sweetie. Just thinking out loud."

"Me and Jen are ready whenever you are."

"Jen and I," Maggie corrected automatically. She picked up her purse and met Buddy at the bedroom door, reaching out and ruffling his hair as she came.

"*Mo*-om!" Buddy protested as he backed out of her reach. "I just got it right."

Maggie laughed. "Sorry, kiddo." She resisted the urge to do it again. It felt good to laugh, she realized as she finger-combed her son's hair back into some semblance of order. She hadn't laughed in days. Not since before she and Rance found the grave.

Not since Rance left her and didn't return.

She sobered again as she and Buddy joined Jennifer in the tiny living room. "You know, you don't have to go if you don't want to. Funerals are not great places for kids, and—" Maggie couldn't finish. The only previous funeral experience her son and daughter had was their father's. Would they be able to separate the two events?

Buddy seemed to be reading her mind. "It's okay, Mom. After Dad's, this one will be a piece of cake." Buddy tried to smile, but the smile faded quickly.

Maggie squeezed her two children to her in a fierce hug. "I'm so lucky to have such grown-up kids. I love you," she finished, her voice cracking.

"I love you, too," two young voices, one male and one female, chimed in unison.

Then Buddy squirmed free. "Do you think we could get this over with?"

Maggie released her children reluctantly and dabbed at an eye with the back of her hand. "Yes, I think we have to." She pasted a smile on her face and opened the door.

"It was such a beautiful service. Especially when you consider that Father Roberts had never met your mama and all," cooed Prudy Meeks. "It was a nice touch to have Reverend Carterette speak as well."

"Yes, it was."

"I never knew your mama, Mr. Montoya," explained Eula Larson, "but it was such a shame she died so young." Mrs. Larson pressed a yellow-squash casserole into Rance's hands and hurried to a knot of people standing by the mantel.

Although most were trying not to look obvious about it,

everybody who'd arrived had made a point of examining the fieldstone fireplace. Some had quietly edged over and quickly moved away. Others, like Eula Larson, headed right to it and stared.

Rance had done the same thing that first time back in the house after Drake Headly admitted what had happened. He had run his fingers over the rocky knob that had caused the life to seep out of Rose Montoya Hightower.

"Let me take that out into the kitchen."

"I'm sorry. What?" Rance gathered his meandering thoughts and focused on Tess Hampton, standing beside him.

"I'll take the casserole into the kitchen. Can I get you something?"

"No." Rance shook his head slowly and tugged at his tie. It was much too tight, and way too hot. He managed what he hoped would pass for a smile. "Not unless you can get some of these folks to clear out."

Tess smiled apologetically.

Lucy Carterette joined them. "Vultures," she muttered. "Half of these people never knew your mother and don't know you. They're only here to get a look at you and the haunted house."

"It isn't haunted anymore," Rance commented sadly, more to himself than to Lucy. He had forced himself to come back after two nights away, and had lain awake all last night, listening for her voice.

"I guess not," Lucy agreed. "If you believe in those things, then Rose's spirit is finally at rest."

"Soul, Lucy," Bobby Carterette corrected. He extended his hand to Rance. When Rance grasped it, he pumped it heartily. "How you holding up?"

"All right, I guess. She hadn't been a part of my life for thirty years, but I always had some hope. Now, that's gone. This was just a ceremony to put an end to it once and for all." Now, just maybe, he could go on. Rance looked around for Maggie, but she wasn't there. He'd seen her at the service, but not since. Maybe she wouldn't come. After all, he'd been avoiding her for days, and she surely knew it. Who would blame her, after the way he'd behaved?

Rance remembered Bobby Carterette standing nearby. "Where's your dad? I want to thank him for saying such nice things about Mama."

"Right here, son." Old Bob came up behind them. "It wasn't hard to say nice things about Rose. She may not have been a member of my congregation, but I knew her well enough. Better than young Roberts anyway." He offered his hand to Rance.

"Well, thank you all the same." Rance gripped Old Bob's hand and held it. "I appreciate it." He appreciated the fatherly hug the old man gave him more.

As the Carterette family moved off, he scanned the throng of well-wishers. He still couldn't find Maggie. Had she decided not to come?

After his disappearing act of the past few days, he couldn't blame her for making herself scarce. Turnabout was fair play, he supposed. He *had* been avoiding her. Not because they'd made love and he was now done with her—he'd meant every minute of that awful, wonderful night—but because he'd needed time to digest everything that he'd discovered in the past few days.

He loved her.

"You were always a dreamy little child," a quavering voice remarked from somewhere near Rance's elbow.

He looked down into the wizened face of Ruby Scarborough. She had been his second-grade teacher at Mattison Consolidated, or so she told him.

"I'm sorry, Mrs. Scarborough. I was thinking of something else."

Mrs. Scarborough chuckled. "Just like when you were mine. Always had your eyes out the window instead of on your work."

"Yes, ma'am. I did learn to concentrate later on."

"I've no doubt you did. Come tell me all about what you've been up to in the last thirty years."

Rance glanced futilely across the room for help, but there was none. He followed Mrs. Scarborough to the chairs and sat down beside her.

Maggie had decided to spare the kids the ordeal at Rance's house and had taken them home. They'd been through it twice with Chet, once at the base chapel in Virginia and once here at home. Maggie figured they were even. She had to pick up the baked ham she'd prepared and sliced that morning. She'd intended it to be a quick trip home and then over to Hightower's Haven, but she had been forced to change clothes.

She wondered if subconsciously she hadn't almost dropped the ham on purpose. She wasn't usually that clumsy, yet she had let the ham slide right off the platter and onto her dress. Only quick thinking and good reflexes had allowed her to save it from falling to the floor, but her heroics had been at the expense of her outfit. She had ruined her black dress in the process of saving the ham by clutching it to her chest.

There had been nothing she could do about the big grease stain except take off the dress and hope it would come clean in the wash. Now she stared into a closet full of brightly colored clothes and wondered what to choose. No matter what she picked, it would be wrong. So, she reasoned, if she was going to provide fodder for the local gossips, she might as well go all the way. Maggie selected a warm apricot shirtwaist dress and pulled it over her head. "There," she said as she buttoned it up. "Let them talk."

She slipped out of the black pumps and into a pair of strappy tan sandals and headed back to the kitchen. She called out some last-minute instructions to the kids, grabbed the plastic-wrapped ham and hurried to the mini-van.

It took just a minute to drive the half mile to Rance's. At least half an hour, or so it seemed, to get from her parking spot partway down the crepe-myrtle-shaded lane. Maggie hurried up the steps and inside.

Poor Rance. He was trapped in a corner with Ruby Scarborough. Maggie had to smile. She hadn't had the dubious pleasure of having Mrs. Scarborough as second-grade teacher, having moved to Mattison when she was older, but her youngest brother, Jack, had. He'd often complained about how possessive his old teacher was whenever they would cross paths. Rance must have been one of her pupils.

Maggie stepped into the room and greeted several acquaintances, all the while edging toward the kitchen. She would just drop off the ham and go back to rescue him. If she could.

She found Lucy, Tess and her mother busily working in the kitchen. Lucy looked up and motioned for Maggie to set her platter down.

"We're setting up a buffet in the formal dining room. Maybe once we've fed all these…people, we can run 'em off."

"I'm sure Rance would appreciate it. He's in the living room, being held hostage by old Mrs. Scarborough." Maggie looked over the abundance of love offerings. "What do you need me to do?"

"Not again. I pulled Ruby off him once already," Daisy joked. "Just start carrying stuff into the dining room. Just as soon as it's all laid out, we'll call 'em in."

It took just a few minutes to set up the buffet. After

Maggie put the final stack of paper plates on the table, she hurried off to rescue Rance.

Mrs. Scarborough meant well, Rance was certain, but he would rather have been anywhere else but where he was at this particular moment. Being trapped under a tractor was looking more and more like a pleasant way to spend the afternoon. Rance stuck his finger behind his tight shirt collar and tugged at it again. He had an unreasonable craving for a cigarette, and he hadn't touched the things in ages.

Rance had grown accustomed to the heat in the old house, but with all the extra bodies blocking the breeze and radiating their own 98.6 degrees, the temperature had risen fast. The ceiling fan made a valiant effort, but it wasn't enough.

A glimmer of hope sprang to Rance's mind. *Maybe they're all as overheated as I am. Once they get too hot, they'll leave.* He looked around the crowd for signs that it was thinning, but saw not the tiniest indication of a reduction in the size of the throng. He still didn't see Maggie.

But he did see, he noticed with dismay, that someone else had just come in. His disappointment turned to curiosity when he realized that it was Sheriff Potts. He was wearing his uniform, so it must mean business.

"There you go wool-gathering again," Mrs. Scarborough's thready voice complained.

Rance tried to look apologetic, but he was afraid he was more irritable than anything. He noticed that Potts was beckoning to him. Gratified for the excuse, he turned back to the elderly lady at his elbow. "I'm sorry, Mrs. Scarborough, but Sheriff Potts is trying to get my attention." He tried not to show his relief.

The woman looked up as the sheriff approached, clutching his hat in his hand.

"I'm sorry, Miz Ruby," Potts apologized in a courtly manner. "I need to have a word with Montoya here. Won't you please excuse us?" Potts, already the owner of a standard-issue southern accent, was slathering it on as thick as honey. "It is official business."

Rance murmured something and got to his feet—not too quickly, he hoped. He followed the sheriff to a relatively quiet corner of the room.

"I thought you could use some rescuing," Potts drawled as soon as he and Rance were out of hearing distance.

Rance nodded gratefully and waited for Potts to tell him what he'd come to say.

"Miss Oxendine from the rest home called me this mornin'. She told me that Headly was admitted to Pittsville Community Hospital. They don't expect him to make it through the day. I don't know if you were dead set on seeing him tried for his part in your mama's death, but it don't look like you're goin' to get the chance."

Rance sucked in a deep breath, a cleansing breath. A freeing breath. He looked toward the fireplace, and then he looked back at Potts. It didn't matter anymore. He had all the answers; he was free.

"I don't guess there was any point prosecuting the old man, anyway. From what he told me, it sounded like an accident." Rance shut his eyes and shuddered. "The guilt he's carried for the last thirty years was punishment enough. Let it go."

Rance had made his peace with Headly that day in the solarium, and that was what mattered most. To Headly and to Rance.

Potts slapped him on the back. "I'm glad you said that. That's just what I figured to do. The coroner's report pretty much backs up what Headly said. A blow to the back of the head. And I can't for the life of me see Drake Headly sneaking up behind her and whopping her." A crackle from the police radio on his hip punctuated the sentence. "I reckon I'll have to go out to the car to hear this. There's too much noise in here."

"Sure. Go on," Rance said as he watched the sheriff go. A flash of color caught his eye, and he turned quickly to see what it was.

It was Maggie, wearing a brightly colored pinkish orange dress. She had finally come.

There was something comfortable and familiar about working in Rance's huge old kitchen, Maggie realized as she swished out another loaned dish and handed it to Rance to dry. Not just because she had worked in the kitchen before, but because she felt she belonged here.

As Lucy had predicted, once the assembled "mourners" had been fed, they dispersed quickly enough. Once their hunger and curiosity had been satisfied, they were willing enough to go. They had drifted off in twos and threes. Soon all that were left were the Carterette and Popwell contingents.

Maggie smiled. Even they had made their excuses after helping with the bulk of the cleanup and had tactfully left Maggie alone with Rance.

Rance chuckled, and Maggie looked up into his dark, dark eyes. She was curious to see what had evoked laughter so soon after his mother's funeral and after the news that Drake Headly had passed quietly away at Pittsville Community Hospital.

He looked so much more relaxed than he had earlier, more like himself. He had removed the tie that had obviously been bothering him all afternoon and had undone several buttons of his shirt, and now Maggie could see the dark swatch of hair that covered his chest. With laughter crinkling his eyes and his shirtsleeves rolled up to show off his powerful, tanned forearms, he looked as if he had been anywhere but to a funeral.

"They weren't exactly subtle, were they?" Rance commented as he looked into Maggie's eyes.

"About what?"

Rance laughed, aloud this time, his rich baritone laughter sending warm thrills through her. "Leaving you and me alone. You realize they've been matchmaking."

Heat burned Maggie's cheeks, and she knew without looking that her face was scarlet. Tess had been pushing her toward Rance since the Fourth of July, but she'd hoped it hadn't been so blatantly obvious. And it wasn't the first time people had discreetly left them together, she realized, remembering the night of the storm, when they'd been left to tend to the dishes.

He'd kissed her then, made love to her, and later they had discovered Rose's grave. And they'd made love again. "Do you mind?" Maggie finally managed.

"No," Rance whispered huskily. He cleared his throat. "Let's finish up here, then we need to talk."

Maggie wasn't certain quite how to take Rance's remark. But she wasn't going to waste time wondering about it. "Okay," she said. Then she gave her decidedly divided attention to the rest of the dishes, so that she could offer it, undivided, to him later.

The lengthening shadows and the setting sun painted Hightower's Haven with dappled light teased by the cooling evening breeze. From the distance, in this magical light, it was hard to imagine all that the stately old house had seen in the past thirty years. It looked much the same as it must have in 1882, when Horace Hightower nailed the first loblolly-pine board in place.

Maggie spoke first. "It's such a beautiful old home."

She sighed as she leaned against Rance's comfortably large body.

"It is beautiful," Rance agreed. "But it's only a house right now. It needs a family to make it a home," he added as he found the soft curve at Maggie's waist and fit his hand to it. She seemed to melt automatically into his grasp, and Rance smiled as he steered her back toward the house.

"You know, my ancestor Horace Hightower envisioned it as a place to be filled with children," Rance said, He stopped for a moment to look up at it. "He did his part to fill it. He had seven kids. But only Morgan survived to adulthood," Rance commented as he resumed his stroll across the weedy lawn. "Morgan only had one son, Marcus, and a daughter. After them there was Justin, and later my father." Rance dug in his pocket for a match. "Then there was me.

"I guess Hightowers weren't meant to be fruitful and multiply, as Horace expected." Rance continued trying to sound glib as he stuck the match into his mouth. He stopped again and stared up at the old family home.

Then he looked down at Maggie. She wore a puzzled expression, as if he had given her a riddle to solve and she couldn't figure it out. He'd hoped she would say something, but she couldn't answer a question that he hadn't yet asked.

Rance plucked the match from his lips and tossed it carelessly away. "I guess I'm going to be the last Hightower here. I worked to get it back," he continued cautiously, "but I don't have a son to hand it down to.

"Unless…" He paused, and Maggie's face lit up as bright as the setting sun. Maybe she did know the answer. Or at least now she knew the question.

"Unless you'd consider marrying me and letting me be father to your kids." Maybe he should have gotten down on his knee or produced a ring, but Rance wasn't exactly used to this kind of thing. He watched a kaleidoscope of emotions flitter across Maggie's face.

Floundering for a way to make her say yes, Rance stumbled over the right thing to say. "I wouldn't blame you for being angry at the way I left you after the other night, but if it helps any, I love you, Margaret Rose," he whispered huskily.

Her reply was as soft as his. "I know that. You can't spend as much time together as we have in the past few weeks and not get to know a person. God, has it only been a few weeks?" She looked up at him and smiled. "I love you," she added. Maggie fixed her remarkable turquoise eyes on his and smiled. "Do you suppose you could kiss me right now? I need you to hold me."

He dragged his lips away a few minutes later, when he felt moisture against his face. Quiet tears ran down Maggie's cheeks. Rance touched a warm drop with the tip of his finger and carefully wiped it away.

"Is the prospect of a life with me so bad?" Rance asked, hoping the answer would be negative.

Maggie smiled another of her sunshine smiles. "That's not it at all." She sniffed and brushed at the drying tears. "I love you. It's just we've been through so much. Who'd have thought we'd have to work so hard to come together? But I'd like nothing better than to marry you." Her voice grew steadier, surer. "And I'd be proud to let you be father to my children." She paused then, and seemed a little uncertain about the next thing she wanted to say. She swallowed and drew in a deep breath. "I would like to be the mother of another Hightower child, who would grow up here and learn to love this house as much as you do," she whispered softly.

Rance's heart slowed, and his breathing stopped. Was she saying what he thought she was? He stared down into Maggie's shining eyes. He drew a deep breath and time started up again. "He wouldn't be a Hightower," he finally said over the lump in his throat.

Maggie smiled. "Names don't matter. He or she would be a Hightower where it counts." She placed her hand on his chest. "Here, in the heart. It isn't the name that makes this place yours. It's the way you love it, and all the land that surrounds us."

"I do love it," Rance whispered huskily. "Almost as much as I love you." Then he bent and kissed her again.

Did he dare hope that Horace Hightower's dream would really come true? Then Rance looked down to the woman in his arms. It wasn't a dream, it was a promise.

* * * * *

Take 4 bestselling love stories FREE

Plus get a FREE surprise gift!

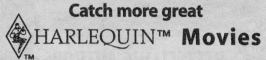

**Look for these titles—
available at your favorite retail outlet!**

January 1998
Renegade Son by Lisa Jackson

Danielle Summers had problems: a rebellious child and unscrupulous enemies. In addition, her Montana ranch was slowly being sabotaged. And then there was Chase McEnroe—who admired her land and desired her body. But Danielle feared he would invade more than just her property—he'd trespass on her heart.

February 1998
The Heart's Yearning by Ginna Gray

Fourteen years ago Laura gave her baby up for adoption, and not one day had passed that she didn't think about him and agonize over her choice—so she finally followed her heart to Texas to see her child. But the plan to watch her son from afar doesn't quite happen that way, once the boy's sexy—*single*—father takes a decided interest in *her*.

March 1998
First Things Last by Dixie Browning

One look into Chandler Harrington's dark eyes and Belinda Massey could refuse the Virginia millionaire nothing. So how could the no-nonsense nanny believe the rumors that he had kidnapped his nephew—an adorable, healthy little boy who crawled as easily into her heart as he did into her lap?

**BORN IN THE USA: Love, marriage—
and the pursuit of family!**

Look us up on-line at: http://www.romance.net

BUSA4

ALICIA SCOTT

**Continues the
twelve-book series—
36 Hours—in March 1998
with Book Nine**

PARTNERS IN CRIME

The storm was over, and Detective Jack Stryker finally had a
prime suspect in Grand Springs' high-profile murder case. But
beautiful Josie Reynolds wasn't about to admit to the crime—
nor did Jack want her to. He believed in her innocence, and he
teamed up with the alluring suspect to prove it. But was he
playing it by the book—or merely blinded by love?

For Jack and Josie and *all* the residents of Grand Springs,
Colorado, the storm-induced blackout was just the beginning of
36 Hours that changed *everything!* You won't want to miss a
single book.

Available at your favorite retail outlet.

Return to the Towers!

In March
New York Times bestselling author

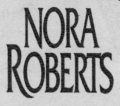

NORA ROBERTS

brings us to the Calhouns' fabulous
Maine coast mansion and reveals the
tragic secrets hidden there for generations.

For all his degrees, Professor Max Quartermain has a
lot to learn about love—and luscious Lilah Calhoun is
just the woman to teach him. Ex-cop Holt Bradford is
as prickly as a thornbush—until Suzanna Calhoun's
special touch makes love blossom in his heart.
And all of them are caught in the race to solve
the generations-old mystery of a priceless
lost necklace…and a timeless love.

Lilah and Suzanna
THE
Calhoun Women

**A special 2-in-1 edition containing
FOR THE LOVE OF LILAH and
SUZANNA'S SURRENDER**

Available at your favorite retail outlet.